Dear Reader,

I really can't express how f[...] grateful I am to Harlequi[...] collection of my published works. It came as a great surprise. I never think of myself as writing books that are collectible. In fact, there are days when I forget that writing is work at all. What I do for a living is so much fun that it never seems like a job. And since I reside in a small community, and my daily life is confined to such mundane things as feeding the wild birds and looking after my herb patch in the backyard, I feel rather unconnected from what many would think of as a glamorous profession.

But when I read my email, or when I get letters from readers, or when I go on signing trips to bookstores to meet all of you, I feel truly blessed. Over the past thirty years, I have made lasting friendships with many of you. And quite frankly, most of you are like part of my family. You can't imagine how much you enrich my life. Thank you so much.

I also need to extend thanks to my family (my husband, James, son, Blayne, daughter-in-law, Christina, and granddaughter, Selena Marie), to my best friend, Ann, to my readers, booksellers and the wonderful people at Harlequin Books—from my editor of many years, Tara, to all the other fine and talented people who make up our publishing house. Thanks to all of you for making this job and my private life so worth living.

Thank you for this tribute, Harlequin, and for putting up with me for thirty long years! Love to all of you.

Diana Palmer

DIANA PALMER

The prolific author of more than one hundred books, Diana Palmer got her start as a newspaper reporter. A multi–*New York Times* bestselling author and one of the top ten romance writers in America, she has a gift for telling the most sensual tales with charm and humor. Diana lives with her family in Cornelia, Georgia.

Visit her website at www.DianaPalmer.com.

THE *Essential* COLLECTION

DIANA

New York Times and USA TODAY Bestselling Author

PALMER

⌒LONG, TALL AND TEMPTED⌒

™ **Harlequin**®

TORONTO NEW YORK LONDON
AMSTERDAM PARIS SYDNEY HAMBURG
STOCKHOLM ATHENS TOKYO MILAN MADRID
PRAGUE WARSAW BUDAPEST AUCKLAND

Recycling programs
for this product may
not exist in your area.

ISBN-13: 978-0-373-36398-8

LONG, TALL AND TEMPTED

Copyright © 2011 by Harlequin Books S.A.

The publisher acknowledges the copyright holder of the individual works as follows:

REDBIRD
Copyright © 1995 by Diana Palmer

PAPER HUSBAND
Copyright © 1996 by Diana Palmer

CHRISTMAS COWBOY
Copyright © 1997 by Diana Palmer

www.Harlequin.com

Printed in U.S.A.

New York Times and USA TODAY
Bestselling Author

Diana Palmer

The Essential Collection
Long, Tall Texans...and More!

AVAILABLE FEBRUARY 2011
Calhoun
Tyler
Ethan
Connal
Harden
Evan

AVAILABLE MARCH 2011
Donavan
Emmett
Regan's Pride
That Burke Man
Circle of Gold
Cattleman's Pride

AVAILABLE APRIL 2011
The Princess Bride
Coltrain's Proposal
A Man of Means
Lionhearted
Maggie's Dad
Rage of Passion

AVAILABLE MAY 2011
Lacy
Beloved
Love with a Long, Tall Texan
(containing "Guy," "Luke" and "Christopher")
Heart of Ice
Noelle
Fit for a King
The Rawhide Man

CONTENTS

REDBIRD

Chapter One

She was there again. Hank Shoeman glared out the window at the figure on the balcony of the ski lodge below. His cabin was on a ridge overlooking the facility, just far enough away to give him the privacy he needed when he was composing. But it wasn't far enough away from the binoculars the slender young woman at the ski lodge was directing toward his living room window.

He shoved his hands into his jeans pockets and glowered at the distant figure. He was used to attention. Leader of the rock group Desperado, and a former linebacker for the Dallas Cowboys, Hank had had his share of adulation from women. In the old days, before his marriage and divorce, it had been flattering and heady to a Texas ranch boy. Now, it was nothing more than a nuisance. He'd had all he wanted of love. And he'd had more than he wanted of star-struck young girls looking for it.

He sighed, the action pulling his silk shirt taut over a hard, impressively muscular chest, and tautening the jeans that outlined powerful long legs and narrow hips. He was thirty-eight, but physically he looked no more than thirty. He had a good body, still fit and athletic. It was his face that frightened people.

He wore a thick beard and a mustache and his dark hair, while scrupulously clean, was unruly and thick around his collar. He wasn't bad-looking, but it was impossible to see that. He liked the camouflage, because it kept all but the most enthusiastic young groupies at bay.

None of the rock group looked much better than Hank with his growth of beard, except for Amanda, of course. The other three male members of the band—Deke and Jack and Johnson—looked as disreputable as Hank did. But Desperado's music won awards, and they were much in demand for public appearances.

The problem with that right now was that Amanda was pregnant. It would be the first child for Amanda and her husband, Quinn Sutton, who lived in Wyoming with his son Elliot. The whole family was anxious because Amanda's pregnancy had been fraught with problems and she'd been forced to take to her bed to prevent a miscarriage. That meant canceled public appearances and vicious rumors that the band was about to break up. It was let people think that, or admit that Amanda was in fierce difficulties with her pregnancy. No one wanted that tidbit of information to get out, and have reporters hounding her. For the moment, they didn't know exactly where in Wyoming she lived. And Hank was here in Colorado, far away from the group's studios—both the one down the hill from Quinn Sutton's ranch in the Tetons, and the one in New York City.

Reporters had hounded him so much that he'd had to escape from the New York studio where the group did some of their recording. It had been impossible to go near Amanda's house, for fear of leading reporters right to her doorstep.

So, this cabin in Colorado was Hank's last resort. He'd come here to work on a new song which he hoped might be a contender for another award. The music had been written, now it was up to Hank to complete the lyrics, but it was slow going. Worrying about Amanda and the future of the group was not conducive to creative effort.

Perhaps he was working too hard, he thought. He needed a break. That woman at the ski lodge was getting on his nerves. If she was a reporter spying on him, he wanted to know it. There had to be some way to get her off his trail and spare Amanda any further media blitz.

He shrugged into his parka and drove to the ski lodge in his white Bronco. The chains made a metallic rhythm on the thick-packed snow covering the road that led to the lodge. Bad weather had plagued the area this January, and there had just been a long period of subzero temperatures and blinding snow, which had made it impossible to ski for the past several days.

When he got to the lodge, it wasn't crowded at all. People who could get out had already gone. Only a handful of hearty, optimistic souls were left in residence, hoping for slightly less arctic temperatures and better skiing when conditions improved.

He walked into the lodge, towering over everyone and attracting a lot of unwanted attention. He went straight to the owner's office.

Mark Jennings got up from his desk and walked around it to shake hands with the visitor.

"What brings you down here, Hank?" he asked with a grin. "Lonesome, are you?"

"I should be so lucky," Hank murmured dryly. "I came down to see which one of your guests is auditioning for the KGB."

Mark's smile faded. "What?"

"You've got a guest with binoculars who spends

a lot of time looking in through my living room window," he replied. "I want to know who she is and what she's looking for."

Mark whistled. "I had no idea."

"It's not your job to watch the guests," the other man said, clapping him on the shoulder with a big hand. "Maybe she's a groupie. I'd like to know, in case she's trying to gather material for the wire services. I've had enough publicity just lately."

"I understand. What can I do to help?"

"I thought I'd hang out in the café for a while and see if she turns up for lunch. I'd recognize her. She's wearing a bright blue parka and a matching cap."

Mark frowned. "Doesn't sound familiar, but I don't get out of this office much lately. We don't have a lot of people staying here, though, so she shouldn't be too hard to spot."

"If you don't mind, I'll have a look around."

Mark nodded. "Help yourself. Any chance that you and the group might sign on next season for entertainment?" he added hopefully.

Hank chuckled. "Ask me again in a few months."

"Don't think I won't!"

Hank shook hands with him and went on into the café, shucking his parka as he walked. It was a bad time to have to hunt down a spy. He was already upset enough about Amanda and the relentless press. Lately his career was playing a bad second to complications of every sort.

He glanced around as he walked into the small café. There were only three women in it. Two of them were drinking coffee at a table overlooking the ski lift. The other was clearing tables. She saw Hank and grinned.

"Hi, Hank," she greeted him, tossing back her blond hair. "Long time no see!"

"I've been busy, Carol," he said with an affectionate smile. She'd been a waitress at Mark's place for several years. There was nothing romantic between them; she was just a friend.

She moved closer, so that they wouldn't be overheard. "Better watch your step down here today," she said confidentially. "One of the women at the side table is a reporter for *Rolling Stone*. I heard her telling the other woman that she'd gotten some juicy gossip about Amanda and that you were in hiding up here. She said she was going to file a really big story with her magazine over her computer modem tonight."

He caught his breath in muted anger and stared at the table intently. One of the women was very petite with short dark hair. The other was a redhead, attractive and full figured. He scowled. "Which is which?" he asked impatiently.

She grimaced. "That's the thing, I couldn't tell. I

dropped a plate and I wasn't looking at them when I overheard her. Sorry, Hank. You know most of their reporters, don't you?"

He nodded. "But I don't recognize either of those women. She could be a stringer or even a free-lancer, hoping to find something worth selling to them on a tentative go-ahead."

"I'll bet it's the redhead," she whispered. "She looks like a reporter."

"And I'd bet on the brunette," he remarked as he suddenly registered the color of her jacket. Royal blue. She was the one who'd been spying on him with the binoculars.

"Could be," Carol replied. "I wish I could be more help. Heard from the rest of the group?"

He shook his head. "We're all taking a rest from public appearances."

"I guess you need one! Give everyone my best, won't you?"

"Sure."

He watched the women from the next room, staying out of sight for a minute, before leaving the lodge. He was easily recognizable these days, with all the media attention, and he couldn't afford to give that reporter a shot at him.

He was going to have to do something, but what? If she filed that story, reporters were going to swarm Amanda like ducks on bugs. He couldn't have that.

Her pregnancy had been one big secret so far, ever since she started to show and the band cut short their tour. They were still recording, but no one knew why they'd left the road so quickly. Where Amanda was, on Quinn Sutton's ranch, no one was likely to be able to get near her. Quinn was a formidable bodyguard, and he loved his pretty blond wife to distraction even if they'd gotten off to one of the world's worst starts.

He leaned against the hood of the Bronco, ignoring the sudden snow flurries and folded his arms over his chest while he tried to decide on a course of action. How was he going to prevent the reporter from filing her story? All sorts of wild ideas occurred to him, the first being that he could cut the telephone wires.

"Great solution," he murmured to himself. "You should try writing fiction."

As he turned over possible solutions to his problem, lo and behold, the brunette came walking out the front door of the ski lodge with a camera and binoculars around her neck and a backpack over one shoulder. She came down the steps and started around the Bronco and Hank when the perfect solution presented itself to him on a silver platter.

Without thinking about consequences, jail terms or FBI intervention, he suddenly walked behind her, picked her up bodily and slid her into the Bronco past the steering wheel. Before she could get over the shock, he had the vehicle headed up the mountain.

Poppy O'Brien stared at him with wide dark eyes full of shock. "Either I'm still asleep and dreaming or I'm being kidnapped by a grizzly bear," she said suddenly.

"I'm not a grizzly bear."

"You look like a grizzly bear."

He didn't look at her. "Insults won't do you any good."

"Listen, I have terrible diseases…" she began, using a ploy she'd heard on a television talk show.

"Don't flatter yourself," he remarked with a speaking glance. "I don't seduce midgets."

"Midgets?" Her dark eyes widened. "I'm five foot five!"

He shrugged. "Okay. So you're a tall midget. You're still too small for a man my size."

She looked at him fully then. His head almost touched the roof of the Bronco. He was huge; not fat, but well built and powerful looking. "Are you one of those wild-eyed mountain men who kidnap hikers?"

He shook his head.

"Hopelessly lonely and desperate for companionship?"

He smiled reluctantly. "Not a chance."

"Then would you like to tell me why you've kid-napped me?"

"No."

She leaned back against the seat. He looked sane, but one could never tell. She studied him with curiosity and just a little apprehension. "What are you going to do with me?" she asked again.

"I don't know."

"That's reassuring."

"I won't hurt you."

"That's even more reassuring." She frowned as she studied him. "You look familiar."

"Everyone says that."

"Have you ever worn a wide-brimmed hat and asked people not to start forest fires?"

He did chuckle then. "Not lately."

"I'm on my way to look for a lost dog. I promised."

"He'll come home."

She glared at him. "After I've found the dog, I have to pack. I'm leaving tomorrow," she informed him.

"Fat chance."

She took in a sharp breath. "Now you listen here, Tarzan of the Snow Country, what you're doing is a federal offense. You could be arrested. You could go to jail."

"Why?"

"Because you're kidnapping me!"

"I'm doing no such thing," he returned, pulling up into the driveway of the cabin. "I'm extending my hospitality to a ski lodge guest who was lost in the mountains."

"I am not lost!" she stormed. "I was at the ski lodge, right in front of the ski lodge…!"

"You looked lost to me. It's snowing. Very hard, too," he remarked as he got out of the truck. In fact, it was worse than snow. It looked like the beginnings of a blizzard. "Come on. Let's get inside."

She folded her arms. "I am not leaving the truck," she informed him bluntly.

"It isn't a truck. It's a four-wheel-drive vehicle."

She lifted her chin. "Oh, details, details! I am not…ohh!"

In the middle of her impassioned resistance, he picked her up and carried her to the cabin.

She was too shocked to resist. She'd been independent most of her life, and at twenty-six she was used to being on her own. She was attractive, and she knew it, but she was also intelligent and studious, traits that didn't endear her to suitors. Her choice of career had made it impossible for her to carry on any sort of affair. She'd spent years in school with midterms and final exams always hanging over her head, with lab after lab eating up her free time. The only people she spent time with were fellow students. The curriculum required for a science degree was so much more difficult than that required for a liberal arts degree that it often seemed she did nothing but study.

And then after graduation, there was the apprenticeship, and that required all sorts of odd hours that none of the other partners wanted. She was the one who spent weekends and holidays and nights at work. Two boyfriends had quickly given her up for women who had nine-to-five day jobs and were geared to nights on the town.

None of that had prepared her for being swept off her feet, literally, by a blue-eyed grizzly bear.

The sheer power and size of his body had her as spellbound as a young girl. She lay in his huge arms like a statue, gaping up at him as he balanced her easily on one knee while he unlocked the cabin door.

He caught that rapt stare and laughed mirthlessly. He was used to the look. His ex-wife had found him fascinating at first. Afterward, it was his best friend and the man's bank account that fascinated her. The divorce was inevitable, with all the time Hank spent on the road. His best friend had probably been inevitable, too. Hank was powerful and talented, but he wasn't handsome. His best friend was. He'd given in to the divorce without a protest, and the parting had been amicable—on the surface, at least. He'd settled a nice amount of money on her. She was grateful. He was alone, as usual. He'd gone home afterward to the Texas ranch that his father and five brothers still owned. It had been comforting there, but he never had fit in. The only horse big enough for him to ride was a Percheron and he'd never been able to spin a rope. He often thought that his brothers despaired of him.

He put the woman down and closed the door, locking it and pocketing the key. Then he took a good, long look at her. She was attractive, pert and pretty and a little irritated. Her dark eyes glared up at him fearlessly.

"You can't keep me here," she informed him.

"Why not?"

"Because I have responsibilities. I have a job. I need a telephone right now, as a matter of fact, so that I can tell someone I'm not looking for that dog."

"Dream on," he said pleasantly. "Can you cook?"

Her eyebrows lifted. "Cook what?"

"Anything."

He was stripping off his parka as he spoke. Her eyes drifted over a magnificent body in jeans and a well-fitting, long-sleeved red shirt. He could have graced a magazine cover. He was perfectly proportioned and huge. He made her feel like a child as he towered over her.

"I can cook toast," she said absently. "How tall are you?"

"Six foot five," he said.

"You must eat like a horse."

He shrugged. "I use up a lot of calories."

She was still staring at him, fascinated. "Who are you?"

He laughed without humor and his blue eyes began to glitter. "Pull the other one."

"I beg your pardon?"

"You might as well get comfortable," he informed her. "You're going to be here for several days."

"I am not. I'll walk back to the lodge."

"Not in that you won't," he said, gesturing toward the window, where snow was coming down outside at a frightening rate.

She gnawed on her lower lip, a nervous habit that often resulted in a sore mouth. "Oh dear," she said uneasily, more worried about the possibility of losing her job than of being sequestered here with a madman.

"You'll be perfectly safe here," he said, mistaking her apprehension. "I won't attack you."

"Oh dear, oh dear," she repeated again. "They'll think I'm having too good a time to come back. They'll think I'm not serious about my job. They didn't really want me in the beginning because they thought I was too young. They'll use this as an excuse to find someone to replace me."

"No doubt," he said irritably. "But what does it matter? You'll find another job."

She glared at him. "Not like this one, I won't!"

"Pays good, does it?" he asked, thinking that reporters always seemed to get a high rate of pay for selling out people's private lives for public consumption.

"Very good," she retorted, "with excellent chances for advancement."

"Too bad."

"You have no right to keep me here," she informed him.

"You had no right to spy on me," he returned.

Her face stiffened. "I beg your pardon?"

"You've had those damned binoculars trained up here for the past few days," he said shortly. "Spying on me."

"Spying...and why, pray tell, would I want to spy on you? Do you think I'm so desperate for a man that I have to peek through windows to get a glimpse of one?"

"You don't need to play games with me," he said coolly. "I'm not likely to be taken in by you. I'm an old hand at fending off groupies."

"This is unreal," she snapped. "Things like this don't happen except in books and movies! Men don't go around kidnapping women unless it's a desert and they're wearing long sheets!"

"Sorry," he said. "I didn't have a sheet handy."

"And what do you mean, calling me a groupie?" She put her hands on her slim hips and glowered up at him with flashing dark eyes.

"Why were you spying on me?"

"Spying…!" She threw up her hands. "I was watching a bald eagle," she said shortly. "They've just released a pair of them ten miles north of the ski lodge, as part of a federal repopulation program. I'd come to see them."

"Oh, my God, tell me you're not one of those animal-loving fanatics!"

"If there were more of us in the world, it wouldn't be in such a mess."

He looked angry as he studied her. "They tried repopulating wolves up north. The damned things are eating lambs and calves all over the mountains, and the people who released them went back home to their apartment buildings."

He said it with such sarcasm and contempt that she almost took a step backward. But she was made of sterner stuff. "Nature exists largely on a system of checks and balances. You've overlooked the fact that without predators, prey multiplies. If you don't believe that, look at Australia where the rabbits hadn't enough natural enemies and overran the country."

"Well then, why don't we ship them some of our leftover wolves?" he asked smugly.

"Show me a wolf who can survive in the desert and it might be a good idea."

"You hotshot animal lovers might consider cross-breeding a wolf with a camel. I hear they're doing some fantastic genetic experiments in labs all over the country."

"To produce healthier animals and disease-resistant strains of plants."

"Hybrids," he scoffed. "Hybrids are sterile, aren't they?"

"I don't deal in experiments," she informed him hotly. "I wouldn't know."

"They turned loose two eagles. Isn't that an experiment?"

She was losing ground. "Why have you brought me here?" She tried again for an answer.

"I'm a lonely man," he said sarcastically. "I don't have any company up here, and I can't get girls. So periodically, I stake out the ski lodge and appropriate their overflow." He lifted an expressive hand. "Think of it as repopulating my bachelor environment with healthy new specimens. That should appeal to someone like you. And think of all the juicy material you can use later."

"Material? Use? For what?"

"Cut it out," he said carelessly. "We both know what you do for a living. I heard it all from Carol at the lodge."

"Carol? Oh, the blond waitress." She sighed. "Well, I guess it doesn't matter if you know, does it? I mean, I wasn't exactly hiding it from anyone."

"Just as I thought. Now. How about something to eat?" He indicated the window. "It's highly doubtful that you could go anywhere right now even if I was willing to let you leave. Which I'm not."

She pursed her full lips and stared up at him curiously. "When the snow clears, I'm heading out," she informed him sweetly. "Or you'll find yourself in jail the minute I can get to a telephone."

"Threats are only useful when you can enforce them."

"And you think I can't?"

"I think that by the time you leave, you won't need any." He was hopeful that he could convince her not to bother Amanda. He was persuasive when he tried to be, and if she liked animals, she had to have a soft center. Knowing the enemy was half the battle. He didn't think he was in for any surprises with her.

Chapter Two

"What's your name?" he asked as he fried bacon.

"Poppy O'Brien," she replied. "And yours?"

He chuckled. She was a game player, all right. "Call me Hank."

"Hank what?"

He glanced toward her with an insolent smile. "Just Hank," he said with faint challenge.

She joined him in the kitchen. "Have it your way. I suppose if I'd kidnapped someone I wouldn't want to give them my real name, either." She started opening cabinets.

"What are you doing?" he demanded. It irritated him that she felt free to rifle through his kitchen.

"I'm going to make biscuits. Unless you think you can."

"I can make biscuits," he said defensively.

"A lot of people can. But can you eat them?" she asked.

He hesitated. After a minute, he paused in his own chore and produced vegetable shortening, flour, milk and a big bowl. "Go for it."

She rolled up the sleeves of her blue sweater and proceeded to make drop biscuits. He'd finished with the bacon and was working on beating eggs in a bowl.

"They'll be cold by the time the biscuits get done if you cook them now," she said pointedly.

He didn't argue. He finished beating the eggs, covered the bowl and put them in the refrigerator. Then he perched himself on the edge of the big table and watched her pat the biscuits into a pan and dab milk onto the tops.

"You do that as if it's a regular thing with you," he commented.

"It is," she said. "I've been feeding myself for a long time. Eating out is expensive. I cook a lot."

"Do you cook for someone?" he probed.

She smiled as she put the biscuits into the oven she'd already had him preheat. "Yes. For myself."

He stuck his hands into his pockets and stared her down.

She lifted a shoulder. "I don't have time for that sort of thing," she said. "I work nights and weekends and holidays. Before I got this job, I was in school."

High school, he figured, by the look of her. She seemed very young. She wasn't hard on the eyes at all, with that trim figure and her big dark eyes and soft oval face. She had a vulnerable manner that appealed to his masculinity. His wife had been a take-charge sort of woman, very businesslike and intelligent, but with hard edges that he could never smooth. She liked being a real-estate executive and she had no thoughts of being a housewife and mother. She didn't like children. She did enjoy pretty clothes and parties, though. His best friend was taking her to a lot of those, he heard.

Poppy glanced at him and saw the expression that narrowed his deep blue eyes. "Do you have someone to cook for?" she asked bluntly. If he could ask questions, so could she.

"I was married," he said flatly. "She took up with my best friend and divorced me. I wasn't home enough to suit her."

"I'm sorry."

"Don't be. It was a friendly divorce. We weren't compatible." He looked down at his hand-tooled leather boots. "I wanted kids. I have a bunch of brothers back home."

She leaned back against the pine counter and

folded her arms across her chest. "I don't have any family left. My mother died when I was born and my father was killed in an airplane crash four years ago."

"Are you an only child?"

She nodded. "It's a good thing I was goal-oriented and self-sufficient, I guess," she confessed. "I threw myself into studying and got over it in time."

"How did you manage to support yourself while you got through high school?" he asked curiously.

"High school?" Her eyes widened. "I was in college." She laughed. "How old do you think I am?"

"Eighteen. Maybe nineteen."

She grinned. "Thanks. I'm twenty-six."

His heavy brows drew together. "Hell!"

"I am. I have a degree."

"In what—"

The thunderous, crashing sound outside cut him off. He rushed to the window and looked out. Snow had come off the mountain above the lodge in a small avalanche, taking down telephone lines and power lines.

"Good thing Mark's got emergency generators," he murmured. "So have I. But those telephone lines are well and truly out until this weather clears a little."

"Do you have a phone?" she asked from beside him.

He looked at her. "No. I've been using the phone

at the lodge. I hate telephones. Unlisted numbers are a farce—there's no such thing. You ought to know that."

She wondered how he did know that her private line was flooded with calls from people at two in the morning whose problems couldn't wait until the office opened.

She laughed. "Well, yes, I do know."

He glanced back out the window. "The lodge is okay, at least. I met a guy in the ski patrol this morning when I went out for supplies. He said they'd checked the slopes earlier and there was no threat. I wonder what caused the avalanche?"

"People skiing outside the safe boundary, a gunshot from an irresponsible hunter, God knows." She grimaced. "I hope that poor dog got found."

"Marshmallow heart," he accused. "The only dog I know of around here is a stray who hangs around the lodge for handouts. He belongs to a retired Austrian skier who lives about a half mile over the hill. That dog knows these mountains better than any human being, and he doesn't get lost. Somebody was pulling your leg." One eye narrowed. "Who sent you out?"

She frowned. "It was one of the younger ski instructors, the one they call Eric. He said that he'd start from the other end of the trail and we'd meet in the middle at some little cabin…" She stopped. "Why are you laughing?"

"Eric Bayer," he said, nodding. "They call him St. Bernard, because he's pulled that lost-dog stunt so many times with pretty young tourists. That cabin is almost a shrine to his prowess as a lover."

She flushed to her hairline. He watched, smiling.

"Where do you come from?" he asked lazily.

"Sioux City, Iowa," she said. "Why?"

"It figures." He moved back into the kitchen just in time to remove the biscuits before they burned. They looked light and fluffy and they were just tanned enough to be tempting. "Nice," he pronounced.

"Thanks." She got butter from the refrigerator while he scrambled the eggs. She made coffee and when the eggs were ready, she poured it into two thick mugs and put them on the small, square kitchen table.

"Forks," he said, handing her one. "I don't fuss with table settings when I'm alone here."

"Ah," she said. "So you're not usually alone?"

"Only when I'm working." He raised his fork and took a mouthful of scrambled egg. "And you should know," he added mockingly, "because *Rolling Stone* prints something about every visit I make here."

Her eyebrows arched. "Rolling Stone? They're a rock group, aren't they? I thought they were in England. Do they have a newsletter?"

"You do that amazingly well," he remarked.

"Do what?"

"The innocent look," he replied, finishing his eggs before he started on the biscuits. "I wish I had some jam. I ate the last of it yesterday and forgot to get more."

"Too bad. What was that about looking innocent?"

"Eat your lunch before it gets cold. These are great biscuits!"

They must have been, he was on his fourth one. She smiled. "Breakfast for lunch," she remarked. "I can't wait to see what you eat for the evening meal."

"Cereal, usually," he remarked. "Or sandwiches. I don't cook much when I'm working. If I get a yen for breakfast in the middle of the day, I have it," he added firmly.

She smiled. "I wasn't complaining. I love breakfast."

Her easy acceptance of the odd meal put him at ease. He finished eating and sat back with the coffee mug in one huge hand and looked at her. She was small. Not tiny, but small, and beautifully proportioned. He liked her soft complexion and those big brown eyes. She had a pretty mouth, too, very full and sweet-looking.

"I feel I should tell you that I know karate."

His eyebrows lifted. "Do you, really?"

She nodded.

He smiled lazily. "Do you really think it would do you any good against someone my size?" he asked gently.

She looked him over. "You ruined it."

"Ruined what?"

"I was going to tell you that I knew karate and several *other* Japanese words."

It took a minute to sink in. When it did, he began to laugh.

She smiled, too. "And to answer that, no, I don't think it would do me a bit of good against someone your size. Even if I knew how to use it." She finished her coffee and put the mug down. "Why did you think I was spying on you?"

"You kept looking in my living room window."

"The eagle was sitting on the top limb of one of those aspen trees behind your house."

He let out a soft whistle. "There really was an eagle?"

"Two of them," she amended. "Beautiful eagles. They're huge birds. I'd never seen any up close before. I thought they were small, but they aren't, and they have pale golden eyes."

"I've seen eagles," he replied. "I spend a lot of time here and in Wyoming."

"I'd love to see Wyoming," she remarked. "I've

always wanted to go to Cheyenne during the rodeo season."

"Don't you animal lovers consider rodeo a cruel sport?" he taunted.

"I'm not a fanatic," she said pointedly. "And I know better than some people how well treated most rodeo stock is. My dad used to handle bulls for the bull-riding events, back in Oklahoma."

"I thought you said you were from Sioux City."

"I live there now. I grew up outside Oklahoma City." She touched the rim of the coffee cup. "Where are you from?"

She was laying it on thick, but he was too tired to question her. He'd been up late for the better part of a week trying to write lyrics that just wouldn't come. "I'm from Texas, up near Dallas."

"Around the cross-timbers country?" She smiled at his surprise. "I've been through there a time or two with Dad, when he went to rodeos."

"It's pretty country. So is this."

The portable generator made a noise and he glared toward the back of the house. "Damn that thing," he muttered. "I knew I should have replaced it. If it goes out, we'll freeze and starve to death in here."

"Hardly," she said. "There's plenty of cut wood out front and you have a fireplace. I know how to cook on a fireplace."

"Good thing," he muttered. "I sure as hell don't."

"I gather that there's no way out of here except down the mountain we just came up?"

He nodded.

She looked out at the blinding snow and rubbed her arms. "You still haven't told me why you brought me up here."

"Does it matter now?" he asked. "You can't leave, anyway. From the looks of that snow, we're going to be cabin-bound for a few days until they can get the snowplows in."

"Well, yes, I think it does matter," she replied. "After all, nobody's ever tried to kidnap me before. I'd like to know what I've done."

"Why do you insist on playing games with me?" he muttered. "I know who you are!"

"Yes, you've already said so."

"Then you know what you've done," he said. "You threatened to call in a story that would damage several careers and possibly cost a woman her child."

"Call in a story." She repeated it again, staring blankly at him. "Call it in to whom? And how would I, since the only things I know how to fill out are medical reports?"

"Medical reports?"

She glowered at him. "Yes, medical reports, prescriptions, medicines, that sort of thing. I have a degree. I'm in practice. That's why I need to be back home, before I lose the partnership I've worked so hard to get!"

"You're a doctor?" he bellowed.

"Yes. Dr. O'Brien!"

He slapped his hand over his forehead. "Oh, God, I got the wrong one!"

"Wrong one. Am I to gather that you meant to kidnap some other poor woman?"

"Yes!" he said impatiently. He ran his hand through his bushy, thick hair. "Damn! Damn, damn, damn, she's probably halfway to New York by now with a heaving bosom full of unsubstantiated facts!"

"She, who?" Poppy demanded.

"That damn reporter!"

"The girl I was sitting with when you came in? But she isn't due to leave for two more days. She's meeting her fiancé in Salt Lake City and then they're going on to Los Angeles."

"She is?"

"That's what she said."

He leaned forward. "This is important. Did she say anything to you about Amanda Sutton?"

"I don't remember any names," she said. "She was talking about a singer who'd vanished from sight and the breakup of a big rock group."

"Which rock group?" he asked.

She grimaced. "Sorry," she said apologetically.

"I don't keep up with pop music. I like classical and opera."

He stared at her, long and hard.

"You needn't look like that," she muttered, sweeping back the fall of hair that dropped onto her brow. "There isn't one thing wrong with symphonies and opera!"

"I didn't know that anyone in the world still listened to them." From his perspective, rock music was all that existed. He spent all his time with people who composed it or played it.

"I see," she returned. "You're one of those MTV fanatics who think that music without a volcanic beat isn't worth listening to."

"I didn't say that."

"I am so *tired* of skeletal men in sprayed-on leather pants wearing guitars for jockey shorts, with their hairy chests hanging out!"

He couldn't hold back the laughter. It overflowed like the avalanche that had brought half a ridge down a few minutes before. "You're priceless."

"Well, aren't you tired of it, really?" she persisted. "Don't you think that there's a place in the world for historical music, beautiful music?"

He sobered quickly. He didn't know how to answer that. It had been a long time since he'd listened to anything classical, and he'd certainly never thought of it in that way. "Historical music?" he asked.

"Yes." She began to smile. "It's like talking to someone who lived a century, two centuries ago. You play the notes they wrote and hear them, just as they heard them. History comes alive in that moment, when you reproduce sounds that were heard in another time."

His heart leapt in his chest. He thought about the history she'd mentioned. Then her wording came back to him.

"You said you play the notes…do you play?"

"Piano," she said. "A little. I only had lessons for five years, and I'm not gifted. But I do love music."

His face softened under its thick covering of hair. "But not rock music," he persisted.

"So much of it is noise," she said. "After you listen to it for a while, it all blurs into steel guitars. But, once in a while, another sort of song sticks its head out and a few people find magic in it." She mentioned one of his songs, one of Desperado's songs. "There were a lot of flutes in it," she recalled, closing her eyes and smiling as she remembered it. "Beyond it was a high, sweet voice that enunciated every word. And the words were poetry." Her eyes opened, dark and soft with memory. "It was exceptional. But it wasn't their usual sort of music, either. The announcer said so. He said the composer did the song on a dare and didn't even want it included on the album, but the other members of the group insisted."

That was true. Hank had been certain that no one would like the soft, folksy song he'd written. And to his amazement, it had won a Grammy. He'd let Amanda accept it for him, he recalled, because he was too embarrassed to take credit for it publicly. "Did you see the video?"

She shook her head. "I've never had time to watch videos. I just listen to the radio when I'm driving."

Incredible. She loved his music and she didn't even know who he was. He wasn't sure if he was insulted or amused. It was the only song of that sort that he'd ever written and he'd sworn that he'd never do another one. A lot of the music critics hadn't liked it. He was trying to break out of the mold and they didn't want to let him. It was a kind of musical typecasting.

"Do you remember the group the reporter was talking about?" he asked, returning to his earlier question.

"She told me, but I was watching the eagle out the window," she confessed sheepishly, and with a grin. "I'm afraid I wasn't listening. She was alone and wanted to talk, and I was the only other person handy when she came in. She was friendly and I didn't mind sharing the table. It was just that the eagle came pretty close to the window..."

"You really do like animals." He chuckled.

"I guess so. I was forever bringing home birds with broken wings and once I found a little snake with its tail cut off by a lawnmower. I couldn't stand to watch things suffer and not try to help."

His blue eyes searched her dark ones for longer than he meant to. She stared back, and he saw the color flood her cheeks. That amused him deep inside and he began to smile.

Poppy felt her heart race. He didn't seem to be dangerous or a threat to her in any physical way, but that smile made her feel warm all over. She hadn't been at a disadvantage, except when he'd carried her inside the cabin. Now she wondered if she shouldn't have fought a little harder for her freedom. He was very big and powerful, and if he wanted to, he could...

"You're amazingly easy to read," he remarked gently. "There's nothing to be nervous about. I don't force women. It's the other way around."

She didn't quite believe him. He had a fantastic physique, but he looked like a grizzly bear. She couldn't imagine him being beset by women.

"Are you rich?" she asked.

His eyes narrowed and the smile faded. "Meaning that I'd have to be rich to attract a woman?" he drawled with muted anger.

He hadn't moved or threatened, but the look in his eyes made her uncomfortable. "I didn't say that."

"Yes, you did."

"I didn't mean to insult you. It's just that you're, well, you're…bushy."

His lips compressed. "Bushy?"

"You look like a grizzly bear!"

"A lot of men wear beards and mustaches!"

"Most of them have some skin on their faces that shows, too!"

He moved away from the window and took a step toward her. She took a step back.

"There's no need to start stalking me," she protested, looking him right in the eye. She stopped. "I won't run. You can't make me run. I'm not afraid of you."

She acted like a woman confronting an attack dog. It would have amused him if he'd been a little less insulted.

"I haven't had to chase women in ten years," he said through his teeth, and kept coming. "They chase me. They hound me. I can't even check into a hotel without having someone search the room. I could have a woman twice a day if I felt like it, and I wouldn't have to pay them for it. I turn down more proposals in a week than you've probably had in your lifetime. But you think I look like a grizzly bear and no woman would want me unless I was rich."

She held up a hand, nervous of him now. "I didn't say that at all," she began soothingly. She came up against something hard, and realized that he'd edged her back against a wall. "Now, see here," she said firmly, "this isn't any way to win an argument, with sheer brute force."

"Isn't that what you think I'd need to get a woman?"

"I didn't mean it," she assured him. She tried to edge past him, but he put an arm that was like a small tree trunk past her on one side and another on the other side and trapped her.

"What makes you think you're qualified to judge?" he continued irritably. "You're almost thin. There's nothing to you. You act as if you've spent your life buried in books. What do you know about men?"

"I date," she said shortly. "In fact, I can go out anytime I like!" And she could, with one of her partner's sons, who seemed to have six hands and used every one of them the time she'd been crazy enough to go to a movie with him. He'd have taken her out again if she liked, but she wouldn't go to the front door with him!

"How much do you have to pay him?" he mocked.

When that sank in, she drew in an angry breath, forgot her embarrassment and fear and raised her hand sharply toward his hairy cheek.

He caught it with depressing ease and pressed it against the side of his face. The hair that grew on it was surprisingly soft, when it looked like steel wool.

"You don't know much about men's egos, do

you?" he asked, bending. "If you don't learn one other thing, you'd better learn right now that insults have consequences. And I'm just the man to show you how many!"

She started to defend herself, and before she could get a single word out, his lips had opened and fitted themselves exactly to the shape of her soft, shocked mouth.

Chapter Three

It hadn't occurred to her that a human grizzly bear would be so good at kissing. He wasn't clumsy or brutal. He was slow and almost tender. Even the huge hands that slid around her waist and brought her lazily against him were all but comforting.

He nibbled at her upper lip where it clung stubbornly to her lower one. "It won't hurt," he breathed softly. "Give in."

"I won't…"

The parting of her lips gave him the advantage he'd been looking for. He eased them open under his with a pressure that was so slow and arousing that she stood, stunned, in his embrace.

He towered over her. At close range, he was even larger than he'd seemed at first. His big hands spread over her back, almost covering both her shoulder blades, and he smiled against her shocked gasp. His teeth gently worried her lower lip while his tongue trailed over it, and she thought dizzily that she'd never known such an experienced caress from the few, the *very* few, men she'd dated.

He felt her stiffen and lifted his head. The blue eyes that searched her dark ones were wise and perceptive. His hand came up and traced the soft color that overlaid one high cheekbone.

"You taste of coffee," he murmured.

It was beginning to dawn on her that he might not be lying about his success with women. And she didn't think it was because he was rich. Not anymore.

He didn't see fear in her face, or experience. He saw a charming lack of it. His big thumb smoothed over her lips and her body seemed to leap into his at the sensation he produced.

"Nothing to say, Poppy?" he asked.

She shook her head, her eyes unblinking as they sought his for reassurance.

"You're perfectly safe," he replied, answering the look. "I'm not a rake, even if I do fit the picture of a kidnapper. But I had noble motives."

"You're...very big, aren't you?" she faltered.

"Compared to you," he agreed. His eyes narrowed as he studied her. She did look very small in his arms. He looked down to her breasts, pressed against his shirt. She barely came up to his chin and she had a fragile build. If he made love to her, it would be touch and go, because she was so much smaller. He scowled.

"What's wrong?" she asked curiously.

He met her eyes. "I was thinking about how careful I'd have to be with you in bed," he said absently.

She flushed and pushed at him. "You'd be lucky!" she raged.

He smiled at her ruffled fury and let her go. "Wouldn't I, though?" he agreed lazily. Her red face told him things she wouldn't. "You're very delicately built. I've deliberately limited myself to tall, buxom women because I'm so big. Do you know, I can't even let myself get into fistfights unless I can find another man my size?"

She studied him, under the spell of a hateful attraction. Her heart was still racing. His shirt was open at the neck and there was a dark, thick nest of hair in it. She wondered what he looked like under his clothes and could have choked on her own curiosity.

"You never told me what you do," she said, diverting her eyes to his face.

"I used to play professional football," he volunteered.

She frowned, searching his features. "I'm sorry. I don't watch it. I'm not much of a sports fan."

"It figures. It was a long time ago."

That explained how he could afford this nice cabin in such a luxury area of the state. He'd probably made a fortune in professional sports and saved a lot of it. It would explain the women, too. All at once, it bothered her to think of him with women.

She wrapped her arms over her breasts. "How long will that last, do you think?" she asked, nodding toward the snowstorm.

"A couple of days," he said. "I'll get you back to the lodge as soon as I can, I promise." He sighed heavily, wondering where that reporter was, and if she'd managed to get out. "I fouled this up really good," he muttered. "Poor Amanda. She'll never forgive me if they get to her."

Amanda? She frowned. "Have I missed something?"

"Probably." He turned away. "I'll check on that generator. I don't have a television here, but there's a piano and plenty of books. You ought to be able to amuse yourself."

"Thanks."

He paused as he shouldered into his parka and

looked at her. "If you don't get back to your job, they won't really fire you, will they?"

"I don't know." It worried her. She interpreted his expression and smiled ruefully. "Don't worry. I'd be stuck at the lodge anyway, even if you hadn't kidnapped me, wouldn't I?"

That seemed to lessen the guilt she read on his face. "Maybe. Maybe not. I'm sorry. I'll make it up to you, if I can. I should have made sure before I acted."

"What were you going to do with that reporter?" she asked.

"I was going to keep her here until I could warn Amanda," he said. "She's not having an easy time of it and all the wire services are after the story. I thought I was safe here, but they can track you down anywhere."

Amanda must be his girlfriend, because he was trying so hard to protect her from the press. She wondered why. "Is she married?" she asked involuntarily.

"Yes," he said solemnly. "I'll be back in a minute."

So that was it, she thought as he left the cabin. He was in love with a married woman and the newspapers were after him. He must be somebody very famous in sports to attract so much media attention even if he didn't play football anymore. She wished she'd paid more attention to sports. He was probably very famous and she'd go home without even knowing his name. She thought whimsically of selling her story to the tabloids— "I was kidnapped by a football star…" But of course she couldn't do that, because she didn't even know his full name.

She wandered out of the huge living room and down the hall. There were two bedrooms, one with a huge, king-size bed and the other with a normal bed. They were nicely decorated and furnished, and each had its own bathroom. Farther down was a room with all sorts of electronic equipment, including speakers and recorders and wires and microphones, a huge keyboard, an electric guitar and a piano. She stood in the doorway, fascinated.

After a minute, she approached the piano, drawn by the name on it. She knew that name very well; it was the sort of instrument even a minor pianist dreamed of being able to afford. It must be his hobby, playing, and he must be very rich to be able to buy something so astronomically expensive to indulge that hobby on.

Her fingers touched the keys and trembled. It was in perfect tune. She sat down on the bench, remembering when she was a child how she'd dreamed night after night of owning a piano. But there had been no money for that sort of luxury. She'd played on other people's pianos when she was invited, and along the way she'd picked up some instruction. Eventually, when her father died, she was left with a huge insurance policy that she hadn't even wanted; she'd wanted her parent back. But the money had put her through college, bought her a small, inexpensive piano and lessons to go with it. And it had made it possible for her to make her own way in the world. She didn't earn a lot just now, but if she could continue in the partnership—if they didn't fire her—she had prospects.

She put her trembling hands on the keyboard, thinking that if she'd had the opportunity to study as a child, she might have made music her life.

She closed her eyes and began to play the *Moonlight Sonata,* softly at first, and then with more power and pleasure and emotion than she'd ever felt before. This magnificent instrument was all hers to enjoy, and enjoy it she did. When the last chord died into the stillness, she came back to her surroundings with a jolt as she realized that she wasn't alone in the room.

She turned around. Hank was there, leaning against the doorway, something in his eyes that she couldn't grasp. He wasn't smiling. His face was somber and oddly drawn.

"I'm sorry!" she stammered, rising quickly to her feet. "I didn't mean to presume..."

"Why aren't you playing professionally?" he asked surprisingly.

She stared at him blankly. "I chose medicine instead of music."

"A noble choice, but you have a gift. Didn't you know?"

She looked around her, embarrassed. "You play, too, I guess? Is it a hobby?"

He smiled to himself. "You might say that."

"I've never thought of a football player as a musician," she said quietly. "It's…surprising."

"Some people think so. I'm too damned big for most hobbies. At least music fits me."

She smiled gently and turned her attention back to the piano. She touched it with loving fingers. "She's lovely, isn't she?" The wonder in her voice was evident. "A real lady."

He was touched and delighted by her unconscious reverence. "That's what I call her," he remarked. "Odd that you'd think the same way, isn't it?"

"I guess a lot of people love music."

"Yes. Even football players."

She laughed self-consciously, because he sounded bitter. "Did that sting? I'm sorry. I didn't mean to sound disparaging. I've never known anybody in sports before. I know a little about baseball, and once I met a minor-league baseball player."

"The thrill of your life?"

"Oh, no, getting my degree was that." She glanced at him uneasily. Some people were immediately hostile when she mentioned her extensive education.

He lifted a bushy eyebrow. "Fitting me for a mold?" he mused. "Will you faint if I tell you that I have a degree of my own?"

Her eyes brightened. "Really?"

"I'm a music major," he said.

"I'll bet that gave the sports announcers something to talk about during games—" She stopped dead. Things she'd read and heard on television, bits and pieces were coming back to her. She didn't follow sports, but there was one sports figure who'd confounded the critics and the fans when he suddenly dropped out of professional football to found of all things a rock group. He'd only had a mustache then, not a full beard and long hair besides. She'd seen his photograph in the paper, and she'd seen an interview on television.

"Oh, my God," she said in a whisper.

"Put it together, did we?" he mused, smiling. "Go ahead."

"Desperado," she said. "You played for the Dallas Cowboys and quit after the best season you'd ever had to go into music. Everybody thought you were crazy. Then you won a Grammy…"

"Several Grammies," he said, correcting her.

"Several. Amanda is your lead singer," she added,

remembering that tidbit. "She's beautiful. But…didn't she marry?"

He chuckled. "Yes. She married a poor Wyoming rancher and she's very, very pregnant and Quinn Sutton is beside himself with worry. She's not having an easy time. We're trying to protect her from the press and it hasn't been easy. We're all afraid that word is going to get out about her problems with the pregnancy and she's going to be covered up by the press."

"We?"

"The group," he said. "She's very special to all of us, although she and Quinn are deeply in love."

"Are you in love with her?" she asked bluntly.

"I was, in the old days," he said easily. "We all were. She's beautiful and talented. But now she's kind of like a kid sister that we try to take care of. I'd do anything to protect her. Even," he added ruefully, "kidnap a reporter."

"That would have been terribly intelligent," she said sarcastically. "What a story it would make!"

"I didn't say I was thinking clearly," he muttered darkly. "I had to act fast, before she could file that story. And look what a great job I did!"

"Anybody can make a mistake. But she doesn't know about Amanda, you know," she added. "She knew that you were here and she was going to tell her office that a man at the lodge said you were about to get engaged to someone you met here. *That's* the hot scoop she had."

He leaned back against the door and laughed delightedly. "Good God!"

"So it doesn't really matter if she gets to a phone, does it?"

"No." He groaned and ran a hand through his thick hair. "Hell, I could have saved myself all this trouble!"

"Not to mention saving me a little," she said irritably.

He looked surprised. "I saved you from St. Bernard."

Her lips protruded. "I don't need saving from a man like that. He had lips like a lizard."

He chuckled. "Did he?"

She closed the lid on the piano. "He wasn't my type at all."

He moved closer and raised the lid. "What is your type?" he asked as he ran his elegant fingers over the keyboard.

"I'll know the minute I find him," she assured him.

He lifted his head and looked into her dark eyes. "You don't like rock music, you said."

"I don't listen to it," she confessed. "Except that one song that I told you about."

"Yes. This one."

He sat down at the piano and began to play it, softly, smoothly, his eyes seeking hers.

"It was you," she said slowly.

He nodded. "Amanda sang it. I don't have a lead voice, only one good enough to second the rest of them. But I can write music. None of them can."

She came to stand just behind him, with a soft hand on his shoulder as he increased the tempo.

"I meant it to be a rock song. Amanda made me slow it down. They ganged up on me and made me put it on the album. I didn't want to."

"Why?"

"Because it's intimate," he said shortly. "It's part of me, when I do something like this. There are things I don't want to share with the world."

"You should share music like this, though," she replied. "It's exquisite."

He smiled at her. "But you like opera. And historical music."

Her fingers became unconsciously caressing on his shoulder. "Yes. But this is beautiful."

He finished the piece and lifted his hands from the keyboard. She hadn't moved.

He reached up and smoothed his fingers over her hand before he lifted it to his mouth.

He swiveled around and caught her by the hips, his eyes darkening, narrowing as they looked up at her.

She felt him move before she saw him. He drew her to him and eased her to her knees between his outstretched legs. Then he framed her face in his big hands and bent to kiss her with slow, tender hunger. She started to protest, but he stayed the instinctive backward movement of her head and kept kissing her, until she gave in to him and slid her arms around his neck.

It wasn't until his hand trespassed onto her soft breast that she stiffened and caught his fingers.

He lifted his head and looked at her flushed face as she fought with his invading hand. There was something very calculating about his expression.

"You're...analyzing me," she accused.

"You aren't used to a man's hand on your breast," he commented, watching her gasp. "You're twenty-six, right? Then why haven't you had a man, Poppy?"

"For heaven's sake!" She pushed at him and he let her go. She scrambled to her feet, pushing back her hair, and stared unseeing out the window while she fought for composure.

He joined her at the window, leaning idly against the window frame with his big hands in his pockets. "Are you physically or emotionally scarred in some way?"

She shook her head.

"Then, why?"

She frowned. "What do you mean, why?"

"Why haven't you slept with anyone yet?"

He seemed to think it was a matter of course, that women had the same freedom that men did and should enjoy it.

"Well, I don't respect men who sleep around just because they want to satisfy a fleeting physical hunger. Why should I want to be that way myself?"

He frowned. "Everyone sleeps around."

"Bull," she said, raising her hand when he started to speak. "And don't quote me statistics. Statistics depend on whom you interview. If you ask two hundred people in New York City what they think of a free sexual life-style, and then you ask the same question of two hundred people in a small town in Iowa, you're going to get a heck of a different set of statistics!"

His big shoulders moved. "I hadn't thought about it that way. But the times are changing."

She only smiled.

"Don't tell me," he chided gently. "You're going to save yourself for the man you marry."

"Of course I am," she said matter-of-factly.

He threw up his hands. "Lunacy," he muttered. "You don't know what you're missing."

"Sure I do. I'm missing all those exciting risks, including the one that can kill you." She pursed her lips as she studied him. "And if we're going to get so personal, how much of a swinger are you?"

"I'm not," he replied, shocked. "Only an idiot sleeps around these days!"

She burst out laughing.

He liked the way she laughed, even the way she lost her temper. "Want to draw straws to see who gets to cook supper?"

She traced his face with soft eyes. "I'll do it, if you'll tell me what you like. Not cereal," she added.

"Steak and baked potatoes and salad, then," he said.

"I like steak, too."

"Two of each for me," he added. "I have to get enough protein."

"I'll bet you're expensive to feed," she remarked.

"Yes. But I'm rich," he added with a meaningful glance.

"I take it all back, what I said about buying women for yourself," she told him pertly.

"Oh?"

The expression on his face was only faintly threatening, but she left him with the piano, just the same.

They shared meals and conversation for two days. He didn't come near her in any sexual way, although she caught his gaze on her. He wasn't feeling well. His skin was flushed and he had a terrible cough. He'd been out working on that generator her first day at the cabin, and he hadn't really been dressed properly for the cold and the vicious snow. He'd caught a cold and it had gone into his chest. She was worried now, because he was obviously feverish and there was no telephone, no way to get him to a hospital. When he went to bed, he refused to take even an aspirin.

She went to bed in the guest room, reluctantly, hoping that he'd be better the next day even when she knew in her gut that he wouldn't.

The third morning, he didn't get up. If only she had access to her supplies back at the clinic in Sioux City, she could have used enough antibiotic to do him some good. As it was, she could only hope that he had a virus or the flu and not pneumonia. If it was a bacterial pneumonia, he could die if help didn't come in time.

She went into his bedroom to check on him, and had to force her legs to carry her the rest of the way. He'd thrashed his way out of the covers and he was lying there totally nude on top of the sheet and blanket. Her embarrassed eyes couldn't leave him. She'd never seen a man in such a condition before. He was beautiful without his clothing, tanned all over, with just enough body hair to make him attractive to the sight and not enough to make him repulsive. It was all on his chest and flat stomach, black and curling hair that ran over his broad chest in a wedge and down over the ripple of powerful muscles to his flat stomach and powerful thighs. Her eyes lingered there with curiosity and fascination and a little fear. She didn't need anyone to tell her that this man was physically exceptional.

He groaned and his eyes opened. He was flushed with fever, his lips dry, his body lifting as he coughed and grimaced from the pain.

"I've picked up that damned bug my band had," he said hoarsely. "Getting chilled working on the generator must have pushed me over the edge." He sat up, realized his condition and with a rueful smile, jerked the sheet over his hips. "Sorry. I must have kicked off the covers. But then, you're a doctor. I don't suppose you're easily shocked by a man's body."

She wasn't about to answer that.

He lay back and coughed again. She moved a little closer, grimacing. "We're going to have a problem if you get worse. Your medicine cabinet is inadequate and I don't have my bag. I don't even have the right medicines or enough of them. The best I'm going to be able to do is mix up a folk remedy for cough and give you aspirin for fever."

"I don't need nursing," he told her.

"Of course not," she agreed. "Oh dear, oh dear."

He closed his eyes, too weary to talk anymore, and fell asleep. She spent the rest of the day sitting by his bedside in a chair, trying to keep his fever down with aspirin and his cough at bay with a mixture of honey, lemon and whiskey. Amazingly the cough remedy seemed to do some good. But the fever didn't go down, despite the aspirin.

The generator was holding, thank God, so it was warm in the cabin. She had to get that fever down. He did at least have a thermometer, but what it registered was hardly reassuring. A high fever could burn up the very cells of the body. She had to stop it.

She got a basin of warm water and a washcloth and towel. With a deep breath as she gathered her nerve, she turned the covers back.

He lay quietly until she began to bathe him, then he groaned harshly and opened his eyes. "What are you doing?" he asked in a weak, raspy tone.

"Trying to get the fever down," she said. "I'm sorry, really I am. But this is the only way I know. The aspirin is only holding it at bay. It's very high. I'll try not to let you get chilled in the process."

"Stroke of luck, kidnapping you," he said with wan humor. "And they say you can't find a doctor when you need one."

She winced, but his eyes had closed again and he didn't see it. She kept on sponging him down, drying him with the towel as she went and feeling his skin slowly begin to cool.

It wouldn't have been so complicated if his body hadn't started reacting to the motion of the washcloth against areas that were normally hidden to the eyes.

He groaned again when she reached his flat stomach and his eyes opened as his powerful body suddenly reacted helplessly—and visibly—to her touch.

She drew her hand back at once and blushed to the roots of her hair. The terrible thing was that she couldn't drag her eyes away. She was paralyzed by the forbidden sight, fascinated and shocked.

"It's all right, Poppy," he said huskily. "Don't be embarrassed. It's a natural reaction, even if it seems shocking to you."

Her wide eyes sought his for reassurance.

"Go ahead," he said gently. "Don't worry about it. We'll both ignore it. Okay?"

She hesitated for a minute, but as the shock wore off, she began to weigh her embarrassment against his state of health. "Sorry," she said as she continued, working her way down his powerful legs.

"You're a doctor," he murmured, but he was watching her narrowly. "Aren't you?"

"Well, yes. Sort of."

His eyebrows lifted. "Sort of?"

She cleared her throat as she finished sponging him down and gently pulled the cover up to his waist, averting her eyes as she did so. "Yes. I am a doctor. I have a degree and a diploma to prove it. But…"

"But?"

"Well…I'm not exactly the sort of doctor you think I am." She put the basin and cloth on the floor by the bed.

"What sort are you?" he persisted.

She bit her lower lip and looked at him guiltily. "I'm a veterinarian," she confessed.

Chapter Four

"You're a what!"

"Please lie down, and don't get excited," she pleaded, pushing him gently back against the pillows. "And it's all right, really, I did have two years of premed, so I'm not a dunce about human anatomy."

"I don't believe this," he groaned, throwing a big arm across his eyes. "My God, I'm being treated by a vet!"

"I'm a good vet," she muttered. "I haven't lost a patient yet. And you shouldn't complain about being treated by a vet, if you insist on looking like a grizzly bear!"

She got up from the bed and walked out with the

basin and cloth and towel, fuming. He acted as if she were guilty of malpractice, and she'd been nursing him all night long!

He must have thought about that, because when she went back into the bedroom, he was more subdued.

"I'm sorry," he said shortly. "It was a shock, that's all. I don't guess you slept all night, did you?"

"I slept in the chair there," she said. "I was nervous about leaving you with such a high fever."

"Thanks."

"I'd have done the same for any sick animal," she replied.

"Rub it in," he said with a wan smile.

She smiled at him. "I'd love to."

He was barely strong enough to glower at her. "What if you catch this stuff?"

"Then I guess you'll have to look after me, if the blizzard doesn't stop," she informed him.

He lifted an eyebrow and let his eyes work their way up and down her slender body with a speaking glance. "I'd get to sponge you down, then, huh?" He smiled wickedly. "What a thrill."

She flushed. "You stop that! I didn't enjoy it!"

"Didn't you? I thought you were familiar with a man's anatomy until I saw that scarlet blush. I wondered if you were going to faint." His blue eyes narrowed. "You haven't seen a naked male like this before, have you?"

She moved restlessly. "I've seen lots of naked male dogs," she said defiantly.

He chuckled, stifling a cough. "It's not quite the same thing."

She could have agreed wholeheartedly with that, but she wasn't going to. She pushed back her hair with a weary hand. "If you'll be all right for a few minutes, I'll heat up some soup."

"You're tired. Why don't we both sleep for a little while, and then you can worry about food."

"Are you sure?"

"I'm sure. I don't feel half as bad as I did last night. Go on. Grab a couple of hours' sleep. I'll wake you if I need you."

"How will I hear you?" she asked worriedly. "The guest room is down the hall…."

"Curl up beside me, if you're concerned about that. It's a big bed."

She wasn't sure, and it showed.

"Don't be silly," he said gently. "I'm too sick to be a threat."

He was. She gave in, smiling shyly as she went around to the other side of the bed and lay down, all too aware of the expanse of his hair-roughened chest, the length of his powerful body. He was really huge this close and she'd never been more aware of her lack of stature. Of course, beside him, a six-foot woman would seem small. She curled up under the covers and stifled a yawn.

"Don't you want to put on something less constraining?" he said. "I won't look."

She smiled. "I'm too tired even to do that. I could sleep for…a week…." Her voice trailed off. She was out like a light.

It was dark when she woke up. A night-light was on and Hank was snoring gently beside her. He'd knocked the covers off again, but it was chilly now. She got up and went around the bed to replace them, pulling them up over his chest and tucking them over him. He looked younger when he was asleep, relaxed and unstressed. She wondered what he was like when he wasn't upset or sick. She'd probably never have the chance to find out, because he was famous and she was a nobody in the veterinary practice back home. It would be something to remember, though, that she'd known someone like him, even briefly. Under normal circumstances, she was certain that they'd never have met at all.

She went into the kitchen and heated some soup. He must be hungry. He was a huge man. He needed nourishment.

She carried the bowl of soup back into the bedroom and put it on the bedside table before she shook him awake.

"Let me take your temperature first, then I'll feed

you," she said, sitting beside him on the bed. She put the thermometer under his tongue and he watched her while she timed it. It beeped just as she'd counted off a minute.

"It's down!" she said, delighted.

"Of course it's down, it was only a virus," he muttered.

"How can you be so sure?"

"Damned if I know. I'm not a vet," he said, drawling out the word.

"I still know more about medicine than you do," she said curtly, reaching for the soup.

"The hell you do. I've had more operations and been in more emergency rooms than you'll ever see over the years."

With all sorts of football injuries, no doubt, she thought, but she didn't argue. He was obviously feeling better and spoiling for a fight.

"Eat," she demanded, holding a spoon of chicken noodle soup to his firm lips.

"I hate chicken soup."

"It's made with real chickens," she said coaxingly.

"Prove it."

She put the spoonful back into the bowl and searched until she found a tiny cube and produced it for him to see. "There!"

"Right. A square chicken. A microscopic square chicken."

"You really must feel better," she said pointedly. "You're being very unpleasant."

"I have a reputation for being very unpleasant," he informed her. "Ask the group."

"You're one of them. They wouldn't admit it. They'd lie for you. They wouldn't want your adoring public to know what a bad man you really were."

"Point taken." He laid back against the propped pillows with a sigh. "Okay. Go ahead. Feed me."

She did, liking the power it gave her. She smiled, enjoying herself. She'd never had anyone to take care of, because her father had never been sick. She took care of animals but it really wasn't the same.

He was enjoying her tender ministrations, too, and hating to admit it. "I'll be back on my feet by tomorrow," he said. "So don't get too fond of this routine."

"God forbid," she agreed.

But he let her feed him the entire bowl of soup, and the warm feeling it gave him wasn't just from the temperature of the liquid. Afterward, he stretched and then relaxed with a long sigh. "God, I'm weak. I feel as if I don't have enough strength to get up." He smiled grimly. "But I've got to, for a minute." He threw back the cover, ignoring her flush, and got to his feet. He staggered a little, and she forgot her discomfort in the rush of concern she felt.

She got under his powerful arm and helped support him.

"Thanks," he said, starting toward the bathroom. "I feel like I've been clotheslined."

"I guess you do. I'm sorry you're sick."

His arm tightened. "You'd better be glad of it," he said grimly as he noticed her shyly appreciative eyes on his body. "I like having you look at me like this. I like it too damn much."

She felt pulsing heat run through her body, and quickly averted her eyes. "I'm not looking," she said at once.

"Of course you're looking. You can't help it. I fascinate you, don't I?"

She glared up at him. "I'll find you some shorts."

"I won't wear them," he returned with a cool smile. "I'm not changing the habit of a lifetime to satisfy some prudish animal doctor."

"I am not a prude!"

"Right."

She refused to notice his amused expression. She helped him to the bathroom door, waited until he called her and then helped him back to bed, averting her eyes while she tugged the sheet up to his waist.

He sighed, his chest rattling a little. He propped

himself up on the pillows and coughed, reaching for a tissue.

"It's a productive cough, at least," she said to herself. "That's a blessing. And if the fever's dropping, hopefully, it's a viral bronchitis and not pneumonia."

He lifted an eyebrow. "Well, you sound professional enough."

"Medicine is medicine," she said pointedly. "Of course, the anatomical structure is a bit different and the pharmacology certainly is, but ways to treat illnesses are basically the same."

He didn't feel like arguing. He yawned widely. "I'm so tired," he said softly. "So tired. I feel as if I haven't had any rest in years."

"From what you've said, I wonder if you've had any rest at all," she remarked. "Perhaps being stuck up here is a godsend."

"I wouldn't say that," he murmured. "The only good thing about it is that reporter doesn't know about Amanda. God forbid that she should cause trouble. Most of that magazine's reporters are topnotch."

"She doesn't work for a magazine," she recalled. "She said she was trying to sell a story that would get her foot in the door. But she was also on the trail of some sports star who was supposed to be hiding out in the Tetons up in Wyoming."

"A hopeful," he said, relieved.

"She was pretty optimistic. And very ambitious."

He fingered the sheet. "Something you should know about."

"I only want to work in a partnership and not have to do all the rough jobs and odd hours," she said wistfully. "I was lucky to get the partnership at all. There are four of us in the practice, but I'm the junior one. So until I prove myself, I can't really expect much free time."

"It sounds to me as if they're the lucky ones," he muttered. "Are they all men?"

She nodded. "All older than me, too. I'm just out of college and full of new ideas, new theories and treatments and they think I'm a hotshot so they won't listen."

"You probably make them feel threatened," he said pointedly. "And as to who's the lucky one, I think it's the other partners, not you. They're getting all the benefits and none of the unpleasant work."

"I could hardly open my own practice fresh out of school," she began.

"Why not? Plenty of people do!"

"I'm not rich," she said. She went to the window and looked out. The snow was still coming down without a break in sight in the sky. "I barely had enough money in the bank to finish school, and part of it was done on government student loans. I have a lot to pay back. That doesn't leave much over for furnishing an office."

"I see."

She shrugged and turned back with a smile. "I don't mind working my way up from the bottom. Everybody has to start somewhere. You did."

It was a nicely disguised question. He adjusted the pillows and leaned back again. "I started as a second guitarist for a group that got lost at the bottom of the pop charts. Eventually I worked up to helping do backup work for some of the better musicians. That's how I met Amanda Sutton—she was Amanda Corrie Callaway back then," he added with a smile. "She and I started working together on a project, along with another guy in the band, and we discovered that Amanda had a voice like an angel. It didn't take us long to put an act together, add a drummer and a second guitarist, and audition for a record company." He shook his head remembering. "We made it on the first try. Amazing, that, when some people take years just to get a record company executive to listen to them."

"Didn't it help that you'd been a football star?"

"Not in music," he replied with a rueful smile. "I was a nobody like the rest of the group until our first hit."

"Why the name Desperado?" she asked.

"You've never seen a group shot of us, I gather?"

She smiled apologetically. "Sorry."

"Look in the top drawer of the desk over there against the wall." He pointed toward it.

She opened it and there was a photograph of four men and a woman.

"Now do you need to ask why?" He chuckled.

"Not really." They were a frightening bunch, the men all heavily bearded and mustached with unruly hair, and they looked really tough. Amanda was a striking contrast, with her long blond hair and dark eyes and beautiful face.

"We've been lucky. Now, of course, we may really have to stop performing. It all depends on how Amanda is doing." He looked briefly worried. "I hope she's all right. I can't even telephone to ask how she is. At least I know Quinn won't let anything happen to her. He's a wild man where Amanda is concerned."

She thought about having someone that concerned for her welfare and wondered how it would feel. Her father had cared about her, but no one else had since he died. She'd been very much alone in the world.

She picked up the soup bowl, but her mind not at all on what she was doing.

He didn't understand the sadness in her face. He reached out and caught her wrist. "What's wrong?" he asked softly.

She shrugged. "I was wondering what it would be like to have someone worry that much about me," she said, and then laughed.

He let go of her wrist. He'd been wondering the same thing. His lean hand smoothed over the bedcover. "I want a bath. Do you suppose you could run some water for me?"

"You're very weak," she cautioned. "And what if you get chilled?"

"It's warm in here. Come on. I can't stand being grungy."

"Grungy?"

He chuckled. "Maybe there's a better word for it somewhere."

"If you get stuck in the tub, how will I ever get you out?" she asked worriedly, measuring him with her eyes. "Heavens, I couldn't begin to lift you!"

"That's a fact. But I wouldn't risk it if I didn't think I could cope. Humor me."

"All right. But if you drown," she advised, "I'm not taking the rap for it."

She went into the bathroom and filled the tub with warm water. It was a Jacuzzi, luxurious and spotless, and she envied him. Her guest bedroom had a nice shower, which she'd used the night before, but nothing like this. She put soap and lotions and towels close to hand and went to help him out of bed and across the tub.

"It's big," he declared as he lowered himself into it. "Why don't you strip off and come in with me?"

She chuckled, trying not to let her faint, remaining embarrassment show. She'd grown used to the sight of his body, although it still intimidated her a bit. "I might fall and break my leg. Where would we be then?"

He stretched his big arms over the sides. "Just as well, I suppose." He sighed, letting his gaze wash over her like warm water. "You aren't the type, are you?"

"What type?"

"For brief interludes," he said seriously. "You're a forever-after girl, despite the fact that forever-after doesn't exist anymore."

"It could, if two people loved each other enough," she said.

"My wife and I loved each other, when we married," he said. "We thought it would last forever." He smiled cynically. "It lasted for a while, then we burned out."

She chewed on her lower lip and frowned a little. "Oh."

"I learned one thing from it. Marriage requires more than a mutual fever. You need common interests, backgrounds, and you need to be friends as well as lovers. That's trite, but it's true."

"It's a hard combination to find," she said.

"People don't have time to look for it anymore." He picked up the cloth and soap and lathered his arms and chest slowly.

"I'd better go…"

"Don't be silly. Sit down."

She perched herself on a chair by the bench that contained a hair blower and electric razor, along with a rack of lotions and powders. She folded her hands together on her jean-clad legs and tried not to look uncomfortable.

"In the old days, people lived in small communities and everyone knew everyone," he said while he bathed. "Now we're all so busy trying to support ourselves that we move around like migrating birds. We don't stay in one place long enough to get to know people."

"Your singer, Amanda. How did she meet her husband?"

He chuckled. "They got snowbound together up in Wyoming," he said. "And he was the ultimate misogynist. He hated Amanda on sight. But she's feisty and she has a kind heart. It was only a matter of time until they fell in love. Unfortunately that happened before he found out who she really was. He went all noble, because he was poor and she was famous. So for her own good, he threw her out. She left and her plane crashed on the way to L.A."

She caught her breath. "He must have been devastated."

"Half out of his mind," Hank replied, remembering the band's nightmare trip back to Wyoming. They'd all left on the bus because Hank and the boys didn't like airplanes. But Amanda had insisted on flying. Hank had felt responsible because he hadn't pushed harder to get her to come with them. "Quinn skied down an unpatrolled ridge into the valley to get her—only a handful of men in the country could have made that run, but he was an Olympic contender in downhill in his younger days. Hell of a trip it was. He found her badly concussed, damn near dead, and he had to have another man ski down to help tow her out of the valley on a litter to a waiting helicopter. There was too much wind for the chopper to land where the crash occurred. As it was, they barely made it in time. Three days after the doctor pronounced her on the mend, they got married, right there in the hospital."

"My goodness!"

"They'd been married for two years when she got pregnant," he recalled. "They were both over the moon about it, but she's a lot more fragile than she looks. It's been a rough pregnancy and she's had to have constant medical care. We'd more or less given up touring when she first married, but we had one commitment we couldn't break, for a charity in New

York. She barely got through it and Quinn put his foot down, hard. He's kept her home since then. He won't even let her do recording sessions now. The rumor is that we're breaking up the group."

"Are you?"

He finished bathing his legs. "I don't know." He looked at her. "The band wouldn't be the same without Amanda. No singer could replace her."

"I don't suppose so," she agreed gently. "But I'm sure the baby is the most important thing to her right now."

He nodded. There was a bitter look on his face that she didn't miss.

"Why didn't your wife want a child?"

He glared at her. "That's none of your business."

He sounded fierce, but she overlooked the bad temper because of the sadness in his blue eyes. "I'm sorry. I didn't mean to pry."

He paused long enough to wash his hair and rinse it before he said anything else. "She said that I wasn't cut out to be a parent," he said shortly. "That I wasn't home enough or patient enough. And besides that, she didn't want a child who might grow up to look like me."

Her eyes lingered on his broad shoulders and chest, on the power and strength of his tanned, hair-roughed skin. "What's wrong with you?" she asked dreamily.

He caught his breath as the surge of desire shot through him like a bolt of lightning.

She saw the tautness of his face and grimaced. "I keep putting my foot in it, don't I?" she said miserably. "Honestly, you make me feel like a babbling adolescent!"

"That isn't how you make me feel," he said with grim humor. "What she meant," he explained, "was that I've got a thick neck and an oversize body and a face that only a mother could love. She said with her luck, she'd have a little girl with a big nose and feet like a duck."

"What a cruel thing to say," she replied, wounded for him. "I expect you'd have a very pretty little girl with blue eyes and brown hair. Except that if you have four brothers, it's a lot more likely that you'd have a little boy."

"So I've heard." He let his narrowed eyes sweep over her. "You're very delicately built," he said quietly. "Slender hips, small breasts, almost a foot shorter than I am. We'd have a hard time just making love, much less having a child together."

She couldn't believe he'd said that. She just looked at him, flustered.

"You know everything there is to know about me, physically." He continued in that same quiet, gentle voice. "But it's one thing to look, and another to consider the problem of intimacy." His eyes narrowed more. "I'll bet you're as small as I am big," he said insinuatingly.

She jumped up from the chair, red faced and shocked. "How dare you!"

"Tell me you haven't thought about how we'd fit together in my bed," he challenged, and he wasn't smiling.

Her fists clenched at her sides. "You can't talk to me like this!"

He searched her outraged eyes with curiosity and faint tenderness. "Another first, hmm?" he mused. "And you're a vet. How did you survive labs?"

"Half the people in my class were women," she informed him. "We forced the men to respect us enough not to make sexist remarks."

"I'm not making sexist remarks," he argued. "I'm indulging in a little sexual logic." He pursed his lips and held her eyes relentlessly. "If I'm very careful, we might try," he said gently.

"Try what?"

"And I can use something. There won't be any risk."

She clenched both fists tighter. "You can stop right there. I'm not sleeping with you!"

He smiled without malice. "You will," he replied. "Eventually."

"I won't be here eventually. The minute the snow

lets up and the snowplow clears the roads, I'm getting out of here!"

"I've never been to Sioux City," he remarked conversationally. "But you're an old-fashioned girl, so I guess I'll have to chase you for a while, won't I?"

"You don't need to start thinking that you'll wear me down. You won't. I have no inclination whatsoever, at all, to...to..."

He stood up slowly in the middle of her tirade, turned off the Jacuzzi and stepped out onto the mat. She couldn't take her eyes off him. It must be some deep-seated weakness, she decided, some character flaw that made her into a blatant Peeping Tom.

And it was worse than ever when he reacted to her appreciative eyes and laughed about it.

She groaned as she pulled a huge bath sheet from the heated towel bar and handed it to him.

He ignored the bath sheet. His hand shot around her wrist and jerked, pulling her completely against his wet body. Even in his weakened condition, he was alarmingly strong.

She started to struggle, the sheet dropping to the floor, but he clamped a big hand around her waist and held her firmly to him, groaning in pleasure as her hips moved sharply in her efforts to escape.

She subsided at once, made breathless by the huge body so intimately close to her. He was so tall that she felt the insistent pressure of him, not against her hips but against her midriff. She caught onto him to keep from reeling, and the feel of that thick mat of hair under her hands paralyzed her with curious pleasure.

"Shrimp," he accused at her temple.

"Giant," she taunted.

His hands swept over her back, burning hot through her thin cotton blouse, flattening her breasts against his diaphragm.

"We don't even fit together like a normal man and woman," he remarked as he looked down at her. "We're like Mutt and Jeff."

But it felt right. It felt as natural as breathing to stand close against his aroused body and be at home. She laid her cheek against his damp chest and just stood there, letting him hold her close, while she tried to deal with the unfamiliar feelings that were overwhelming her. It felt like more than physical attraction. It felt like…love.

Chapter Five

"**I**'m out of my mind," he said pleasantly. "I must be, even to consider such a thing with a midget like you. We'd be totally incompatible in bed."

She closed her eyes and relaxed against him, feeling him tauten in response. "No, we wouldn't. I studied anatomy. I'd have to be a foot shorter than I am to be worried. A woman's body is very elastic."

"Is yours elastic enough to accommodate mine?" he asked quietly.

She lifted her head and looked up into his blue, blue eyes. She felt the hunger all through her, burning and hot. "I think so," she said involuntarily.

His jaw clenched as he searched her face. "Then, let me."

She swallowed. Her fingers went up to touch his hair-roughened face. His lips were the only bit of skin visible below his cheekbones and his blue eyes. "I can't."

He scowled. "Those damned old-fashioned ideas again! This is the nineties, for God's sake!"

"I know." She traced his hard mouth and wanted so much to lie in his arms and learn what it was to love. But it wasn't what she wanted. "I'm not emotionally strong enough for brief affairs. That's why I don't have them. I really do want a home and children, Hank. I want my husband to be the first. If that's outdated, I'm sorry. I don't feel inferior or out of step just because I put a high value on my chastity. I hope the man I marry will feel the same way about his body."

His hands loosened. "In other words, you don't want a permissive man for a husband."

She lowered her eyes to his broad chest. "I suppose a lot of women think a man like that can reform, that he can be faithful. But if he's had a hundred women, he's already proven that he can't. He sees sex as an itch to scratch. He'll probably always consider it that casual, so he'll feel free to sleep around after he marries. And it will probably surprise him if his wife objects."

His big hands smoothed up and down her arms.

"I guess I've given you the impression that I'm that way with women."

She looked up. "Yes."

He took a slow breath and smiled tenderly. "You don't think I might one day value a woman enough to become faithful rather than risk losing her?"

"I don't know you," she said solemnly.

"No. You really don't." He hesitated for another minute, but then he let her go and bent to pick up the bath sheet she'd dropped.

She moved away while he dried himself, finding a robe hanging behind the door that she handed to him when he was through. He put it on without a protest and let her help him back to the bedroom.

"Your hair is still damp," she said.

"It dries fast. Don't bother about the blower." He started toward the bed, but she diverted him into the chair.

"I want to change the sheets first. You'll be more comfortable."

He smiled. "Thanks."

"Where are they?"

He told her where to look and sat like a lamb while she remade the bed and then helped him out of his robe and into the bed.

"Are you all right?" she asked, because he looked so tired.

"I'm just weak. I think I may sleep for a while."

"That would be the best thing for you. Do you need anything?"

He shook his head. He studied her blouse for a long time, and she wondered why until she looked down and flushed. It had gotten so damp while she was standing against him that it had become see-through, and she wasn't wearing anything under it because her bra and the clothes she'd put on yesterday were in the load of laundry she'd started earlier.

Her arms came up over her body and she looked at him defensively.

"They're very pretty," he said with quiet reverence, and no mockery.

"Marshmallows," she muttered with self-contempt.

"Stop that," he said sharply. "I don't like big women."

Her eyebrows lifted. "All men do…"

"Not me," he repeated. "You're perfect just the way you are."

He eased her inferiority complex quite a lot, because he obviously wasn't lying about the way he felt. She managed a self-conscious smile. "Thanks."

He arched his arms behind his head and shifted with an oddly sensuous movement of his body. His eyes cut into hers, faintly glittering. "Open your blouse and come down beside me. I'll put my mouth on them and show you ten different ways to moan."

She flushed, jumping to her feet. "No doubt you

could. I'm grass green that way. But I wouldn't thank you for reducing me to that condition, even if a dozen other women have."

She walked toward the door and heard him mutter under his breath.

"I haven't had a hundred women," he said angrily.

"Oh, sure." She laughed as she put her hand on the doorknob.

"I've had one. My wife. And she left me impotent."

The shock that tore through her spun her around to face him. He wasn't joking. It was all there, in his drawn face, his bitter eyes, even in the taut line of his mouth.

"But you're not impotent!" she blurted.

"Not with you," he said, chuckling softly. "You can't imagine what a shock it was to find out. I've been putting off women for years because I was sure that I couldn't perform in bed."

She leaned back against the door. Her legs felt weak. "You weren't married for very long, though, were you?"

"Six years," he told her. "Before that, I gave everything in me to football. I lived in the gym. I had no interest in seducing scores of women, however prudish that sounds. I was like you, bristling with idealism and romance. I saved myself for the right woman. Except she wasn't the right woman," he said shortly. "We burned each other up in bed, but we had nothing to talk about in broad daylight."

"Did she…know?"

"No," he replied. "Because by the time we decided to get married, I discovered that I was one in a line. She'd had one lover after another until I came along, and never wanted to marry any of them. She said that she didn't think she could ever be faithful to one man, but I was certain that she could. More fool me," he added bitterly. "Amusing, isn't it, that you know already that permissive people find it difficult to be faithful, and I had to learn it the hard way."

"I wasn't in love," she reminded him. "You were."

"I should have known. Permissive people don't seem to make faithful lovers."

"But if she was like that," she began, moving closer to the bed, "experienced, I mean…how did you become impotent?"

"I stopped being able to want her after she had her third extramarital affair," he said honestly. "And without a lifetime of experience behind me, I thought that meant that I was permanently demanned. So I didn't try."

She saw him quite suddenly in a different light. Not as a playboy of the music world, but as an intense,

deeply emotional man who felt things right down
to his soul.

"Feeling sorry for me, Poppy?" he taunted as she
paused by the bed.

"Oh, no. I'm feeling sorry for her," she said. "How
sad to have someone love you so much and to be able
to feel nothing in return."

"She's happy. She has a husband who doesn't require faithfulness, and plenty of money to spend."

"That wouldn't make me happy."

He smiled. "What would?"

"Being loved. Having a home. Having children.
I'd still practice, of course. I guess I'd have to marry
a man who was willing to sacrifice a little so that I
could, but I'd make sure he never regretted it."

"Do you have hang-ups about sex?" he asked
curiously.

"Just about having it before I get married," she
replied, and grinned at him. "Deep-seated principles
aren't easily uprooted."

"People shouldn't try to uproot them," he replied.
"I'm sorry about that. It was a delicious surprise to
find myself so quickly capable with you. I wanted to
explore it." He shrugged. "But I shouldn't have put
pressure on you."

"I want to," she said sincerely. "I'll bet you're a
wonderful lover. But I want it all, the white wedding

gown, the wedding night, the honeymoon...I'm greedy."

He smiled. "Don't sound as if you're apologizing for it. You're a breath of fresh air to a cynic like me." He frowned quizzically at her. "Has it occurred to you that in a few days we've become as intimate as a married couple except in one respect?"

"We still don't know each other."

"You'd be surprised at what I know about you," he remarked gently. "You like to go barefoot on the carpet. You're neat, but not fanatical about it. You like to cook, but you don't like to clean up. You're intellectual so no situation comedies for you. You like nature specials and news and politics and music. You have a kind heart and you like animals and children, but underneath all that is a passionate nature held under very tight control." His eyes narrowed on her body. "You'll be a demanding lover, little Poppy, and some lucky man will probably find you next to insatiable in bed."

She lifted both eyebrows. "Stop that."

"I wish it was going to be me," he replied. "But I've already messed up one marriage by leaping in with my eyes closed after a one-week courtship. I'm not going to do it twice in one lifetime."

"Neither would I, although you didn't ask."

"Sit down." He pulled her down on the bed and drew her hand to his chest, holding it there. "I'm on the road six months out of the year, recording and making business deals, doing interviews and talk shows and working with underprivileged inner-city kids. It's a project of mine, finding volunteers to work with them once a week to help keep them out of trouble," he added with a grin. "When I'm home, and home is Texas, I compose to the exclusion of everything else. Sometimes I go for a whole day without eating, because I'm so wrapped up in my work that I forget to cook." He smoothed his thumb over the back of her hand. "I'd make a lousy husband. In fact, I did. I can't really blame her—"

"I can." She interrupted him. "If you love someone, you accept it all, the separations, the good times, the bad times, the illnesses. It's all part of marriage."

"You've already had the illness part," he mused.

"I'd have done that for anyone," she protested.

"You did it for me, though," he replied. "Blushing all the way. You don't do it so much anymore, though," he added amusedly. "You're getting used to me, aren't you?"

"You're very nice, when you forget to grumble."

"I have my faults. A quick temper is the worst of them. But I don't drink or gamble, and when I'm not working, I'm fairly easy to get along with." He searched her eyes. "Why are you called Poppy?"

"My father told me that my mother loved flowers," she recalled. "But he added that when I was born, the first thing she thought of was a poem about poppies growing in Flanders Fields where the veterans of World War I were buried. She went into the hospital to have me on Veterans Day and they were selling Buddy Poppies…." She smiled.

"Muddled, but I get the idea," he said. "My name is Henry, but everyone called me Hank from the time I was in grammar school."

"It's a nice name."

"So is yours." He drew her hand to his lips and kissed it softly. "Thank you for taking care of me."

The gentle caress was thrilling. She smiled. "It was very educational."

One blue eye narrowed. "Just don't start experimenting with men who aren't sick," he said.

Her eyebrows went up.

He laughed and let go of her hand. "Now I know I must be delirious with fever."

"I guess so," she murmured dryly. "I'll finish the wash then clean up the kitchen while you nap."

"You don't have to do that," he said gently.

"We both need some clean clothes. It's no trouble."

"Thanks, then."

She shrugged, smiled and went back to her chores. All the while she was thinking about Hank and how easily they seemed to fall into living together. Not that it was the normal sort of living together, she reminded herself.

But it was exciting all the same, and there was a closeness here that she'd never known. She liked just being with Hank, listening to his deep voice as he talked. He was intelligent and kind, and not at all the unprincipled rounder she'd thought he was. She thought of him in a totally different light now, and she knew that she was going to miss him terribly when the weather broke enough to let them out of this cabin.

She tried to put it out of her mind while she did the chores. She was beginning to feel very much at home here. The views were spectacular and she enjoyed the solitude. It would have been the ideal place to live, with the right man.

It occurred to her that Hank was the right man, the one she'd been looking for all her life. But it was impossible. You couldn't fall in love in four days, not the sort of love you needed to get married. Besides, Hank had a failed marriage behind him and he didn't want to risk a second. All that would have been left for them was an affair, which she couldn't accept.

She finished the washing and put the clothes into the dryer, wondering how it was going to be when she got back home. Probably she'd put this adventure into perspective and forget about it in a few months. Of course she would.

Hank slept for the rest of the afternoon, while Poppy amused herself with the piano, lowering the volume to keep from disturbing the man in the master bedroom. The song he was working on was lying on the table beside the piano. She glanced over the tune and began to pick it out, slowly, smiling as the beautiful melody met her ears.

He didn't have more than a few words on paper, rhyming words mostly and not in any sort of order. Love, he'd written, when the feeling stirred fluttered like a…and he'd crossed out two words that didn't quite rhyme with it.

"A bright redbird," she mumbled, "playing in the snow."

"That's it!"

She jumped and caught her breath. Hank was leaning against the doorframe in his bathrobe. His blue eyes were glimmering, and he was laughing.

"I couldn't get the rhyme or any sort of reason to go with those words," he explained. "But that's it, that's exactly it…!"

He moved to the piano and slid onto the bench beside her. He played the song with a deep bass beat that emphasized the sweetness of the high melody.

"Love when the feeling stirred, fluttered like a redbird, playing in the snow," he sang in his deep, soft voice, looking at her and grinning. "Flew like an arrow through the sky, higher than a redbird flies, left me all aglow."

Only words, she thought, but when the music was put with them, major and minor chords intermixing, when he sang the words, when the deep, throbbing counterrhythm caught her up—it was going to be a hit. She knew it and felt goose bumps rise on her arms at the power and beauty of it.

"You feel it, too, don't you?" he asked, stopping. "It's good, isn't it? Really good."

"The best yet," she had to agree. "Who did the music?"

One corner of his mouth tugged up just a fraction of an inch and she laughed. "Silly question," she murmured. "Sorry."

"It will take some more work, but that's the melody." He chuckled. "Imagine that, I'd been sitting in here for a solid week trying to come up with something, anything…and all I needed was a veterinarian to point me in the right direction." He grinned at her. "I suppose you treat birds, too, don't you?"

She nodded. "Parrots and canaries and parakeets, for lung infections. Birds are mostly lung, you know." She searched his face. "You shouldn't be up. It's too soon."

"I heard you playing my song," he explained. "I had to come and see what you thought of it."

"I think it's great."

He smiled. "Thanks." She was slowly touching the keys again and some soft sadness in her face touched him. "What's wrong?" he asked.

She looked up. "The snow's stopped."

He looked out the window. He hadn't noticed. He got up from the bench and walked to stare out the other window down at the road. It had stopped, and the sun had come out. "Great skiing weather now," he murmured. "The snowplows will dig us out by tomorrow." He stuck his hands into the pockets of his robe. "You'll be free."

What an odd way to put it. "I don't plan to rush out and file kidnapping charges against you," she said pointedly.

He turned. "That wasn't how I meant it, although I will apologize handsomely for kidnapping you by mistake." His eyes swept over her very slowly, almost possessively. "I suppose you'll be rushing back to your practice."

"I need to."

"What if you don't have a job to go back to?" he persisted seriously.

She blew out a soft breath. "Well, I suppose they'll repossess my car and my apartment first…"

"Is there somewhere else you could work, if you had to?"

"Of course!" she said, laughing. "Sioux City isn't that small. There are other practices. I could find something, but it wouldn't be as a partner. I'd have to start at the bottom again."

"Honey, I don't think you've realized that you're at the bottom right now."

The endearment made her heart race. She dropped her eyes before he could read the pleasure it gave her.

"Sorry. That slipped out," he said, teasing.

"Oh, I liked it," she replied. "Nobody ever called me honey except the mailman, and he was seventy."

He burst out laughing. "I'll have to make up for that. You can't leave until morning, anyway, not unless they get those roads cleared early."

"I wouldn't leave until you were well, regardless," she said, surprised at his assumption that she couldn't wait to get out.

His face smoothed. All expression went out of it. "I see."

"You needn't look shocked," she said. "You'd do it for me."

"Yes, I would." He began to realize how much he'd do for her. Under different circumstances, they might have had a real beginning. But it was the wrong time, the wrong place, and he was still afraid of the risk.

"It's been an experience I'll never forget," she said absently. "I'll listen to your tapes from now on. I suppose I was a bit of a musical snob."

"Maybe I was, too. I think I'll buy an opera tape or two."

She smiled. "That's nice. You might try Puccini."

"Is he that Italian singer?" he asked.

"He's the composer. He's dead. But Domingo and Pavorotti sing the operas he wrote. My favorite opera is *Turandot*."

"*Turandot*." He smiled back. "I'll remember."

She got up from the piano. "How about something to eat?"

"You took the words right out of my mouth!"

She went into the kitchen and made potato pancakes and steak and biscuits with a side salad. When she went to call Hank, he was out of bed and dressed in jeans and a green pullover shirt. Despite that overshadowing growth of hair that covered his face, concealing its shape, he looked wonderful to Poppy.

"Are you sure you feel like eating at the table?" she asked worriedly.

"Yes. I'm still a little weak, but I'm on the mend." He smiled. "Doesn't it show?"

She nodded. "I guess it does."

They ate at the small table in the kitchen. His appetite was much better, and he was only coughing occasionally now. He ate heartily. Considering the speed of his recovery, it didn't take much guesswork to tell that overall, he was in great shape.

"How did you learn to cook like this?" he asked.

"From my dad. He was a chef. He really was good at it, too. He taught me how to make pastries and sauces. I enjoy cooking."

"It shows. This is delicious."

"Thank you!"

They were silent until they finished eating. They drank their second cup of coffee at the kitchen table, and Hank stared into his mug pensively.

"You're brooding, aren't you?" she asked.

He nodded. He looked up into her eyes and held them for a long, static moment. "I haven't had anyone around me, close like this, for a long time. You've grown on me, Poppy," he mused half-humorously. "I'm going to miss you."

She smiled back, a little sadly. "I'm going to miss you, too. I haven't had anyone to look after or care about since my dad died. It's been lonely for me."

He turned the coffee mug idly on the table's glossy surface. "Then suppose we keep in touch," he suggested without looking at her.

Her heart leapt. "Oh, that would…" She calmed her tone. "That would be nice. I'd like that."

He smiled at her. "So would I. I'll give you the address here and in Texas. Write to me when you get back."

"Are you terrible about answering letters?" she asked.

He shook his head. "I'm very good about it, in fact. I answer most of my own fan mail with the help of a secretary."

"I see."

"No, you don't." He corrected her, interpreting her expression accurately. "I don't leave her to do the answering, I dictate the replies. And I won't let anyone answer your letters. I'll do it myself."

Her stiff posture relaxed. "Then I'll write."

"And don't assume that if you don't hear back immediately that I've forgotten you or that I'm ignoring you," he added. "I'm on the road a lot, I told you. It may take a week or two, sometimes longer, for my mail to catch up with me."

"I'll remember," she promised.

He reached out and covered her soft hand with his big one. "One more thing," he said gently, coaxing her eyes up to meet his. "Find another job."

She gaped at him. "My job is my business."

"Your job is a joke," he returned. "They're using you, sweetheart, dangling the idea of a partnership so that they can get someone to take over the jobs they don't want. There won't be any partnership. One day they'll find someone more useful and you'll be out on your ear, perhaps at the most inconvenient time."

"You're very cynical," she remarked.

He nodded. "I'm an expert on people who use other people," he told her. "I've been used a time or two myself."

She wiggled her eyebrows. "Can I have three guesses about how they did it?"

He glowered at her. "I'm serious."

She finished her coffee. "Okay. I'll think about it."

"You do that."

She got up and put the dishes in the dishwasher. "Is there anything else that needs doing?"

"Yes." He came up behind her and slipped his lean arms around her, hugging her back against him. "I need to be ravished."

She laughed with pure delight. "I'm not up to your weight," she reminded him, looking up over her shoulder with sparkling dark eyes. "And besides, I'd never be able to overpower you."

"I'll help."

She shook her head. "No. I expect that you're as addictive as caffeine. One taste of you wouldn't be enough. I'd get withdrawal symptoms."

He chuckled and hugged her closer for a minute.

"So would I. And I'm probably still a little contagious," he added with a sheepish grin as he let her go. "No matter," he mused, watching her. "When I'm well and truly back on my feet, I'll come calling. Then, look out."

The soft warning kept her going, all through the rest of the day, and through the anguish of the parting the next morning, when he had to take her to the ski lodge and leave her with barely more than an affectionate hug.

She worried about him all the way to the airport on the lodge's shuttle bus, because even though the snowplows had been along, the roads were still treacherous. But as the shuttle passed the road to his cabin, she saw that his Bronco was safely parked at the door and smoke was coming out of the fireplace. He'd made it home, and hopefully, he'd be fine. She settled back into her seat, trying not to cry. It was amazing, she thought, how five days in Colorado had altered the rest of her life. Her last thought as they left the snow-covered valley behind was how would she survive until she saw Hank again?

Chapter Six

Poppy began to realize very quickly after her return to Sioux City, Iowa, that Hank had been right about her supposed partnership. The vets with whom she worked seemed to have plenty of free time and yet they made three times her salary. She was always the one to work nights and weekends and holidays, and whenever the weather was particularly bad, it was Poppy who had to go out on large-animal calls. That could be very difficult indeed when she was asked to deliver a calf or a foal, or treat a mean-tempered bull for a cut.

She had bruises all over her, a bad cold and there was no mention of an increased salary or a partnership two months later. She was getting fed up. And not only with the veterinary practice.

She'd written twice to Hank. So far, there hadn't been even a postcard in reply. On one of the music talk shows, which she'd started watching, there had been one tidbit about Amanda Sutton being in a hospital in Wyoming awaiting the birth of her first child and some more rumors about the breakup of her group, Desperado. But that was all the news there had been. Remembering how fond Hank was of Amanda, Poppy hoped she was all right and that her child had been born healthy.

She tried very hard to remember what Hank had said about not being upset if she didn't hear from him right away. But when two months rolled into three, she began to put the past in perspective. The time she'd spent with Hank had been a five-day interlude and nothing serious had really happened, except for a few kisses. He'd told her he wanted nothing less than another marriage, so what had she expected? Perhaps he'd decided that even friendship with her was too much of a risk, and he'd withdrawn.

She couldn't blame him. He hadn't had an easy time of it where women were concerned. But the last thing on her mind had been trapping him into a relationship he didn't want. When she thought about it, it seemed likely that he'd had his share of ambitious women stalking him because he was rich and famous.

She wasn't like that, but he wouldn't know. He didn't know her at all. Apparently he didn't want to.

Poppy tried to put him out of her mind, but his new song, "Redbird," had just been released on an album along with several other newly recorded tracks. It meant that Amanda had to be working again, because her sweet, clear soprano could be heard above the deep bass voices of her group. The song that Poppy had given him the inspiration for was as beautiful as it had sounded in the cabin, and it was a surprise to find that her first name was mentioned in the dedication of the album, jointly to Carlton Wayne Sutton—very obviously the new baby—and herself. She tingled all over at the thought that Hank had remembered her even that well. She was a nobody, after all, hardly his sort of woman. The terrible thing was that she had no close girlfriends, no one to share the thrill with. She mentioned it to a clerk in the nearby record shop, but he only smiled and agreed that it was a great honor. She was sure that he didn't believe her.

Her stamina was giving out. Despite her youth, the practice was really getting her down. Eventually she couldn't take it anymore and she went looking for another job.

She found it in a very small practice in a town twenty miles outside Sioux City, in a farming community. The elderly veterinarian there had one young partner but needed someone to take care of the office while the two of them were out on large-animal calls. Poppy wasn't overly eager, but she was pleasant and had qualifications that they liked.

"What about experience?" Dr. Joiner, the elder partner, asked gently.

"I'm working for a group practice in Sioux City," she explained, "but I have to do all the large-animal calls and work nights and holidays and weekends." She smiled sheepishly. "I'm sorry. I suppose that sounds as if I'm lazy. I'm not, and it is a great opportunity to learn how a practice works. But I'm so tired," she concluded helplessly.

Dr. Joiner exchanged a speaking glance with his young partner, Dr. Helman. "It isn't quite so busy here," he explained. "But we have enough work for three people. The thing is, I can't offer you a partnership. You'd be a salaried employee and nothing more."

"Oh, that's all right," Poppy said, relieved. "I don't think I've got enough stamina for another partnership."

Dr. Joiner chuckled. "Dr. O'Brien, you're a peach. I'll be happy to have you aboard. When can you start?"

She explained that she'd have to give two weeks' notice, and that she'd make sure she got a reference from her partners. She thanked Dr. Joiner again, smiled at Dr. Helman and set off to her office with a lighter heart.

* * *

The partners weren't surprised when she announced her resignation, and they gave her a good recommendation as well. They apparently expected that no junior partner was going to last very long with what was expected of her or him. But they were interviewing other new graduates the last few days Poppy worked for them. She couldn't even warn the excited prospective employees. They'd have to find out the truth the same harsh way she had. But it would teach them a good lesson. Heaven knew, she'd learned hers.

She kept her apartment. It was only a twenty-five-minute drive to the new office, and she'd have to have time to look for a new place to live that was closer, if her new job worked out.

The job itself, after the long, strenuous practice she'd left, was wonderfully uncomplicated and enjoyable. She didn't have to work every weekend. The other vets alternated with her. Each one was on call a different night, so she didn't have to work every night, either. Holidays were shared. It was heavenly and the odd thing was that she made just as much money as she'd made in the practice. She felt at home after just one week on the job. She decided that moving closer was a pretty safe bet, considering how well they all worked together.

She found a room in a nice, comfortable boarding

house and paid a week's rent in advance. Then she went to pack up her things and have them moved to her new home.

It didn't take long, because she didn't have much. She made two trips in her car and was just packing it for the third time when the telephone rang inside. It was supposed to be disconnected already, so she ignored it. The last few calls had been salespeople doing promotions. She couldn't imagine who might be looking for her, short of her old partners. Certainly, she knew, it wouldn't be Hank Shoeman. It had been over four and a half months and he'd surely forgotten all about her by now. She'd faced that fact, without much enthusiasm, because her memories of him were sweet.

She settled in her new apartment in the boarding house and got more comfortable in her job over the next week. She'd just finished examining and inoculating a three-month-old poodle puppy when she heard the waiting-room door open. She was alone in the office, because it was just after hours and the receptionist had gone home. Drs. Joiner and Helman were out on calls.

"I'll only be a minute!" she called out. She finished with the poodle, assured the owner that he was in excellent health and that he'd be automatically notified when to bring the dog back for his next round of shots.

He thanked her and she smiled happily as she watched him leave. She finished writing up the chart and went out into the waiting room, hoping that it was going to be something uncomplicated so that she could go home and eat.

She opened the outer office door with her professional smile, and stopped there, frozen in place.

The man looked familiar, and not familiar. He was wearing a gray suit. His hair was conventionally cut. He had a mustache, nothing more. The rest of his lean, handsome face was clean-shaven, and except for a couple of thin scars and a crooked nose, it was an appealing face. Blue eyes twinkled out of it as he studied her in her neat white lab coat.

"Nice," he said pleasantly. "You haven't lost a pound, have you? And I gather that this new job doesn't require your life's blood."

"Hank?" she asked uncertainly.

He nodded.

"Your hair...your beard," she began.

"I'm changing my image," he explained. "I'm tired of looking like a refugee from a cave."

"You look very nice," she said.

"So do you. How about supper?"

"There aren't any restaurants around here," she told him. Her heart was beating madly. "You didn't answer my letters."

"It's a long story," he said. "I'll tell you everything you want to know. But for now, I'd enjoy a good meal. I've spent two days tracking you down and except for breakfast at the hotel and a couple of sandwiches, I'm running on empty."

"There are lots of restaurants in Sioux City," she said.

"Then we'll go there. Do you need to stop by your apartment first?"

She shook her head, bemused by the sight of him. He looked unspeakably elegant and sexy. She wanted to throw herself into his arms and tell him to forget about explanations, it was enough that he was here. But she couldn't do it. He was probably on his way to or from Texas and had only stopped in because he wondered what had happened to her. It wasn't a proposal or a proposition; it was just a visit. She had to remember that and not let her imagination run away with her.

She took off her lab coat and slid her arms into the deep pink cotton jacket she wore over her pale pink blouse. She took time to run a brush through her hair and refreshen her makeup before she rejoined Hank in the outer office.

"I have to lock up," she explained, and took time to do that, too. When the lock was secure and checked, and the burglar alarm set, she walked with Hank to his car. But she stopped short when she saw it, and her uplifted face was wary and a little scared.

He reached down and took her hand, holding it tightly in his. "It's all right," he said gently.

The driver came around, smiling, and opened the door of the big white stretch limousine for them. Hank helped Poppy inside and slid in next to her. The driver closed them in and went around to get behind the wheel.

Hank had already told him where to go. He took off without a word, and Hank closed the curtains between front and back and turned on the interior light.

Poppy's expression fascinated him. She looked at everything, explored the CD deck, the television, the well-stocked bar, the telephone...

"Six people could ride in here," she remarked, smoothing her hand over the burgundy leather seat.

"Six people usually do," he replied, stretching out lazily to study her. "Like it?"

She grinned. "I love it. I only wish I had a friend that I could brag about it to."

"Surely you have one or two."

She shook her head. "I don't make long-lasting friends that easily. Only casual ones. My best friend married years ago, and we lost touch."

He crossed one long leg over the other. "Did you see the song on the charts?"

"Yes! It was great! Thank you for the dedication."

He waved her thanks away. "Thanks for the help. Everyone loved it, especially Amanda."

"How is she?"

"Blooming," he said with a smile. "She and Quinn and Eliott are all moonstruck over that baby. They take him everywhere, even to recording sessions with the group." His eyes were sad and faintly wistful. "I've always envied them that closeness. Now I envy them the baby."

"The album was dedicated to him, too," she recalled.

"He's a good-looking kid," he said. "Even cries with rhythm. We're all going to buy him a set of drums when he's two."

"Do they still hang people in Wyoming?" she asked meaningfully.

He got the joke at once and chuckled. "Quinn might just do that to me." He locked his hands behind his head, pulling his suit coat pleasantly taut over the powerful muscles of his chest and arms while he looked at her. "I've been tying up loose ends, settling business affairs, getting recording contracts and publicity tours finalized. I'm free for the next two months."

"You're not in town on business, then?" she asked conversationally.

His blue eyes narrowed. "You know why I'm in town, Poppy."

Her heart jumped but her face gave nothing away. "Actually I don't. I wrote you two letters, neither of which was ever answered. There wasn't a telephone call or any communication for months. You don't ignore people for almost half a year and then just drop by as if you saw them yesterday."

"You're mad." He sighed. "Yes, I was afraid you would be. I kept trying to put down what I felt on paper, and failing miserably. I couldn't boil it down to a telephone call, either. Just when I thought I'd fly out here, something kept coming up. It's been a long five months, honey. The longest five months of my life. But I'm here now, and you're going to have hell getting rid of me."

"Don't you have contractual obligations to fulfill?" she asked.

He shook his head, slowly. "That's why it took me so long to come after you. I didn't want any interruptions."

She shifted back against the leather seat. "I won't have an affair with you, so if that's why you came, I'll save you the time."

He began to smile. "Have you forgotten what a low boiling point you have with me?"

"Yes," she said uncomfortably. "And that should

bother you. One more groupie might be more than you could take."

"Not if she was you," he said pointedly. "I'd love having you throw yourself at me and hang on for dear life."

"Why?"

"That's something we'll talk about for the next few days." He stretched again and yawned. "I haven't slept. You're a hard woman to track down. Eventually I phoned every single veterinarian's office in the city. Do you know how many there are?"

"I have a fairly good idea," she replied, shocked. "Couldn't you have had your secretary or someone do that for you?"

"Why, no," he said, surprised at the question. "It wouldn't have occurred to me to trust something so important to another person."

She flushed. "You'd forgotten all about me, surely? I've seen some of the photos on your other albums. You attract beautiful women."

"Beauty isn't everything," he replied. "And sometimes it isn't anything at all. You're beautiful to me, Poppy, because you have the kindest heart of any woman I've ever known. I've never had anyone want to take care of me when I was sick until you came along. And under those circumstances, too, when I'd practically kidnapped you. You'd have been perfectly justified in walking out and leaving me there to cough myself to death."

"I couldn't have done that," she protested.

"Not even if you'd hated me. Yes, I know. But I don't think you hated me, Poppy," he mused, watching her like a hawk. "In fact, I think you felt something quite different on that last day we spent together."

"Compassion," she said abruptly.

"Compassion." He smiled. "Is that all I get?"

"What do you want?"

He leaned forward with his hands clasped loosely over his long legs. "I want you to love me, Poppy," he drawled deeply. "I want you to become so obsessed with me that you grow pale if I'm out of your sight for an hour. I want you to hate women who look at me or touch me. I want you to ache for me in your bed at night, and go hungry for the feel of me in your arms."

She already felt that way. She wasn't telling him so, however. She cleared her throat. "Well!"

"And before you start raging at me about indecent proposals before dinner," he added slowly, "I want a hell of a lot more than one night with you."

Her eyebrows levered up. "An affair is still…"

"I want a baby, Poppy," he said in a deep, soft whisper. "I want a son of my own, so that I don't have to stand over Amanda and Quinn and covet theirs."

Her body reacted to the statement in an unexpected

way, so that she had to fold her arms over her breasts to keep him from noticing.

He noticed anyway, and his eyes gleamed with feeling. "You want it, too, don't you?" he said coaxingly. "A home, a husband, a family of your own. Maybe a few pets to look after, too."

"My job…"

"Whatever," he said easily. "If you want to keep on practicing, that's all right with me. It will give you and the kids something to do when I'm out of town."

Her heart was racing wildly in her chest. He looked sane. Perhaps he had a fever again.

"I'm not crazy," he explained. "I'm just lonely. So are you. So if we get married and make a family together, neither of us will ever have to be lonely again."

"There are plenty of women who would be willing…"

"I want you," he said simply. "You can't imagine how empty my cabin has been since you left." He laughed, but without mirth. "All my life I've been self-sufficient, independent. Women have chased me for years, before and after my marriage. But here you come, spend less than a week in residence, and you're living with me still, here and here." He touched his head and his heart. "I can't get rid of you. And believe me, I tried. I tried for five months."

She glared at him. "Maybe I had more success at it than you did," she taunted.

"Maybe you didn't."

He reached across the space that separated them and lifted her body right into his arms.

"Now, you see here…!"

His mouth hit hers while she was getting the last word out. He wasn't brutal or rough, but the action was amazingly effective. She went under without a protest. Her arms went around his neck and she lifted to the slow, soft caress of his hands even as her mouth opened to accept the deep, hard thrust of his tongue inside it.

Her legs trembled where they lay over his. He drew her closer and deepened the kiss even more, held it until he felt her begin to shudder. His hand smoothed up over her thighs, her flat stomach, her breasts. She moaned.

"You got over me, right?" he whispered against her mouth. "It's really noticeable, how completely you've gotten over me. Open your mouth again…"

She barely heard him above the wild throb of her heart. She clung to him while one kiss led to another, each more arousing than the one before. He turned her so that her hips pressed deeply into his own, so that his arousal was suddenly blatantly threatening. But she wasn't afraid.

"You're so small," he groaned as he let his mouth slide onto her throat. "Too small!"

She kissed his cheek, his temple, his closed eyelids with quick, warm lips. "I'll fit you," she promised. "I'll fit you like a glove."

"Poppy," he groaned again in anguish.

"Do stop worrying," she whispered as she found his mouth. "I love you."

"No more than I love you," he whispered back, holding her closer. "Are you going to marry me, complications and all?"

"I don't seem to have any choice. How else can I protect you from scores of sex-crazed beautiful women?"

He chuckled and kissed her again, murmuring his agreement against her soft, welcoming mouth.

And they were married, six months to the day after Hank had abducted Poppy to his mountain cabin. The whole group of Desperado was there as witnesses in the small Wyoming church where Amanda had married Quinn Sutton several years before. They spoke their vows and exchanged rings. The look Hank gave his new bride would have melted snow, but fortunately it was summer.

"Where are you going for your honeymoon?" Amanda asked them when they'd changed and were ready to get into the limousine.

"That's our secret." Hank chuckled. He kissed

Amanda's cheek, and the baby's, and shook hands with Quinn Sutton and Elliot.

"Well, write when you get time," Quinn asked. "Let us know you're okay."

"I'll do that. Take care of each other. We'll be in touch."

The Suttons all stood close together, waving until Poppy and Hank were out of sight.

"They're a very special couple, aren't they?" Poppy asked, sliding as close to Hank as she could get.

"A very special family," he agreed. "We're going to be one, too. I'll prove that to you tonight," he said, his voice deepening, lowering. There had been nothing more than kisses all during the time they waited for their wedding day. Now the time had come for all the secrets to be unveiled for Poppy and she was as excited as she was apprehensive. She loved him. That had to be enough, she reminded herself. She slid her small hand into his big one and snuggled close.

But she was less comfortable after they ate a leisurely supper and cleared away the dishes. Her disquiet showed on her face, too.

He tossed aside the dishcloth and pulled her gently in front of him. "Weddings are traumatic at best," he said quietly. "We can wait until you're rested and feel more like a new experience."

She nibbled at the skin on her lower lip. "I'm not usually so cowardly," she began.

He took her face in his big hands and tilted it up to his tender eyes. "I don't have anything that you haven't already seen," he reminded her.

"But I do," she said miserably. She plucked at his shirt. "And I'm grass green and inhibited...!"

"And five minutes from now, you won't know your own name," he whispered as his mouth searched for her lips and opened on them.

Actually it took less time than that for him to reduce her to insensibility. Her desire for him matched his for her, and by the time he carried her into the bedroom, she was fighting her way to his bare chest through the confining shirts that separated them.

"Slowly," he whispered as he put her down and slid onto the bed beside her. "Slowly, darling, we have all the time in the world. Nice and easy, now. Let's not rush."

She was shivering with new sensations, new expectations, but he gentled her until she lay drowsily in his big arms and let him undress them. She didn't have the will to protest or the sense to be embarrassed as he studied her pink nudity with covetous, possessive eyes. His hands were slow and thorough, like his warm mouth. He aroused her and excited her, and when she was whimpering softly with the overwhelming pleasure of his ardor, he moved into total possession.

She stiffened a little and gasped, but his mouth

savored hers, and pressed reassuring kisses over her closed eyelids as he coaxed her into accepting the raw intimacy of his body.

"You are...very much a virgin," he whispered against her trembling lips, and he smiled. "Is it all right? Am I hurting you?"

"No," she managed to say. Her nails dug into his shoulders as he moved again, very tenderly.

"It stings, doesn't it?"

"Yes."

"Only a little farther," he said half to himself, and his mouth crushed down hard on hers, his tongue shooting deeply into her mouth. The action shocked her so much that she relaxed and allowed him complete and total access to the soft warmth of her body.

She cried out, surprised, because it was the most profound experience of her entire life. Her eyes opened wide and she looked straight into his.

"Yes," he whispered huskily. "It's a miracle, isn't it? Man and woman, fitting together so closely, so completely, that they form one person." He kissed her damp face gently as he began to move, each tender shift of his body bringing a sudden, sharp pleasure that lifted her to him in delight. "Feel the rhythm and move with me," he coaxed, smiling as she began to match him. "Think of it as composing a symphony, making music...that's it. Hard now, baby. Cut loose and move to the beat. Move hard. Real hard...!"

She lost control of herself completely then and

although she heard his urgent whispers, she seemed outside her body, watching it dance to his tune, contort and convulse with pleasure that seemed to feed on itself. Finally there was a hot burst of it that made her cry out against the unbearable sensations deep within her body. She buried her face against his throat and moaned endlessly as it went through her in waves. Somewhere in the heat of it, she heard him, felt him, as he joined her in that surreal existence with a hard shudder that arched his powerful body down roughly against hers.

Minutes later, the dazzling heat and color began to fade away and she found tears falling down her cheeks.

"It stopped," she whispered miserably.

He rolled onto his side and gathered her very close. "We'll get it back again when we've rested." He kissed her gently. "For a first time, it was fairly volcanic, wasn't it?" he mused. He laughed delightedly. "And we fit, don't we?"

"Oh, yes." She nuzzled closer, shivering with pleasure and love. "Hank…"

His mouth slid over hers. "We've just said all there is to say, and we never spoke a word," he whispered into her mouth. "I'm glad you waited for me, Poppy. I wish that I'd been able to wait for you, all my life."

She hugged him closer. "I'll settle for the rest of our lives," she said gently, "and everything that's ahead of us."

His big arms folded her close. "Love, then. Years and years of it."

She smiled against his chest. "And children to share it with."

"Yes." He tugged the cover over them, because it was chilly at night this high up in the mountains. "I'm glad I didn't apologize for abducting you," he murmured. "It was the only sensible thing I've done in the past few years."

"All the same, you can't abduct anyone else, ever."

"Oh, I'm reformed," he promised her with a grin. "The only thing I expect to abduct in the future is a piano now and again, so that I can compose an occasional song."

Her eyes fell to his mouth. "I particularly like the way you compose in bed. Would you like to try a new theme? Something on the order of a blues tune?"

He rolled over, smoothing her body against his in the growing darkness. "I think I can manage that." He chuckled. "How about you?"

She whispered that she had no doubts at all; about that, or about the future with him. It was going to be wonderful. And she told him that, too.

* * * * *

PAPER HUSBAND

Chapter One

The summer sun was rising. Judging by its place in the sky, Dana Mobry figured that it was about eleven o'clock in the morning. That meant she'd been in her present predicament for over two hours, and the day was growing hotter.

She sighed with resigned misery as she glanced at her elevated right leg where her jeans were hopelessly tangled in two loose strands of barbed wire. Her booted foot was enmeshed in the strands of barbed wire that made up the fence, and her left leg was wrapped in it because she'd twisted when she fell. She'd been trying to mend the barbed-wire fence to keep cattle from getting out. She was using her father's tools to do it, but sadly, she didn't have his strength. At times like this, she missed him unbearably, and it was only a week since his funeral.

She tugged at the neck of her short-sleeved cotton shirt and brushed strands of her damp blond hair back into its neat French braid. Not so neat now, she thought, disheveled and unkempt from the fall that had landed her in this mess. Nearby, oblivious to her mistress's dilemma, her chestnut mare, Bess, grazed. Overhead, a hawk made graceful patterns against the cloudless sky. Far away could be heard the sound of traffic on the distant highway that led around Jacobsville to the small Texas ranch where Dana was tangled in the fence wire.

Nobody knew where she was. She lived alone in the little ramshackle house that she'd shared with her father. They'd lost everything after her mother deserted them seven years ago. After that terrible blow, her father, who was raised on a ranch, decided to come back and settle on the old family homeplace. There were no other relatives unless you counted a cousin in Montana.

Dana's father had stocked this place with a small herd of beef cattle and raised a truck garden. It was a meager living, compared to the mansion near Dallas that her mother's wealth had maintained. When Carla Mobry had unexpectedly divorced her husband, he'd had to find a way of making a living for himself, quickly. Dana had chosen to go with him to his boyhood home in Jacobsville, rather than endure her mother's indifferent presence. Now her father was dead and she had no one.

She'd loved her father, and he'd loved her. They'd been happy together, even without a huge income. But the strain of hard physical labor on a heart that she had not even known was bad had been too much. He'd had a heart attack and died in his sleep. Dana had found him the next morning when she went in to his room to call him to breakfast.

Hank had come immediately at Dana's frantic phone call. It didn't occur to her that she should have called the ambulance first instead of their nearest, and very antisocial, neighbor. It was just that Hank was so capable. He always knew what to do. That day he had, too. After a quick look at her father, he'd phoned an ambulance and herded Dana out of the room. Later he'd said that he knew immediately that it was hours too late to save her father. He'd done a stint overseas in the military, where he'd seen death too often to mistake it.

Most people avoided Hayden Grant as much as possible. He owned the feed and mill store locally, and he ran cattle on his huge tracts of land around Jacobsville. He'd found oil on the same land, so lack of money wasn't one of his problems. But a short temper, a legendary dislike of women and a reputation for outspokenness made him unpopular in most places.

He liked Dana, though. That had been fascinating from the very beginning, because he was a misogynist and made no secret of the fact. Perhaps he considered her safe because of the age difference. Hank was thirty-six and Dana was barely twenty-two. She was slender and of medium height, with dark blond hair and a plain little face made interesting by the huge dark blue eyes that dominated it. She had a firm, rounded chin and a straight nose and a perfect bow of a mouth that was a natural light pink, without makeup. She wasn't pretty, but her figure was exquisite, even in blue jeans and a faded checked cotton shirt with the two buttons missing, torn off when she'd fallen. She grimaced. She hadn't taken time to search for a bra in the clean wash this morning because she'd been in a hurry to fix the fence before her only bull got out into the road. She looked like a juvenile stripper, with the firm, creamy curves of her breasts very noticeable where the buttons were missing.

She shaded her eyes with her hand and glanced around. There was nothing for miles but Texas and more Texas. She should have been paying better attention to what she was doing, but her father's death had devastated her. She'd cried for three days, especially after the family attorney had told her about that humiliating clause in the will he'd left. She couldn't bear the shame of divulging it to Hank. But how could she avoid it, when it concerned him as much as it concerned her? Papa, she thought miserably, how could you do this to me? Couldn't you have spared me a little pride!

She wiped stray tears away. Crying wouldn't help. Her father was dead and the will would have to be dealt with.

A sound caught her attention. In the stillness of the field, it was very loud. There was a rhythm to it. After a minute, she knew why it sounded familiar. It was the gait of a thoroughbred stallion. And she knew exactly to whom that horse belonged.

Sure enough, a minute later a tall rider came into view. With his broad-brimmed hat pulled low over his lean, dark face and the elegant way he rode, Hank Grant was pretty easy to spot from a distance. If he hadn't been so noticeable, the horse, Cappy, was. Cappy was a palomino with impeccable bloodlines, and he brought handsome fees at stud. He was remarkably gentle for an ungelded horse, although he could become nervous at times. Still, he wouldn't allow anyone except Hank on his back.

As Hank reined in beside her prone body, she could see the amused indulgence in his face before she heard it in his deep voice.

"Again?" he asked with resignation, obviously recalling the other times he'd had to rescue her.

"The fence was down," she said belligerently, blowing a strand of blond hair out of her mouth. "And that stupid fence tool needs hands like a wrestler's to work it!"

"Sure it does, honey," he drawled, crossing his forearms over the pommel. "Fences don't know beans about the women's liberation movement."

"Don't you start that again," she muttered.

His mouth tugged up. "Aren't you in a peachy position to be throwing out challenges?" he murmured dryly, and his dark eyes saw far too much as they swept over her body. For just an instant, something flashed in them when they came to rest briefly on the revealed curves of her breasts.

She moved uncomfortably. "Come on, Hank, get me loose," she pleaded, wriggling. "I've been stuck here since nine o'clock and I'm dying for something to drink. It's so hot."

"Okay, kid." He swung out of the saddle and threw Cappy's reins over his head, leaving him to graze nearby. He squatted by her trapped legs. His worn jeans pulled tight against the long, powerful muscles of his legs and she had to grit her teeth against the pleasure it gave her just to look at him. Hank was handsome. He had that sort of masculine beauty about him that made even older women sigh when they saw him. He had a rider's lean and graceful look, and a face that an advertising agency would have loved.

But he was utterly unaware of his own attractions. His wife had run out on him ten years before, and he'd never wanted to marry anyone else since the divorce. It was well-known in the community that Hank had no use for a woman except in one way. He was discreet and tight-lipped about his liaisons, and only Dana seemed to know that he had them. He was remarkably outspoken with her. In fact, he talked to her about private things that he shared with nobody else.

He was surveying the damage, his lips pursed thoughtfully, before he began to try to untangle her from the barbed wire with gloved hands. Hank was methodical in everything he did, single-minded and deliberate. He never acted rashly. It was another trait that didn't go unnoticed.

"Nope, that won't do," he murmured and reached into his pocket. "I'm going to have to cut this denim to get you loose, honey. I'm sorry. I'll replace the jeans."

She blushed. "I'm not destitute yet!"

He looked down into her dark blue eyes and saw the color in her cheeks. "You're so proud, Dana. You'd never ask for help, not if it meant you starved to death." He flipped open his pocketknife. "I guess that's why we get along so well. We're alike in a lot of ways."

"You're taller than I am, and you have black hair. Mine's blond," she said pointedly.

He grinned, as she knew he would. He didn't smile much, especially around other people. She loved the way his eyes twinkled when he smiled.

"I wasn't talking about physical differences," he explained unnecessarily. He cut the denim loose from the wire. It was a good thing he was wearing gloves, because the barbed-wire was sharp and treacherous. "Why don't you use electrified fence like modern ranchers?"

"Because I can't afford it, Hank," she said simply.

He grimaced. He freed the last strand and pulled her into a sitting position, which was unexpectedly intimate. Her blouse fell open when she leaned forward and, like any male, he filled his eyes with the sight of her firm, creamy breasts, their tips hard and mauve against the soft pink mounds. He caught his breath audibly.

Embarrassed, she grasped the edges of her shirt and pulled them together, flushing. She couldn't meet his eyes. But she was aware of his intent stare, of the smell of leather and faint cologne that clung to his skin, of the clean smell of his long-sleeve chambray shirt. Her eyes fell to the opening at his throat, where thick black hair was visible. She'd never seen Hank without his shirt. She'd always wanted to.

His lean hand smoothed against her cheek and

his thumb pressed her rounded chin up. His eyes searched her shy ones. "And that's what I like best about you," he said huskily. "You don't play. Every move you make is honest." He held her gaze. "I wouldn't be much of a man if I'd turned my eyes away. Your breasts are beautiful, like pink marble with hard little tips that make me feel very masculine. You shouldn't be ashamed of a natural reaction like that."

She wasn't quite sure what he meant. "Natural... reaction?" she faltered, wide-eyed.

He frowned. "Don't you understand?"

She didn't. Her life had been a remarkably sheltered one. She'd first discovered her feelings for Hank when she was just seventeen, and she'd never looked at anyone else. She'd only dated two boys. Both of them had been shy and a little nervous with her, and when one of them had kissed her, she'd found it distasteful.

She did watch movies, some of which were very explicit. But they didn't explain what happened to people physically, they just showed it.

"No," she said finally, grimacing. "Well, I'm hopeless, I guess. I don't date, I haven't got time to read racy novels...!"

He was watching her very closely. "Some lessons carry a high price. But it's safe enough with me. Here."

He took her own hand and, shockingly, eased the fabric away from her breast and put her fingers on the hard tip. He watched her body as he did it, which made the experience even more sensual.

"Desire causes it," he explained quietly. "A man's body swells where he's most a man. A woman's breasts swell and the tips go hard. It's a reaction that comes from excitement, and nothing at all to be ashamed of."

She was barely breathing. She knew her face was flushed, and her heart was beating her to death. She was sitting in the middle of an open field, letting Hank look at her breasts and explain desire to her. The whole thing had a fantasy quality that made her wide-eyed.

He knew it. He smiled. "You're pretty," he said gently, removing her hand and tugging the edges of the blouse back together. "Don't make heavy weather of it. It's natural, isn't it, with us? It always has been. That's why I can talk to you so easily about the most intimate things." He frowned slightly. "I wanted my wife all the time, did I ever tell you? She taunted me and made me crazy to have her, so that I'd do anything for it. But I wasn't rich enough to suit her. My best friend hit it big in real estate and she was all over him like a duck on a bug. I don't think she ever looked back when she left me, but I didn't sleep for weeks, wanting her. I still want her, from time to time." He sighed roughly. "And now she's coming back, she and Bob. They're going to be in town for a few weeks while he gets rid of all his investments. He's retiring, and he wants to sell me his racehorse. Hell of a gall, isn't it?" he muttered coldly.

She felt his pain and didn't dare let him see how much it disturbed her. "Thanks for untangling me," she said breathlessly, to divert him, and started to get up.

His hand stayed her. He looked studious and calculating. "Don't. I want to try something."

His fingers went to the snaps of his chambray shirt and he unfastened it all down his chest, pulling the shirttail out of his jeans as he went. His chest was broad and tanned, thick with hair, powerfully muscled.

"What are you doing?" she whispered, startled.

"I told you. I want to try something." He drew her up on her knees, and unfastened the remaining buttons on her shirt. He looked searchingly at her expression. She was too shocked to protest, and then he pulled her close, letting her feel for the first time in her life the impact of a man's seminudity against her own.

Her sharp breath was audible. There was wonder in her eyes as she lifted them to his in fascinated curiosity.

His hands went to her rib cage and he drew her

lazily, sensuously, against that rough cushion of his chest. It tickled her breasts and made the tips go harder. She grasped his shoulders, biting in with her nails involuntarily as all her dreams seemed to come true at once. His eyes were blazing with dark fires. They fell to her mouth and he bent toward her.

She felt the hard warmth of his lips slowly burrow into hers, parting them, teasing them. She held her breath, tasting him like some rare wine. Dimly she felt his hand go between them and tenderly caress one swollen breast. She gasped again, and his head lifted so that he could see her eyes.

His thumb rippled over the hard tip and she shivered all over, helpless in his embrace.

"Yes," he whispered absently, "that's exactly what I thought. I could lay you down right here, right now."

She barely heard him. Her heart was shaking her. His fingers touched her, teased her body. It arched toward him, desperate not to lose the contact.

His eyes were all over her face; her bare breasts pressed so close against him. He felt the touch all the way to his soul. "I want you," he said quietly.

She sobbed, because it shouldn't have been like this. Her own body betrayed her, giving away all its hard-kept secrets.

But there was a hesitation in him. His hand stilled

on her breast, his mouth hovered over hers as his dark eyes probed, watched.

"You're still a virgin, aren't you?" he asked roughly.

She swallowed, her lips swollen from the touch of his.

He shook her gently. "Tell me!"

She bit her lower lip and looked at his throat. She could see the pulse hammering there. "You knew that already." She ground out the words.

He didn't seem to breathe for a minute, then there was a slow, ragged exhaling of breath. He wrapped her up in his arms and sat holding her close, rocking her, his face buried in her hot throat, against her quick pulse.

"Yes. I just wanted to be sure," he said after a minute. He released her inch by inch and smiled ruefully as he fastened her blouse again.

She let him, dazed. Her eyes clung to his as if they were looking for sanity.

Her mouth was swollen. Her eyes were as round as dark blue saucers in a face livid with color. In that moment she was more beautiful than he'd ever known her to be.

"No harm done," he said gently. "We've learned a little more about each other than we knew before. It won't change anything. We're still friends."

He made it sound like a question. "Of...of course," she stammered.

He stood up, refastening his own shirt and tucking it back in as he looked at her with a new expression. *Possession.* Yes, that was it. He looked as if she belonged to him now. She didn't understand the look or her own reaction to it.

She scrambled to her feet, moving them to see if anything hurt.

"The wire didn't break the skin, fortunately for you," he said. "Those jeans are heavy, tough fabric. But you need a tetanus shot, just the same. If you haven't had one, I'll drive you into town to get one."

"I had one last year," she said, avoiding his eyes as she started toward Bess, who was eyeing the stallion a little too curiously. "You'd better get Cappy before he gets any ideas."

He caught Cappy's bridle and had to soothe him. "You'd better get her out of here while you can," he advised. "I didn't think you'd be riding her today or I wouldn't have brought Cappy. You usually ride Toast."

She didn't want to tell him that Toast had been sold to help settle one of her father's outstanding debts.

He watched her swing into the saddle and he did likewise, keeping the stallion a good distance away. The urge to mate wasn't only a human thing.

"I'll be over to see you later," he called to her. "We've got some things to talk over."

"Like what?" she asked.

But Hank didn't answer. Cappy was fidgeting wildly as he tried to control the stallion. "Not now. Get her home!"

She turned the mare and galloped toward the ranch, forgetting the fence in her headlong rush. She'd have to come back later. At least she could get out of the sun and get something cold to drink now.

Once she was back in the small house, she looked at herself in the bathroom mirror after a shower and couldn't believe she was the same woman who'd gone out into the pasture only this morning. She looked so different. There was something new in her eyes, something more feminine, mysterious and secretive. She felt all over again the slow, searching touch of Hayden Grant's hard fingers and blushed.

There had been a rare and beautiful magic between them out there in the field. She loved him so much. There had been no other man's touch on her body, never another man in her heart. But how was he going to react when he knew the contents of her father's will? He didn't want to marry again. He'd said so often enough. And although he and Dana had been friends for a long time, he'd drawn back at once when he made her admit her innocence. He'd wanted an affair, obviously, but discovered that it would be impossible to justify that with his conscience. He couldn't seduce an innocent woman.

She went into her bedroom and put on blue slacks and a knit shirt, leaving her freshly washed and dried hair loose around her shoulders. He'd said they would talk later. Did that mean he'd heard gossip about the will? Was he going to ask her to challenge it?

She had no idea what to expect. Perhaps it was just as well. She'd have less time to worry.

She walked around the living room, her eyes on the sad, shabby furniture that she and her father had bought so many years ago. There hadn't been any money in the past year for reupholstery or new frills. They'd put everything into those few head of beef cattle and the herd sire. But the cattle market was way down and if a bad winter came, there would be no way to afford to buy feed. She had to plant plenty of hay and corn to get through the winter. But their best hand had quit on her father's death, and now all she had were two part-time helpers, whom she could barely afford to pay. A blind woman could see that she wouldn't be able to keep going now.

She could have wept for her lost chances. She had no education past high school, no real way to make a living. All she knew was how to pull calves and mix feed and sell off stock. She went to the auctions and knew how to bid, how to buy, how to pick cattle for conformation. She knew much less about horses, but that hardly mattered. She only had one left and the part-time man kept Bess—and Toast, until he was sold—groomed and fed and watered. She did at least know how to saddle the beast. But to Dana, a horse was a tool to use with cattle. Hayden cringed when she said that. He had purebred palominos and loved every one of them. He couldn't understand anyone not loving horses as much as he did.

Oddly, though, it was their only real point of contention. In most other ways, they agreed, even on politics and religion. And they liked the same television programs. She smiled, remembering how many times they'd shared similar enthusiasms for weekly series, especially science fiction ones.

Hank had been kind to her father, too, and so patient when a man who'd given his life to being a country gentleman was suddenly faced with learning to be a rancher at the age of fifty-five. It made Dana sad to think how much longer her father's life might have been if he'd taken up a less exhaustive profession. He'd had a good brain, and so much still to give.

She fixed a light lunch and a pot of coffee and thought about going back out to see about that downed fence. But another disaster would just be too much. She was disaster-prone when Hank was anywhere near her, and she seemed to be rapidly getting that way even when he wasn't. He'd rescued her from mad bulls, trapped feet in corral fences, once from a rattlesnake and twice from falling bales of hay. He must be wondering if there wasn't some way he could be rid of her once and for all.

It was nice of him not to mention those incidents when he'd rescued her from the fence, though. Surely he'd been tempted to.

Tempted. She colored all over again remembering the intimacy they'd shared. In the seven years they'd known each other, he'd never touched her until today. She wondered why he had.

The sound of a car outside on the country road brought her out of the kitchen and to the front door, just in time to see Hank's black luxury car pull into the driveway. He wasn't a flashy sort of man, and he didn't go overboard to surround himself with luxurious things. That make of car was his one exception. He had a fascination for the big cars that never seemed to waver, because he traded his in every other year—for another black one.

"Don't you get tired of the color?" she'd asked him once.

"Why?" he'd replied laconically. "Black goes with everything."

He came up onto the porch, and the expression on his face was one she hadn't seen before. He looked as he always did, neatly dressed and clean-shaven, devastatingly handsome, but there was still a difference. After their brief interlude out in the pasture, the atmosphere between them was just a little strained.

He had his hands in his pockets as he glanced down at her body in the pretty ruffled blue sundress.

"Is that for my benefit?" he asked.

She blushed. She usually kicked around in jeans or cutoffs and tank tops. She almost never wore dresses around the ranch. And her hair was long and loose around her shoulders instead of in its usual braid.

She shrugged in defeat. "Yes, I guess it is," she said, meeting his eyes with a rueful smile. "Sorry."

He shook his head. "There's no need to apologize. None at all. In fact, what happened this afternoon gave me some ideas that I want to talk to you about."

Her heart jumped into her chest. Was he going to propose? Oh, glory, if only he would, and then he'd never even have to know about that silly clause in her father's will!

Chapter Two

She led the way into the kitchen and set out a platter of salad and cold cuts and dressing in the center of the table, on which she'd already put two place settings. She poured coffee into two mugs, gave him one and sat down. She didn't have to ask what he took in his coffee, because she already knew that he had it black, just as she did. It was one of many things they had in common.

"What did you want to ask me, Hank?" she ventured after he'd worked his way through a huge salad and two cups of coffee. Her nerves were screaming with suspense and anticipation.

"Oh. That." He leaned back with his half-drained

coffee cup in his hand. "I wondered if you might be willing to help me out with a little playacting for my ex-wife's benefit."

All her hopes fell at her feet. "What sort of acting?" she asked, trying to sound nonchalant.

"I want you to pretend to be involved with me," he said frankly, staring at her. "On this morning's showing, it shouldn't be too difficult to look as if we can't keep our hands off each other. Should it?" he asked with a mocking smile.

Everything fell into place; his odd remarks, his "experiment" out there in the pasture, his curious behavior. His beloved ex-wife was coming to town and he didn't want everyone to know how badly she'd hurt him or how he'd grieved at her loss. So Dana had been cast as his new love. He didn't want a new wife, he wanted an actress.

She stared into her coffee. "I don't guess you ever want to get married again, do you?" she asked with studied carelessness.

He saw right through that devious little question. "No, I don't," he said bluntly. "Once was enough."

She grimaced. Her father had placed her in an intolerable position. Somehow, he must have suspected that his time was limited. Otherwise why should he have gone to such lengths in his will to make sure that his daughter was provided for after his death?

"You've been acting funny since your father died," he said suddenly, and his eyes narrowed. "Is there something you haven't told me?"

She made an awkward motion with one shoulder.

"Did he go into debt and leave you with nothing, is that it?"

"Well…"

"Because if that's the case, I can take care of the problem," he continued, unabashed. "You help me out while Betty's here, and I'll pay off any outstanding debts. You can think of it as a job."

She wanted to throw herself down on the floor and scream. Nothing was working out. She looked at him in anguish. "Oh, Hank," she groaned.

He scowled. "Come on. It can't be that bad. Spit it out."

She took a steadying breath and got to her feet. "There's a simpler way. I think…you'd better read Dad's will. I'll get it."

She went into the living room and pulled out the desk drawer that contained her father's will. She took it into the kitchen and handed it to a puzzled Hank, watching his lean, elegant hands unfasten the closure on the document.

"And before you start screaming, I didn't know anything about that clause," she added through her teeth. "It was as much a shock to me as it's going to be to you."

"Clause?" he murmured as he scanned over the will. "What clause... Oh, my God!"

"Now, Hank," she began in an effort to thwart the threatened explosion she saw growing in his lean face.

"God in heaven!" He got to his feet, slamming the will back on the table. His face had gone from ruddy to white in the space of seconds. "What a hell of a choice I've got! I marry you or I end up with a stock car racetrack on the edge of my barn where my mares foal! Moving the damned thing would cost half a million dollars!"

"If you'll just give me a chance to speak," she said heavily. "Hank, there may be a way to break the will—"

"Oh, sure, we can say he was crazy!" His black eyes were glittering like diamonds.

She flushed. He was flagrantly insulting her. She might love him, but she wasn't taking that kind of treatment, even from him. She got to her own feet and glared up at him. "He must have been, to want me to marry you!" she shouted. "What makes you think you're such a prize, Hank? You're years too old for me in the first place, and in the second, what sane woman would want to marry a man who's still in love with his ex-wife?"

He was barely breathing. His anger was so apparent that Dana felt her knees go wobbly, despite her spunky words.

His black eyes slewed over her with contempt. "I might like looking at your body, but a couple of kisses and a little fondling don't warrant a marriage proposal in my book."

"Nor in mine," she said with scalded pride. "Why don't you go home?"

His fists clenched at his sides. He still couldn't believe what he'd read in that will. It was beyond belief that her father, his friend, would have stabbed him in the back this way.

"He must have been out of his mind," he grated. "I could have settled a trust on you or something, he didn't have to specify marriage as a condition for you to inherit what's rightfully yours!"

She lifted her chin. "I can hardly ask what his reasoning was," she reminded him. "He's dead." The words were stark and hollow. She was still in the midst of grief for the passing of her parent. Hank hadn't considered that she was hurting, she thought, or maybe he just didn't care. He was too angry to be rational.

He breathed deliberately. "You little cheat," he accused. "You've had a crush on me for years, and I've tolerated it. It amused me. But this isn't funny.

This is low and deceitful. I'd think more of you if you admitted that you put your father up to it."

"I don't give a damn what you think of me," she choked. Her pride was in tatters. She was fighting tears of pure rage. "When you've had time to get over the shock, I'd like you to see my attorney. Between the two of you, I'm sure you can find some way to straighten this out. Because I wouldn't marry you if you came with a subscription to my favorite magazine and a new Ferrari! So I had a crush on you once. That's ancient history!"

He made a sound through his nose. "Then what was that this morning out in the pasture?" he chided.

"Lust!" she threw at him.

He picked up his hat and studied her with cold contempt. "I'll see what I can do about the will. You could contact your mother," he added pointedly. "She's wealthy. I'm sure she won't let you starve."

She folded her arms across her breasts. "I wouldn't ask my mother for a tissue if I was bleeding to death, and you know it."

"These are desperate circumstances," he said pointedly, a little calmer now.

"My circumstances are no longer any of your business," she said in a voice that was disturbingly calm. "Goodbye, Hank."

He slammed his hat over his eyes and went to

the front door, but he hesitated with the doorknob in his hand and looked over his shoulder. She was pale and her eyes were shimmering. He knew she was grieving for her father. It must be scary, too, to have her inheritance wrapped around an impossible demand. If he didn't marry her, she was going to lose everything, even her home. He winced.

"Goodbye," she repeated firmly. Her eyes startled him with their cold blue darkness. She looked as if she hated him.

He drew in a short breath. "Look, we'll work something out."

"I'm twenty-two years old," she said proudly. "It's past time I started taking care of myself. If I lose the ranch, I'll get a grant and go back to college. I've already completed the basic courses, anyway."

He hadn't thought that she might go away. Suddenly his life was even more topsy-turvy than before. Betty was on her way back to town, Dana's father had tried to force him into a marriage he didn't want and now Dana was going away. He felt deserted.

He let out a word that she'd never heard him use. "Then go, if you want to, and be damned," he said furiously. "It will be a pleasure not to have to rescue you from half a dozen disasters a day."

He slammed the door on his way out and she sank into a chair, feeling the sudden warm wetness of the tears she'd been too proud to let him see. At least now she knew how he felt about her. She guessed that she'd be well-advised to learn to live with it.

The rest of the day was a nightmare. By the end of it, she was sick of the memories in the house. Grief and humiliation drove her to the telephone. She called Joe, the oldest of her two part-time workers on the ranch.

"I'm going away for a couple of days," she told him. "I want you and Ernie to watch the cattle for me. Okay?"

"Sure, boss lady. Where you going?"

"Away."

She hung up.

It only took her a few minutes to make a reservation at a moderately priced Houston hotel downtown, and to pack the ancient gray Bronco she drove with enough clothes for the weekend. She was on her way in no time, having locked up the house. Joe had a key if he needed to get in.

She spent the weekend watching movies on cable and experimenting with new hairstyles. She drifted around the shops downtown, although she didn't buy anything. She had to conserve her money now, until she could apply for a grant and get into college. On an impulse she phoned a couple of colleges around the area and requested catalogs be sent to her home address in Jacobsville.

The runaway weekend had been something of

an extravagance, but she'd needed to get away. She felt like a tourist as she wandered around all the interesting spots, including the famed San Jacinto monument and the canal where ships came and went into the port city. Heavy rain came on the second day, with flash flooding, and she was forced to stay an extra day or use her Bronco as a barge, because the streets near the hotel were too flooded to allow safe travel.

It was late Monday before she turned into the long driveway of her ranch. And the first thing she noticed as she approached the farmhouse was the proliferation of law-enforcement vehicles.

Shocked, she pulled up and turned off the ignition. "What's happened? Has someone broken into my home?" she asked the first uniformed man she met, a deputy sheriff.

His eyebrows went up. "You live here?" he asked.

"Yes. I'm Dana Mobry."

He chuckled and called to the other three men, one of whom was a Jacobsville city policeman. "Here she is! She hasn't met with foul play."

They came at a lope, bringing a harassed-looking Joe along with them.

"Oh, Miss Mobry, thank the Lord," Joe said, wringing her hand. His hair was grayer than ever, and he looked hollow-eyed.

"Whatever's wrong?" she asked.

"They thought I'd killed you and hid the body!" Joe wailed, looking nervously at the law officers.

Dana's eyes widened. "Why?"

"Mr. Grant came over and couldn't find you," Joe said frantically. "I told him you'd gone away, but I didn't know where, and he blew up and started accusing me of all sorts of things on account of I wouldn't tell him where you were. When you didn't come back by today, he called the law. I'm so glad to see you, Miss Mobry. I was afraid they were going to put me in jail!"

"I'm sorry you were put through this, Joe," she said comfortingly. "I should have told you I was going to Houston, but it never occurred to me that Mr. Grant would care where I went," she added bitterly.

The deputy sheriff grinned sheepishly. "Yeah, he said you'd had an argument and he was afraid you might have done something drastic…"

She glared at him so furiously that he broke off. "If that isn't conceit, I don't know what is! I wouldn't kill myself over a stuck-up, overbearing, insufferable egotist like Mr. Grant unless I was goofy! Do I look goofy?"

He cleared his throat. "Oh, no, ma'am, you don't look at all goofy to me!"

While he was defending himself, Hank came around the side of the house to see where the search party had disappeared to, and stopped when he saw

Dana. "So there you are!" he began furiously, bare-headed and wild-eyed as he joined her. "Where in hell have you been? Do you have any idea how much trouble you've caused?"

She lifted her chin. "I've been to Houston. Since when is going to Houston a crime? And since when do I have to inform you of my whereabouts?"

He snorted. "I'm a concerned neighbor."

"You're a royal pain in the neck, and I left town to get away from you," she snapped. "I don't want to see you or talk to you!"

He straightened his shoulders and his mouth compressed. "As long as you're all right."

"You might apologize to poor Joe while you're about it," she added pointedly. "He was beside himself, thinking he was going to jail for doing away with me."

"I never said any such thing," he muttered. He glanced at Joe. "He knows I didn't think he'd done you in."

That was as close as he was likely to come to an apology, and Joe accepted it with less rancor than Dana would have.

"Thanks for coming out," Hank told the deputy and the others. "She was missing for two days and I didn't know where she was. Anything could have happened."

"Oh, he knows that," the city policeman, Matt

Lovett, said with a grin, jerking his thumb at the deputy sheriff. "He and his wife had an argument and she drove off to her mother's. On the way her car died. She left it on the river bridge and caught a ride into town to get a mechanic."

"Matt…!" the deputy grumbled.

Matt held up a hand. "I'm just getting to the best part. He went after her and saw the car and thought she'd jumped off the bridge. By the time she got back with the mechanic, the civil defense boys were out there dragging the river."

"Well, she might have been in there," the deputy defended himself, red-faced. He grinned at Hank. "And Miss Mobry might have been eaten by one of her young steers."

"Or carried off by aliens," Matt mused, tongue in cheek. "That's why our police force is always on the job, Miss Mobry, to offer protection to any citizen who needs it. I'd dearly love to protect you at a movie one night next week," he added with twinkling green eyes. "Any night you like. A good movie and a nice big burger with fries."

Dana's eyes were twinkling now, too.

Hank stepped in between her and the policeman. "I think she'll need some rest after today's excitement, but I'm sure she appreciates the offer, Matt."

The words didn't match the dark threat in his eyes. Matt had only been teasing, although if he'd really wanted to take Dana out, all the threats in the world wouldn't have stopped him.

"You're probably right," Matt agreed. He winked at Dana. "But the offer stands, just the same."

She smiled at him. He really was nice. "Thanks, Matt."

The law enforcement people said their farewells and went off to bigger tasks, leaving Dana and Joe and Hank standing aimlessly in the front yard.

"I'll get home now, Miss Mobry. So glad you're all right," Joe said again.

"Thanks, Joe," she replied. "I'm sorry for all the trouble you had."

"Not to worry."

He ambled off. Dana folded her arms over her breasts and glared furiously at Hank.

He had his hands deep in his pockets. He looked more uncomfortable than she'd ever seen him.

"Well, how was I to know you hadn't done something desperate?" he wanted to know. "I said some harsh things to you." He averted his eyes, because it disturbed him to remember what he'd said. In the few days Dana had been missing, he'd done a lot of remembering, mostly about how big a part of his life Dana was, and the long friendship he'd shared with her. He'd had no right to belittle the feelings she had for him. In fact, it had rocked his world when he realized how long he'd been deliberately ignoring them. He was torn between his lingering love for Betty and his confused feelings for Dana. It was an emotional crisis that he'd never had to face before. He knew he wasn't handling it very well.

Dana didn't budge an inch. "I've already decided what I'm going to do, in case you had any lingering worries," she told him coolly. "If you can find a loophole, a way for us to break the will, I'm going to sell the place and go back to school. I have catalogs coming from three colleges."

His face went rigid. "I thought you liked ranching."

She made an amused, bitter sound. "Hank, I can't even use a fence tool. I can't pull a calf without help from Joe or Ernie. I can feed livestock and treat wounds and check for diseases, but I can't do heavy lifting and fix machinery. I don't have the physical strength, and I'm running out of the financial means to hire it done." She threw up her hands. "If I even tried to get a job at someone else's ranch, with my lack of skills, they'd laugh at me. How in the world can I run a ranch?"

"You can sell it to me and I'll run it for you," he said curtly. "You can rent the house and stay here."

"As what?" she persisted. "Caretaker? I want more than that from life."

"Such as?" he asked.

"Never you mind," she said evasively, because a

ready answer didn't present itself. "Did you talk to my lawyer?"

"No."

"Then would you, please?"

He stuck his hands into his pockets. "Listen, Dana, no court in Jacobsville is going to throw out that will on the grounds that your father was incompetent. His mind was as sound as mine, and he knew business inside out."

Her heart fell. "He might have been temporarily upset when he inserted that clause."

"Maybe he was," he agreed. "Maybe he'd had some chest pain or a premonition. I'm sure he meant it as a way to make sure you weren't left alone, with no support, after he was gone. But his reasons don't matter. Either you marry me or we both stand to lose a hell of a lot of money."

"You don't want to marry me," she reminded him with painful pleasure. "You said so."

He drew in a long, weary breath and searched her wan little face. "God, I'm tired," he said unexpectedly. "My life is upside down. I don't know where I'm going, or why. No, Dana, I don't want to marry you. That's honest. But there's a lot riding on that will." He moved his shoulders, as if to ease their stiffness. "I'd rather wait a few weeks, at least until Betty's visit is over. But there's a time limit as well. A month after your father's death, I believe, all the conditions of the will have to be fulfilled."

She nodded miserably.

"In a way, it would suit me to be married right now," he reflected solemnly. "I don't want Betty to see how badly she hurt me, or how much I still want her. I might be tempted to try and break up her marriage, and that's not the sort of man I want to be."

"What about her husband?"

"Bob doesn't care what she does," he replied. "He's totally indifferent to her these days, and he's no longer a financial giant. I don't think it would take too much effort to get her away from him. But she left me because he had more money, don't you see?" he added pointedly. "My God, I can't let myself be caught in that old trap again, regardless of what I feel for her!"

She felt sorry for him. Imagine that. She linked her hands together over her stomach. "Then what do you want to do, Hank?" she asked quietly.

"Get married. But only on paper," he added deliberately, his dark eyes steady and full of meaning. "Despite the physical attraction I felt for you out in the pasture that day, I don't want a physical relationship with you. Let's get that clear at the outset. I want a document that gives you the right to sell me that land. In return, I'll make sure the figure you receive is above market price, and I'll put you through college to boot."

It sounded fair enough to Dana, who was wrung out from the emotional stress. "And I get to stay here, in my own house," she added.

"No."

Her eyebrows shot up.

"I'll want you to stay up at the homeplace with me," he replied, "as long as Betty and Bob are in town. Even though this is a legal marriage, I don't want Betty to know that I'm only a paper husband."

"Oh, I see," she replied. "You want us to pretend that it's a normal arrangement."

"Exactly."

She didn't want to agree. He'd hurt her feelings, made horrible remarks, insulted her and embarrassed her with today's womanhunt. But she needed to be able to sell the ranch. It would be her escape from the emotional poverty of loving where there was no hope of reciprocation.

"Okay," she said after a minute. "Will we have to get a blood test and a license at the courthouse?"

"We'll fly to Las Vegas and get married out there," he told her. "As soon as we've completed the legal maneuvers and Betty is safely out of my hair, we'll get a divorce there, which will be just as easy."

Easy marriage. Easy divorce. Dana, with her

dreams of returned love and babies to raise, felt the pain of those words all the way through her heart.

"An annulment will spare you any hint of scandal afterward," he continued. "You can get your degree and find someone to spend your life with. Or part of it," he added with a mocking smile. "I don't think anybody has illusions about marriage lasting until death these days."

Her parents had divorced. Hank had divorced. But Dana had seen couples who'd stayed together and been in love for years. The Ballenger brothers with their happy marriages came instantly to mind.

"I'm not that cynical," she said after a minute. "And I think that children should have both parents while they're growing up if it's at all possible. Well," she added, "as long as it isn't a daily battleground."

"Was your family like that?" he asked gently.

She nodded. "My mother hated my father. She said he had no ambition, no intelligence, and that he was as dull as dishwater. She wanted parties and holidays all the time. He just wanted to settle down with a good book and nibble cheese."

She smiled sadly, remembering him, and had to fight the easy tears that sprang so readily to her eyes.

"Don't cry," he said shortly.

She lifted her chin. "I wasn't going to," she said roughly. She remembered him holding her at her father's funeral, murmuring comforting words softly at her ear. But he had little patience with emotion, as a rule.

He took a deep breath. "I'll set everything up and let you know when we'll go," he said.

She wanted to argue, but the time had long passed for that. She nodded. He waited, but when she didn't say anything else, he went back to his car, got in and drove away.

Chapter Three

Las Vegas sat right in the middle of a desert. Dana had never been there, and the sight of it fascinated her. Not only was it like a neon city, but the glitter extended even to the people who worked at the night spots. Dana found the way women dressed on the streets fascinating and almost fell out the window of Hank's hired luxury car trying to look at them. It wasn't until he explained what they did for a living that she gave up her surveillance. It was interesting to find that what they did was legal and that they could even advertise their services.

"Here we are," he said gruffly, stopping at one of the all-night wedding chapels.

It looked flashy, but then, so did the rest of them. Hank offered her an arm but she refused it, walking beside him with her purse tight in her hand. She was wearing a simple off-white suit. She didn't have a veil or even a bouquet, and she felt their omission all the way to her toes. It was so very different from the way she'd envisioned her wedding day.

Hank didn't seem to notice or care. He dealt with the preliminaries, they signed a document, he produced a ring that she didn't even know he'd bought. Five minutes later, they were officially married, ring, cool kiss and all. Dana looked up at her husband and felt nothing, not even sorrow. She seemed to be numb from head to toe.

"Are we flying right back?" she asked as they got into the car once more.

He glanced at her. She seemed devoid of emotion. It was her wedding day. He hadn't given her a choice about her wedding ring. He hadn't offered to buy her a bouquet. He hadn't even asked if she wanted a church wedding, which could have been arranged. He'd been looking at the whole messy business from his own point of view. Dana had deserved something better than this icy, clinical joining.

"We can stay at one of the theme hotels overnight, if you like, and take in a show."

She didn't want to appear eager. The only show she'd ever seen was at a movie theater in Victoria.

"Well," she said hesitantly.

"I'll introduce you to the one-armed bandit," he added, chuckling at her expression.

"If you think we could," she murmured, and that was as far as she was willing to commit herself. "But I didn't pack anything for an overnight stay."

"No problem. The hotel has shops."

And it did. He outfitted her with a gown, a bag and everything in the way of toiletries that she needed. She noticed that he didn't buy any pajamas, but she thought nothing of it. Surely they'd have separate rooms, anyway.

But they didn't. There were too many conventions in town, and they got the last suite the hotel had—one with a king-size bed and a short sofa.

Hank stared at the bed ruefully. "Sorry," he said. "But it's this or sleep on the floor."

She cleared her throat. "We're both adults. And it's only a paper marriage," she stammered.

"So it is," he mused, but his dark eyes had narrowed as they assessed her slender, perfect figure and he remembered the sight of her in the pasture with her blouse open and the feel of her breasts pressed hard into his bare chest.

She glanced up, meeting that hot, intent stare. She flushed. "I'm not having sex with you, Hank," she said shortly.

His eyebrows went up. "Did I ask?" he drawled

sarcastically. "Listen, honey, the streets are full of prime women, if I'm so inclined."

Her eyes blazed at him. "Don't you dare!" she raged. "Don't you dare, Hank!"

He began to smile. "Well, well, aren't we possessive already?"

"That's not the point. You made a vow. Until we have it undone, we're married." She stared at her shoes. "I wouldn't go running to some gigolo on my wedding night."

"Of course you wouldn't." He moved closer, his hands finding her small waist, and brought her gently to him. His breath feathered her forehead. "I can hear you breathing," he whispered. "Nervous?"

She swallowed. "Well…yes…a little."

His lips brushed her hair. "There's no need. It's a big bed. If you don't want anything to happen, it won't."

She felt disappointed somehow. They were legally married. She loved him. Did he really not want her at all?

He tilted her face up to his dark, curious eyes. "On the other hand," he said softly, "if you want to know what it's all about, I'll teach you. There won't be any consequences. And you'll enjoy it."

She felt the words to the very tips of her toes. But she wasn't going to be won over that easily, even if she did want him more than her next breath.

"No dice, huh?" he mused after a minute. "Okay. Suppose we go downstairs and try our luck?"

"Suits me," she said, anxious to go anywhere away from that bed.

So they went the rounds in the casino and played everything from the one-armed bandits to blackjack. The glittery costumes of the dancers on stage fascinated Dana, like everything else about this fantasy city. She ate perfectly cooked steak, watched the shows, and generally had a wonderful time while Hank treated her like a cherished date. In fact, that's what it was. They'd never been out together in all the years they'd known each other. During that one evening they made up for lost time.

They returned upstairs just after midnight. Dana had gone overboard with piña coladas, the one drink she could tolerate. But she'd underestimated the amount of rum the bartender put in them. She was weaving at the door, to Hank's patent amusement.

He slid the coded card into the slot and when the blinking green light indicated that it was unlocked, he opened the door.

"Home again," he murmured, standing aside to let her enter.

She tugged up the strap of her black dress that had slipped off her shoulder. Like the rest of her abbreviated wardrobe, it was the result of the afternoon's quick shopping trip. In addition to the knee-length cocktail dress and hose, she had a far too revealing black nightgown and no robe. She hoped Hank was agreeable to letting her undress in the dark.

"You can have the bathroom first," he invited. "I'll listen to the news."

"Thanks." She gathered her gown and underwear and went into the bathroom to shower.

When she came out, Hank was sitting on the edge of the bed. He'd removed everything except his slacks. He got up, and she had to suppress a shiver of pleasure at the sight of him bare from the waist up. He had muscular arms and a sexy dark chest with a wedge of curling black hair running down it. His hair was mussed and down on his forehead. He looked rakish because he needed a shave.

"Good thing I packed my razor," he mused, holding up a small pouch that had been in the attaché case he always carried when he traveled. "I have to shave twice a day." His dark eyes slid over her body in the abbreviated gown, lingering where her arms were crossed defensively over the thin fabric that didn't quite cover her breasts from view. "We're married," he reminded her. "And I've seen most of you."

She cleared her throat. "Which side of the bed do you like?" she asked shyly.

"The right, but I don't mind either one. You can have first pick."

"Thanks."

She put her discarded clothing on a chair and climbed in quickly, pulling the covers up to her chin.

He lifted an eyebrow. "Stay just like that," he coaxed, "and when I come out, I'll tell you a nice fairy tale."

She glared at him through a rosy haze. "I'll probably be asleep. I haven't ever had so much to drink."

He nodded slowly. "That may be a good thing," he said enigmatically, and went into the bathroom.

She wasn't asleep when he came out. She'd tried to be, but her mind wouldn't cooperate. She peered through her lashes and watched him move around the room turning out lights. He had a towel hooked around his hips and as he turned out the last lamp on his side of the bed, she saw him unhook the towel and throw it over the back of the vinyl-covered chair.

She stiffened as he climbed in beside her and stretched lazily.

"I can feel you bristling," he murmured dryly. "It's a big bed, honey, and I don't sleepwalk. You're safe."

She cleared her throat. "Yes, I know."

"Then why are you shivering?"

He rolled over and moved closer. She could feel the

heat of his body through her thin gown. She trembled even more when his long leg brushed against hers.

"Shivering," he continued, moving closer, "and breathing like an Olympic runner." He slid a long arm under her and brought her sliding right over against him. "I haven't forgotten the signs when a woman wants me," he whispered as his hands smoothed the gown right down her body. "And you want me, Dana."

She started to protest, but his mouth was already covering hers. He turned and pulled her to him, so that she felt his nude body all the way down hers. He was warm and hard, and even in her innocence she was aware that he wanted her badly.

His lean hands smoothed over her flat belly, tracing down to the juncture of her long legs. His thumb eased between them and he touched her softly in a place that she hadn't dreamed he would.

She jerked.

"No," he said gently. "Don't pull back. This isn't going to hurt. It's only going to make it easy when I take you." His fingers were slow and sensual and insistent. She shivered, and the pressure grew. His mouth teased over her parted lips while he taught her body to yield to building pleasure.

"Does it feel good?" he whispered.

"Yes," she sobbed.

"Don't fight it," he breathed. His mouth slid down

to her breasts and explored them in a silence that grew tense as the movement of his hand produced staggering sensations that arched her body like a bow.

He was doing something. It wasn't his finger now, it was part of his body, and he was easing down and pushing, penetrating...!

"It hurts," she whispered frantically.

"Here," he whispered, shifting quickly. He moved again, and she shivered, but not with pain. "Yes, that's it," he said quickly. "That's it, sweetheart!"

She was unconsciously following his lead, letting him position her, buffet her. She felt his skin sliding against her own, heard the soft whisper of it even as the sensations made her mind spin. She was making sounds that she didn't recognize, deep in her throat, and clinging to him with all her strength.

"I...wish...!" she choked.

"Wish what?" he bit off, fighting for breath. "What do you want? I'll do anything!"

"Wish...the light...was on," she managed to say.

"Oh, God..." he groaned.

He tried to reach the light switch, but just at that moment, a shock of pleasure caught him off guard and bit into his body like a sweet, hot knife. He gave up any thought of the light and drove against her with all his might, holding her thrashing hips as she went with him on the spiral of pleasure. He heard her cry out and thanked God that she was able to feel anything, because his only sane thought was that if he didn't find release soon, he was going to die...

"Dana!" he cried out as he found what he craved, shuddering and shuddering as he gave himself to the sweetness of ecstasy.

Her hands soothed him as she came back down again, shivering in the aftermath. She stroked his hair and his nape, pressing tender kisses on his cheeks, his eyes, his nose.

"It was good," she whispered. "It was so good, so sweet. Oh, Hank, do it again!"

He couldn't get enough breath to laugh. "Sweetheart, I can't," he whispered huskily. "Not just yet."

"Why? Did I do something wrong?" she asked plaintively.

He turned his head and kissed her soft mouth. "A man's body isn't like a woman's," he said gently. "I have to rest for a few minutes."

"Oh."

He kissed her lazily, stretching his strained muscles and drawing a deep breath before he laced her close against him again and sighed.

"Did it hurt very much?" he murmured drowsily.

"A little, at first." She stretched against him. "Heavens, it's just like dying," she remarked with wonder. "And you don't care if you die, because it's so good." She laughed wickedly. "Hank, turn on the light," she whispered.

"I thought you were a prude," he taunted.

"No, I think I'm a voyeur." She corrected him. "I want to look at you."

"Dana!"

"And don't pretend to be shocked, because I know you aren't. I'll bet you want to look at all of me, too."

"Indeed I do."

"Well, then?"

He turned on the light and peeled the covers away. She looked at him openly, coloring just a little at the sight of his blatant nudity. He didn't blush. He stared and stared, filling his eyes with her.

"God, what a sight," he murmured huskily. He held out his arms. "Come here."

She eased into them, felt him position her and lift her, and then bring her down over him to fit them together in a slow, sensual intimacy.

"Now," he whispered huskily, moving his hands to her hips. "Let's watch each other explode."

"Are we...going to?" she whispered back, moving slowly with him.

He nodded, because he couldn't manage words. His black eyes splintered as the sensations began to build all over again. His last sane thought was that he might never be able to get enough of her....

* * *

He was distant the next morning. Dana had expected a new and wonderful closeness because of their intimacy in the night, but Hank was quiet and reserved in a way he'd never been before.

"Is something wrong?" she asked worriedly.

He shrugged. "What could be wrong?" He checked his watch. "We'd better get a move on. I have an appointment in the office late this afternoon, and I can't afford to miss it. Got your stuff together?"

She nodded, still a little bewildered. "Hank…you aren't sorry about last night, are you?" she asked uneasily.

"Of course not!" he said, and forced a smile. "I'm just in a hurry to get home. Let's go."

And so they left and went home.

Chapter Four

Dana peered again at the thick gold wedding ring on her hand. They'd been back in Jacobsville for two weeks, and she was living in his big sprawling brick mansion now. The housekeeper, Miss Tilly, had been with Hayden for a long time. She was thin and friendly and secretly amused at the high-handed manner Hayden had managed his wedding, but she didn't say a word. She cooked and cleaned and kept out of the way.

Dana was uneasy at first. Her brand-new husband didn't wear a wedding band, and she didn't like to suggest it to him for fear of sounding possessive. But it made her uncomfortable to think that he didn't want to openly indicate his wedded state. Surely he wasn't thinking of having affairs already?

That was a natural thought, because despite his ardor in Las Vegas on their wedding night, he hadn't touched her since. He'd been polite, attentive, even affectionate. But he hadn't touched her as a lover. He was like a friend now. He'd insisted on separate bedrooms without any explanations at all, and he'd withdrawn from her physically to the point that he wouldn't even touch her hand. It wore on Dana's nerves.

His behavior began to make sense the next morning, however, when Tilly went to answer the doorbell and a strange couple entered the house as if they belonged there.

"Where's Hank? He saw Bob at the bank and invited him to lunch," the woman, a striking brunette, announced flatly. "Didn't he say he'd be back by this time, Bob?" she asked the much older, slightly balding man beside her. He looked pale and unhealthy, and he shrugged, as if he didn't much care. He glanced at Dana with an apologetic smile, but he seemed sapped of energy, even of speech.

"I don't know where he is. I just got home," Dana said. She was very conscious of her appearance. She was wearing jeans and boots and a dusty shirt, because she'd been down to her own place to check on her small herd of cattle. She smelled of horses and her hair wasn't as neat in its braid as it had started out.

"And who are you, the stable girl?" the woman asked with a mocking smile.

Dana didn't like the woman's attitude, her over-polished look, or the reek of her expensive perfume that she must have bathed in.

"I'm Mrs. Hayden Grant," she replied with curt formality. "And just who do you think you are, to come into my home and insult me?" she added for good measure, with sparks in her blue eyes.

The woman was shocked, not only by the name she'd been given, but by that quick hostility.

She fumbled her words. "I'm Betty Grant. I mean, Betty Collins," she amended, rattled and flushed. "I didn't know Hank…had remarried! He didn't say anything about it."

"We've known each other for years, but we've only been married a few weeks," Dana replied, furious at Hank for putting her in this position so unexpectedly. He hadn't said anything about his ex-wife paying a visit. "Tilly, show them into the living room," she told the thin housekeeper. "I'm sure Hank will be along," she added curtly. "If you'll excuse me, I have things to do." She spared the man a smile, because he hadn't been impolite, but she said nothing to Betty. Her feelings had been lacerated by the woman's harsh question.

She walked to the staircase and mounted it without a backward glance.

"She isn't very welcoming," Betty told her husband with a cold glance toward the staircase.

"She wasn't expecting you," Tilly said with irritation. She'd never liked the ex-Mrs. Grant and she liked her even less now. "If you'd like to wait in here, I'll bring coffee when Mr. Grant comes."

Betty gave the housekeeper a narrow-eyed look. "You never liked me, did you, Tilly?"

"I work for Mr. Grant, madam," she replied with dignity. "My likes and dislikes are of concern only to him. And to Mrs. Grant, of course," she added pointedly.

As the blood was seeping into Betty's cheeks, the housekeeper swept out of the room and closed the door. She went down the hall to the kitchen and almost collided with Hayden, who'd come in the back door.

"Whoa, there," he said, righting her. "What's got you so fired up?"

"Your ex-wife just slithered in, with her husband," she said grimly, noticing the pained look the statement brought to his face. "She's already had a bite of Mrs. Grant, which she got back, with interest," she added with a smile.

He sucked in his breath. "Good Lord, I forgot to

phone and tell Dana I'd invited them. Is she very upset?"

"Well, sir," Tilly chuckled, "she's got a temper. Never raised her voice or said a bad word, but she set Betty right on her heels. Betty asked if she was the stable girl."

His face grew cold and hard. "How does she look?"

"Dana?"

He shook his head. "Betty."

"She looks very rich, very haughty and very pretty, just as she used to." She frowned. "Sir, you aren't going to let her knock you off-balance again, are you?"

He couldn't answer that. The memory of Betty in his bed had tormented him ever since the divorce, despite the ecstasy Dana had given him that one night they'd had together.

"No," he said belatedly. "Certainly I'm not going to give her any rope to hang me with."

"Might think about telling Dana that," Tilly mused. "She won't take kindly to the kind of shock she just got. Especially considering the sleeping arrangements around here."

He opened his mouth to reply hotly, but she was already through the door and into the kitchen. He glared after her. Tilly's outspokenness was irritating at times. She was right, which didn't help the situation.

"Bring a tray of coffee to the living room," he bellowed after her.

There was no reply, but he assumed that she heard him. So, probably, had half the county.

He strolled into the living room, trying not to think about how it was going to affect him to see Betty. He wasn't as prepared as he'd thought. It was an utter shock. She'd been twenty when she left him, a flighty girl who liked to flirt and have men buy her pretty things. Ten years had gone by. That would make her thirty now, and she was as pretty as ever, more mature, much more sensuous. The years rolled away and he was hungry for this woman who'd teased him and then taken him over completely.

She saw his reaction and smiled at him with her whole body. "Well, Hank, how are you?" she asked, going close.

With her husband watching, she reached up and kissed him full on the mouth, taking her time about it. She laughed softly when he didn't draw back. She could feel the tension in him, and it wasn't rejection.

He hated having her know how he felt, but he couldn't resist the urge to kiss her back. He did, thoroughly. His skill must have surprised her, because he felt her gasp just before he lifted his head.

"My, you've changed, lover!" she exclaimed with a husky laugh.

He searched her eyes, looking for emotion, love. But it wasn't there. It never had been. Whatever he felt for her, Betty had never been able to return. Her victorious smile brought him partially back to his senses. Ten years was a long time. He'd changed, so had she. He mustn't lose sight of the fact that despite her exquisite body and seductive kisses, she'd left him for a richer man. And now Hank was married. Dana was his wife, in every sense of the word.

He blinked. For the space of seconds he'd kissed his ex-wife, Dana had gone right out of his mind. He felt guilty.

"You look well," he told Betty. His eyes shifted from her to his friend Bob in the distance. He held out his hand. "How are you, Bob?" he asked, but without the warmth he could have given the man before the divorce.

Bob knew it and his smile was strained as he shook the proffered hand. "I'm doing all right, I guess," he said. "Slowing down a little, but it's time I did. How've you been?"

"Prosperous," Hayden replied with a faint, mocking smile.

"So I've seen," the older man said congenially. "You've made quite a stir among breeders, and I hear one of your two-year-olds will debut this year at the track."

"That's the long and short of it. How's the poultry business?"

"I've divested myself of most of my holdings," Bob said. He grimaced. "I was so busy traveling that I didn't realize I'd lost control until there was a proxy fight and I lost it," he added, without looking at Betty. "Then I had a minor stroke, and even my shares weren't worth the trouble. We're living comfortably on dividends from various sources."

"Comfortably is hardly the word," Betty scoffed. "But we've got one prize possession left that may put us in the black again. That's one reason we're here today." She smiled flirtatiously at Hank, who looked very uncomfortable, and deliberately leaned back against his desk in a seductive pose. "When did you get married, Hank? When you heard we were moving back here?"

His face hardened. "That's hardly a motive to get married."

"I wonder. Your new bride is frightfully young, and she seems to prefer the great outdoors to being a hostess. She wasn't very friendly. Is she the little farm girl whose father just died? She's not even in your league, socially, is she?"

"Oh, I wouldn't say that," came a voice from the doorway.

Hank turned his attention to his wife and didn't recognize her. Her blond hair was down around her shoulders, clean and bright, and she was wearing a silk sundress that even made Bob stare.

She was wearing just enough makeup, just enough perfume. Hank's eyes went down to her long, elegant legs and he felt his whole body go rigid as he remembered how it felt to kiss her. His face reflected the memory, to Betty's dismay.

Dana walked in, her body swaying gracefully, and took Hank possessively by the arm. She was delighted that she'd bought this designer dress to wear for Hank. The occasion hadn't arisen before, so she'd saved it. "I thought you'd forgotten the invitation," she said idly, glancing at Betty. "We're so newly married, you see," she added with indulgent affection.

Betty's face had flushed again with temper. She crossed her legs as she leaned back further into the desk. Her eyes narrowed. "Very newly married, we hear. I was just asking Hank why the rush."

Dana smiled demurely and her hand flattened on her stomach. "Well, I'm sure you know how impetuous he is," she murmured huskily, and didn't look up.

The gesture was enough. Betty looked as if she might choke.

Hank was surprised at his wife's immediate grasp of the situation, and her protective instincts. He'd been horrible to her, and here she was saving his pride. He'd been set to go right over the edge with Betty again, and here was Dana to draw him back to safety. Considering his coolness to her since their marriage, and springing this surprise on her today, it was damned decent of her.

His arm contracted around her waist and he smiled down at her with genuine appreciation. "A child was our first priority, but we sort of jumped the gun," he added, lying through his teeth as he helped things along. "We're hoping for a son."

Bob looked wistful while Betty fumed. "I'd have liked a child," he told them. "It wasn't on the cards for us, though."

"Children are a nuisance," Betty murmured. "Little irritations that grow."

"Aren't you lucky that your mother didn't have that opinion?" Dana returned smoothly.

Betty stood up. She'd been expecting a pushover, and she was getting one until the venomous child bride walked in and upset her cart. Things weren't going at all according to her plan. "Has Bob asked you about the racehorse? He hoped you might be willing to come down to Corpus Christi with us and take a look at him, Hank," she said, getting straight to the point. "He's a proven winner, with good bloodlines, and we won't rob you. We'll make you a good price."

Why hadn't he realized that Betty might have had an ulterior motive when Bob had all but invited himself and Betty for lunch? He'd thought she'd put Bob up to it because she wanted to see him again, perhaps because she'd regretted the divorce. But it was just like old times. She was after money and saw him as a way to feather her nest—and Bob's. Her body had blinded him again. Angrily he drew Dana closer. "I don't think Dana would feel up to traveling right now," Hank replied, continuing with the fiction of pregnancy.

"We don't have to take her with us," Betty said curtly.

Bob laughed. "Betty, they're newlyweds," he said with noticeable embarrassment. "What are you trying to do?"

"That would have been *my* next question, Mr. Collins," Dana replied quietly. "Although I'll tell you right now that my husband doesn't travel without me." She caught his hand in hers, and he was surprised at how cold it was, and how possessive.

"Oh, you don't surely think *I'm* after your husband," Betty scoffed. "I...we...only want to see our racehorse placed in good hands. Nobody knows thoroughbred horses like Hank." She shifted her posture, for effect. She had a perfect figure and she didn't mind letting it show whenever possible, if it was to her benefit. "You must be very insecure in your marriage, dear, if you don't trust your husband out of your sight with a married woman and her husband. And that's rather a sad statement about your relationship."

Dana flushed. She could tell that Hank was suddenly suspicious. He looked down at her with narrowed eyes, as if he'd taken Betty's taunt to heart. And his hand was dead in hers, as if he felt nothing when he touched her.

Dana felt his withdrawal. She drew her fingers away. So much for the pretense, she decided. "Hank and I have only been married for two weeks," she said.

"Yes, dear, but if you're pregnant, it hardly means you've only been sleeping together since you married, or can't I count?" she asked pointedly.

Which put Dana between a rock and a hard place. She couldn't admit that she and Hank had only slept together since their wedding, unless she wanted to make herself a liar about the pregnancy. She glanced at Hank, who'd started the fabrication, but he wasn't helping her now. In fact, he looked as if he hated being tied to her when Betty was within his grasp. Her husband didn't seem to be jealous at all. It was a frightening thought to a woman in love with a husband whose motives for the marriage had been suspect from the start, and who had admitted that he still felt something powerful for his ex-wife. He'd said, too, that he had no love to offer Dana; only affection.

"Besides, it isn't as if I'm trying to break up your marriage," Betty continued. "Bob and I are in terrible financial shape. That's one reason we're having to give up our holdings all over Texas and our racehorse. Even if Hank doesn't want to buy the horse, he might be able to help us find someone who'll want him. Surely you don't begrudge us a little advice, for old times' sake? It's only Corpus Christi, after all, not some foreign country. It would only mean a night away from home."

Hank was wavering, so Betty advanced on Bob and draped herself against him with a seductive smile, as if she was making him an offer. "Tell him, honey," she drawled seductively.

Bob's face burned with color as he looked at her and he shifted restlessly. "Come on, Hank," he said. "The stable where this horse is kept is right down the road, about ten miles from where we live. We've got plenty of room. You can spend the night and come back tomorrow." He smiled weakly. "We really can't afford to wait any longer. I've had some health problems, so I have to get this settled now. We were good friends once, Hank."

You're being suckered, Dana wanted to scream. *She's using him to get to you, she's bribing him with*

her body to coax you down to Corpus Christi so she
can seduce you into buying that horse.

Hank felt Dana's tension. His eyes narrowed as he
looked down at her and recognized the jealousy, the
distrust. He was feeling much too threatened already
by Betty, and he was puzzled by the stormy indecision
his own feelings brewed inside him. He felt trapped
between two women, one whom he wanted to the
point of madness and the other who'd discarded his
heart and now seemed to want him again—despite
her husband.

He glanced from Dana's set, angry face to Betty's
coaxing one and felt himself wavering.

"Your wife doesn't have you on a leash or something, does she?" Betty asked pointedly.

That did it.

Chapter Five

Male pride asserted itself. "I can spare a day or two," Hayden told Bob with a meaningful glare down into Dana's flushed face. "After all, we're civilized people. And the divorce was years ago. It's stupid to hold a grudge."

Betty beamed. She'd won and she knew it. "What a nice thing to say, Hank. But you always were sweet."

Dana felt left out. The other two took over the conversation, and in no time, they were recalling old times and talking about people Dana had never met. She poured the coffee that a disgruntled Tilly had brought on a tray, with cake, and served it to the guests. But she might have been invisible, for all the attention Hank paid her. After a few minutes she excused herself and left the room, without being really sure that he'd even noticed her absence.

Tilly was headed toward the kitchen with her tray right ahead of Dana's retreat, muttering to herself about men who couldn't see their own noses. Normally Tilly amused Dana by talking to herself, but she was far too preoccupied today to notice.

She went up the stairs to the room she occupied alone and began to pack. If Hank was going away, so was she. She'd had enough of being an extra person in his life, in his house. If she'd had any hopes that he might one day learn to love her, they'd been killed stone dead with the arrival of his ex-wife. Anyone could see how he still felt about her. He was so besotted that he hadn't even noticed Dana once Betty flashed that false smile at him. Well, let him leave with his ex-wife, on whatever pretext he liked, and good luck to him!

It took her ten minutes to pack. She threw off the sundress and put on jeans and a knit top and her boots. She braided her hair and looked in the mirror. Yes, that was more like it. She might have been a society girl once, but now she was just a poor rancher. She could look the part if she liked, and Hank surely wouldn't miss her if she left, not when Betty was ready, willing and able.

Apparently it didn't matter at all to Hank that Betty was still married, avaricious, and only using Hank to make a profit on that horse. God knew he could afford to buy it, and the woman looked as if she wouldn't mind coming across with a little payment in kind to reimburse him.

She was going through drawers to make sure she hadn't left anything when the door opened and Hank walked in.

He'd expected to find her crying. She had a sensitive nature and he'd been unkind to her, especially downstairs in front of their guests. Betty's remarks had made him feel like a possession of Dana's, and he'd reacted instinctively by shutting Dana out. Now he was sorry. His conscience had nipped him when she walked out with such quiet dignity, without even looking at him, and he'd come to find her, to comfort her, to apologize for making her feel unwelcome. But apparently it was going to take a little more than an apology, if those suitcases were any indication of her intentions.

"Going somewhere?" he asked politely, and without a smile.

"I'm going home," she said with quiet pride. "You and I both know that this was a mistake. You can get a divorce whenever you like. The will only required a paper marriage. The property is now mine and I promise you that I won't sell it to any enterprise that might threaten your horses."

He hadn't been prepared for this. He stared at her with mixed feelings.

"It's a big house," he said, because he couldn't think of anything else to say.

"You and Tilly won't miss me. She's busy with domestic things and you're never here, anyway." She didn't meet his eyes as she said that, because she didn't want him to see how much his frequent absences had made her feel unwanted. "I thought I might get a dog."

He laughed coldly. "To replace a husband?"

"It won't be hard to replace a husband who won't even sleep with me...!" She stopped dead, cold, as she realized that the door was standing open and Betty was right there, listening.

Her abrupt cessation of conversation and her horrified gaze caused him to turn, too.

Betty wasn't even embarrassed. She smiled victoriously. "I was looking for a bathroom. Sorry if I interrupted anything."

"The bathroom's down the hall, as you know, third door on the right," Hank said shortly.

"Thank you, darling." Her eyes swept over the suitcases and Dana's pale face, and she smiled again as she left them.

Hank's face had no expression in it at all. Dana

picked up her suitcase. "I'll take this with me. If you wouldn't mind, could you have one of the men drop off the rest of my things? I've still got my Bronco in the garage, I hope?"

"I haven't done anything with it."

"Thanks."

She walked past him. He caught her arm, feeling the stiffness, the tension in her.

His breath was warm at her temple. "Don't," he said through his teeth.

She couldn't afford to weaken, to be caught up in some sordid triangle. Betty wanted him, and he'd always loved her and made no secret of it. Dana was an extra person in his life. She didn't fit.

Her dark blue eyes lifted to his brown ones. "Pity isn't a good reason to marry. Neither is breaking a will. You don't love me, any more than I love you," she added, lying through her teeth, because she'd always loved him. Her eyes lowered. "I don't want to stay here anymore."

His hand dropped her arm as if it was diseased. "Get out, then, if that's what you want. I never would have married you in the first place except that I felt sorry for you."

Her face was even paler now. "And there's the way you feel about your ex-wife," she returned.

He stared at her blithely. "Yes. There's Betty."

It hurt to hear him admit it. She went past him

without looking up. Her body was shaking, her heart was bursting inside her. She didn't want to leave but she had no choice, it had been made for her. Even as she went down the staircase, she could hear Betty's softly questioning voice as she spoke to Hank.

Dana headed for the front door, and a voice called to her from the living room.

"Good Lord, you aren't leaving, are you?" Bob asked, aghast. "Not because of us?"

She stared at him without expression. "Yes, I'm leaving. You're as much a victim as I am, I guess," she said.

His mouth opened to refute it, and the sadness in his eyes killed the words. He shrugged and laughed shortly. "I guess I am. But I've lived with it for ten years, with taking Betty away from Hank with my checkbook. Funny how life pays you back for hurting other people. You may get what you want, but then you have to live with it. Some choices carry their own punishment."

"Don't they just?" she replied. "So long."

"She doesn't really want him," he said softly, so that his voice didn't carry. "She wants a way to live as high as we used to, on an unlimited budget. I've lost my bankroll so I've become expendable. It's his money she wants, not the man. Don't give up if you love him."

She lifted her chin. "If he loved me, I'd stay, I'd

fight her to my last breath," Dana replied. "But he doesn't. I'm not brave enough to have my heart torn out by the roots every day of my life, knowing that he looks at me and wants her."

Bob winced.

"That's what you've done for ten years, isn't it?" she continued perceptively. "You're much braver than I am, Mr. Collins. I guess you love her so much that it doesn't matter."

"It isn't love," he said coldly, with the most utter self-contempt she'd ever heard in a man's voice.

She sighed. The needs of men were alien and inexplicable to her. "I guess we're both out of luck." She glanced toward the staircase with eyes that grew dark with pain. "What a fool I was to come here. He told me he had nothing to give me. Nothing except wealth. What an empty, empty life it would have been."

Bob Collins scowled. "Money means nothing to you, does it?" he asked, as if he couldn't comprehend a woman wanting a poor man.

She looked at him. "All I wanted was for him to love me," she said. "There's no worse poverty than to be bereft of that, from the only person you care about in the world." She made a little face and turned away. "Take care of yourself, Mr. Collins."

He watched her go, watched the door close, like

the lid on a coffin. *Oh, you fool*, he thought, *you fool, Hank, to give up a woman who loves you like that!*

Dana settled back into her house without any great difficulty, except that now she missed more than just her father. She missed Hank. He hadn't been home much, probably because he was avoiding her, but at least he'd given her the illusion of belonging somewhere.

She looked at her bare hands as she washed dishes. She'd left the rings behind, both of them, on her dresser. She wondered if he'd found them yet. She had no reason to wear wedding rings when she wasn't a wife anymore. Hank had married her because he didn't want Betty to know how he felt about her. But his ex-wife was so eager to have him back that a blind man could see it. He'd never made any secret of his feelings for Betty. What an irony, that his wife should come back now, of all times, when Dana might have had some little chance to win his heart. Betty had walked in and taken him over, without a struggle. She wondered if she could ever forget the look in Hank's dark eyes when he'd stared at his ex-wife with such pain and longing. He still loved her. It was impossible not to know it. He might have enjoyed sleeping with Dana, but even so, he'd never shown any great desire to repeat the experience.

She put away the dishes and went to watch the evening news. Her father had liked this time of the day, when he was through with work, when they'd had a nice meal and he could sit with his coffee and listen to the news. He and Dana would discuss the day's events and then turn off the television and read. She'd missed that at Hank's elegant house. It was empty and cold. The television was in his study, not in the living room, and she'd never felt comfortable trespassing in there to watch it. She had none of her own favorite books, and his were all about horses and livestock and genetics. He read biographies, too, and there were some hardcover bestsellers that looked as if they'd never been opened at all.

Hank didn't make time to read for pleasure, she supposed. Most of his material seemed to be business-related.

She curled up in her father's armchair with tears stinging her eyes. She hadn't given way to tears in all the time she'd been married, and she wasn't going to cave in now, either, but she felt entitled to express a little misery while there was no one to see her.

She dabbed at tears, wondering why Hank had tried to stop her from leaving since he'd said he didn't want her anymore. Maybe it was the thought of ending their brief marriage so soon. It would be hard on the pride of a man like that to have failed more than once as a husband.

After a while, she got up and turned on a movie. It was one she'd seen half a dozen times but she only wanted the noise for company. She had to consider what she was going to do for the rest of her life. At this point, she was certain that she couldn't go on trying to keep the wolf from the door while she fought to maintain the small cattle ranch. She didn't have the working capital, the proper facilities or the money to trade for more livestock. The best way to go would be to just sign the whole thing over to Hank before it bankrupted her, and use the trust fund her mother had given her to pay for a college education. With that, she could find a job and support herself. She wouldn't need help from anyone; least of all from a reluctant husband. There was no alimony in Texas, but Hank had a conscience and he'd want to provide for her after the divorce. She wanted to be able to tell him she didn't want it.

Her plans temporarily fixed in her mind, she turned her attention to the movie. It was nice to have things settled.

Hayden Grant didn't have anything settled, least of all his mind. He was on the way to Corpus Christi with Bob and Betty, only half listening to the radio as he followed behind the couple, they in their Mercedes, he in his Lincoln.

He could have gone in the car with them; something he thought Betty was secretly hoping for. But he wanted to be alone. His ex-wife had fouled everything up with her untimely reappearance. Her taunts had caused him to be cruel to Dana, who'd had nothing from him except pain. He'd forced her into marriage whether she wanted it or not, seduced her in a fever of desire, and then brought her home and literally ignored her for two weeks. Looking back, he couldn't explain his own irrational behavior.

Since the night he'd been with Dana, his only thought had been of how sweet it was to make love to her. He hadn't dreamed that he could want anyone so much. But his feelings had frightened him because they were so intense, and he'd withdrawn from her. Betty's intervention had been the coup de grace, putting a wall between himself and Dana.

But desire wasn't the only thing he felt for his young wife, and for the first time he had to admit it. He remembered Dana at the age of sixteen, cuddling a wounded puppy that some cruel boy had shot with a rifle and crying with anger as she insisted that Hank drive her to the vet's. The puppy had died, and Hank had comforted the young girl whose heart sounded as if it might break. Dana had always been like that about little, helpless things. Her heart embraced the whole world. How could he have hurt her so, a woman like that?

He groaned out loud. He wondered if he'd lost his reason with Betty's return. He'd dreaded it because he thought he was still in love with Betty. He wasn't. He knew it quite suddenly when he saw Dana with tears in her eyes and her suitcase in her hand. Dana had lived with him for two weeks, and he hadn't even touched her since their wedding night. He thought of it with incredulity. Now he realized what his behavior had masked. He'd been afraid of falling so deeply in love with her that it would be as it had been with Betty. Except that Dana wasn't mercenary. She wanted him, and seemed to be ashamed of feeling that way. But she had a tender heart, and she'd cared about him. If he'd tried, he might have made her love him. The thought, once dreaded, was now the essence of heaven.

It was too late, though. He'd let her leave and he wouldn't be able to get her back. He'd lost her. What the hell was he doing driving to Corpus Christi with two people he didn't even like?

As he thought it, he realized that they were already driving into its city limits. It was too late to turn back now. He'd do what he'd promised, he thought, but after that, he was going home to Dana. Whatever it took, he was going to get her back.

If only it had been that easy. They'd no sooner gotten out of the car at the Collins's white brick mansion when Bob groaned and then fell. He died right there on the green lawn before the ambulance could get to him, despite Hank's best efforts to revive him. He'd had another stroke.

Betty went to pieces and Hank found himself in

the ironic position of arranging a funeral for his ex-wife's second husband; and his former friend.

Back home, Dana heard about Bob Collins's death; it was all over the radio. He'd been a prominent man in the state's poultry industry and was well-known and liked. His funeral was very big and many important people attended it. Dana saw newspaper clippings of Hank supporting the grieving widow. She couldn't imagine that cold-eyed woman grieving for her husband. If Betty was crying, it was because Bob's life insurance policy had probably lapsed.

Dana chided herself for her uncharitable thoughts and threw the newspaper into the trash. Well, one thing was certain, Hayden Grant would be asking for a divorce so that he could remarry the woman he really loved. If Betty was what he wanted, he should have her. Dana remembered what she'd said to Bob Collins about not wanting to eat her heart out for the rest of her life with a man who wanted someone else. Poor Bob, who'd done exactly that, steadfastly, for ten long years. Dana offered a silent prayer for him. At least now perhaps he would have peace.

Two long weeks passed, with no word from Hank. The next morning, Dana went to see the family lawyer and asked him to initiate divorce proceedings. It would mean dipping into her small trust fund to pay for it, but that didn't matter. She wanted Hank to be happy.

"This isn't wise," the attorney tried to advise her. "You've been upset and so has he. You should wait, think it over."

She shook her head. "I've done all the thinking I care to. I want the deeds made up for my signature and delivered to Hank, along with the divorce papers. I'm throwing in the towel. Betty's free now and Hank deserves a little happiness. God knows he's waited long enough to get her back."

The attorney winced as he looked at the vulnerable, pale woman sitting in front of him. She'd suffered, judging by the thinness of her face and those terrible shadowed blue eyes. He couldn't imagine a man crazy enough to turn down a love that violent and selfless. But if she was right, that's exactly what Hayden Grant had already done. He sighed inwardly. Talk about throwing gold away in favor of gloss! Some men just didn't know their luck.

"I'll have everything ready by tomorrow morning. You're absolutely sure?"

She nodded.

"Then consider it done."

She thanked him and went home. The house was very empty and she felt the same. There would be a new life ahead of her. She was closing a very firm door on the old one, starting tomorrow. That thought was fixed firmly in her mind until the morning came and she began to throw up as if she were dying. She made it to the attorney's office to sign the papers, but she was too sick to travel.

Fearful that she had some virus that would prevent her plans to move, she made an appointment to see Dr. Lou Coltrain, a newly married member of the local medical community.

Lou examined her, asked pertinent questions and began to whistle softly while Dana looked at her with horror.

"It must have been some wedding night," Lou said, tongue in cheek, "because you've only been married a month and I know Hayden Grant. He wouldn't have touched you until the ring was in place."

"Lou, you're awful!" Dana groaned, flushing.

"Well, I'm right, too." She patted the younger woman on the shoulder. "It's two weeks too early for tests to tell us anything positive. Come back then. But meanwhile, you watch what medications you take and get plenty of rest, because I've seen too many pregnancies to mistake one. Congratulations."

"Thanks. But you, uh, won't tell anyone, right?" Dana asked gently.

"Your secret is safe with me." The doctor chuckled. "Want to surprise him, I guess?"

"That's right," Dana said immediately, thinking what a surprise it would have been.

"Come back and see me in two weeks," Lou repeated, "and I'll send you to Jack Howard up in

Victoria. He's the best obstetrician I know, and it's a lot closer than Houston."

"Thanks, Lou."

"Anytime."

Dana went home in a cloud of fear and apprehension and joy. She was almost certainly pregnant, and her marriage was in tatters. But she knew what she was going to do. First she had to find her way to Houston, get an apartment and find a job. She'd handed the deeds to her father's property and the divorce petition over to the attorney for disposition. Presumably, he'd have already forwarded them to Hank in Corpus Christi in care of the bereaved Mrs. Collins. She'd burned her bridges and there was no going back.

Unaware of what was going on in Corpus Christi, Dana set out for Houston the next morning, painfully working out a future without Hank while a tall man with shocked dark eyes was served a divorce petition and cursed her until he went hoarse.

Hank jerked up the phone, oblivious to Betty's shocked stare, and dialed the phone number of the attorney, who was also a friend of his.

"Luke, what the hell's going on?" he demanded, shaking the divorce papers at the receiver. "I didn't ask her for the deeds to the ranch, and I sure as hell don't remember asking for a divorce!"

"There, there, old fellow, calm down," Luke said

firmly. "She said it was the best thing for both of you. Besides, you're going back to Betty anyway."

"I am?" he asked, shocked.

"That's what Dana told me. See here, Hank, you're throwing over a good woman. She never thought of herself once. It was what you wanted, what you needed to make you happy that she considered when she arranged all this. She said it would give you a head start on all the happiness you'd missed out on ten years ago, and she was glad for you."

"Glad for me." He looked at the papers and glanced irritably at Betty, who'd been practicing bereavement for two weeks while trying to entangle Hank in her web again. She hadn't succeeded. He was untangling Bob's finances for her, and they were in one major mess. It had taken time he didn't want to spend here, but for Bob's sake he'd managed it. Now he only wanted to go home and reclaim his wife, but he was holding proof that she didn't want to be reclaimed.

"She knew you'd be happy to have the matter dealt with before you came back," he continued. "Listen, if you don't contest the divorce—and why should you, right?—I can get it through in no time."

Hank hesitated, breathing deliberately so that he wouldn't start swearing at the top of his lungs. The words on the pages blurred in his sight as he remembered the last time he'd seen Dana. He mentally replayed the cruel, hateful things he'd said to her. No wonder she was divorcing him. She didn't know how he felt; he'd never told her. She thought he hated her. What a laugh!

"Can you hold it back for a few weeks?" he asked the attorney. "I've got some things to untangle down here for Bob's widow, and I can't get back home for a week, possibly longer."

"I can, but she won't like it," Luke said.

"Don't tell her."

"Hank…"

"Don't tell her," he repeated. "Leave it alone until I get back."

There was a heavy sigh. "If she asks me, point-blank, I won't lie to her."

"Then make sure she doesn't have the opportunity to ask you."

"I'll try."

"Thanks."

He hung up. He felt sick. God, what a mess he'd made of his life!

Betty sidled close and leaned against his arm, wearing a wispy negligee. "Poor old dear, is she leaving you?" she asked softly. "I'm sorry. Why don't you come upstairs with me and I'll kiss you better?"

He looked at her as if he hadn't heard correctly. "Betty, your husband was buried week before last," he said.

She shrugged. "He'd run out of money and he was

barely able to get around by himself." She smiled in a shallow, childlike way, and he realized that she was just that—childlike. She had no depth of emotion at all, just a set of wants and needs that she satisfied the best she knew how, with her body. He'd lived with her for two years, ached for her for ten more, and he'd never known the sort of person she really was until he became involved with Dana. Now he could see the real difference between the two women.

He removed her hand from his arm. "I have some things to finish," he told her. "We'll talk later. Okay?"

She smiled. "Okay, lover."

Chapter Six

It took all of another ten days for Hayden to wrap up the odds and ends of Bob's life and get his affairs safely into the hands of a good local attorney. Bob had an attorney, but the man had been evasive and almost impossible to locate. Finally it had taken the threat of litigation to get him to turn over needed documents. And afterward, the man—who had a degree in law from an interesting but unaccredited law school overseas—had vanished. It was no wonder that Bob had lost most of his money. The charlatan had embezzled it. Fortunately there would be enough left, added to the life insurance, to keep Betty fairly secure if she was careful.

It was only as he explained things to her and she realized that he wasn't going to propose marriage that she came apart for real.

"But you love me," she exclaimed. "You always have. Look at how quickly you married that child just so I wouldn't think you were carrying a torch for me!"

"It might have started that way," he replied quietly. "It didn't end that way. I can't afford to lose her now."

"Oh, she's got money, I guess."

He frowned. "No. She hasn't a dime in the world. Do you always ascribe mercenary reasons to every decision?"

"Of course I do," she said, and smiled faintly. "Security is the most important thing in the world. I didn't have anything when I was a child. I went hungry sometimes. I promised myself it would never happen to me." She made an awkward gesture with her shoulder. "That's why I left you, you know. You were heading into debt and I was scared. I did love you, in my way, but there was Bob and he had a lot of money and he wanted me." She smiled. "I had no choice, really."

"I don't suppose you did." He was remembering that Dana had nothing, and she was giving him the only thing of worth in her possession, those deeds to the land, so that he wouldn't face the threat of some dangerously noisy neighbor. He could have kicked himself for letting her walk out of the house in the first place.

"I felt sort of sorry for her," she added thoughtfully. "She isn't sophisticated, is she? She was afraid of me." Her eyebrows met. "Why won't you sleep with her?"

He averted her eyes. "That's none of your business."

"It is, in a way. You won't sleep with me, either. Why?"

He grimaced. "I don't want you," he admitted reluctantly. "I'm sorry."

"You used to," she recalled. "You wanted me all the time. I thought it was going to kill you when I walked out."

"It damned near did. But things have changed." His eyes were sad and quiet. "I am sorry, Betty. For your loss, for everything."

"Bob wasn't a bad man," she said. "I was fond of him. I guess I'll miss him, in a way." She looked up. "You're sure about not wanting me?"

He nodded.

She sighed and smiled again. "Well, that's that. At least I'll have enough money to make ends meet, thanks to you. And I'm still young enough to make a good third marriage!"

On that note, he said his goodbyes and went back

to the motel where he'd been staying. It felt nice to have the weight of Betty's disastrous finances off his shoulders, although he'd enjoyed untangling the mess. Now he was going to go home and work on his own problems.

He looked at the divorce petition and the deeds and his eyes narrowed. Dana had wasted no time at all turning over the ranch to him. He began to frown. Where was she going to live without her house?

He picked up the phone and dialed the attorney's number, but he was told that Luke was in court on a case and couldn't be reached. Really worried now, he dialed the Mobry ranch number. It rang twice and the line was connected. He started to speak. Just as he did, a mechanical voice informed him that the number had been disconnected.

Frustrated and worried, his next call was to his own house, where he found Tilly.

"All right, what the hell's going on? Where did Dana go?" he demanded without preamble.

"She wouldn't let me call you," Tilly said stiffly. "I begged, but she wouldn't budge. I gave my word. Couldn't break it."

"Where is she?"

"She's left," came the terse reply. "Said you had the deeds and that Joe and Ernie would keep watch over the place until you made other arrangements, but you'd have to pay them."

"Oh, to hell with the ranch!" he snapped. "Where is she?"

"Took a cab to the bus station. Got the bus to Houston. I don't know where she went from there."

Hope raised its head. "Houston! Tilly, you're a wonder!"

"There's, uh, something else. The nurse who works for Dr. Lou Coltrain is a cousin of mine. Seems Dana went to see Lou before she left town. If you don't find her pretty soon, you're going to be looking for two people instead of one," she said, and hung up.

He stared at the telephone blankly and felt all the blood draining out of his face. Dana was pregnant? He counted back to their wedding night and realized that neither of them had even thought about precautions. His Dana was going to have a baby, and she'd left him! What an idiot he'd been!

He called the airport. Houston was a good place to start, thanks to Tilly, who'd saved him hours of tracking. But it was a big city, and he didn't even know where to start. He cursed himself for every painful thing he'd ever said to her. It couldn't be too late to convince her how much he cared, it just couldn't!

He soon realized how impossible it was going to be to locate Dana in Houston. She had a little money, but it would soon run out if she didn't get a job. He had to find her quickly, so he went straight to one of the better-known Houston detectives, and told him everything he knew about Dana including a description.

"Do you have a photo of your wife, Mr. Grant?" Dane Lassiter asked the man across the desk from him. A former Texas Ranger, Dane had built his agency from scratch, and now it had a fine national reputation for doing the impossible.

The question startled Hank, who hadn't expected it. He looked uncomfortable. "No," he said.

The other man didn't comment, but his eyes were steady and curious. No wonder, because the table behind Lassiter's desk carried a family photo of the detective, his attractive wife and two young sons who looked just like him.

"We're newlyweds," Hayden felt constrained to explain. "It was a quick marriage."

Dane didn't say a word. He was busy writing things down. "Did she run away, Mr. Grant?" he asked suddenly, and his black eyes pinned the other man.

Hayden took a sharp, angry breath. "Yes," he said through his teeth. "I did something stupid and I deserve to lose her. But I don't think I can stand to, just the same." He leaned forward and rested his forearms on his splayed legs in a defeated position. "And she's pregnant," he added through his teeth.

Hank's predicament sounded very familiar to

Dane Lassiter. He knew all about pregnant women who ran away.

"We'll find her," Dane told the man, not so distant now. "You've given us some good leads, we'll check them out. Where can I reach you?"

Hayden gave the name of a local hotel. "I'll be here until I hear from you," he added, and he had the look of a man who planned to stay there until the turn of the century if that's how long it took.

"Okay. I'll get right on it." He stood up and shook hands. "Women need a lot of tenderness. They get hurt easily, and they keep secrets," he said surprisingly. "But if it helps, you learn how to cope with it after a while."

Hayden smiled. "Thanks."

Dane shrugged. He smiled back. "I've been married a long time. Nobody starts out in paradise. You sort of have to work up to it."

"I'll remember that. I hope I get the chance to find out firsthand."

It took two days for Dane to track Dana to a small boarding house outside Houston. During that time, Hayden lost sleep and thought torturously of all the things that could have happened to his errant, pregnant wife. It didn't improve his temper, or his heartache.

When Dane called, he was over the moon. He

wasted no time at all getting to Mrs. Harper's Boarding House, but when he pulled up at the front steps in the Lincoln he'd rented at the airport on his arrival in Houston, he didn't know quite what to say. He stared at the big white house with longing and apprehension. His wife was in there, but she didn't want him. She'd tried to divorce him, had moved here and she'd made a good effort to erase her presence from his life. She hadn't even said a word to him about her pregnancy. How did he talk to her, what did he say to cancel out all the hurts he'd dealt her?

He got out of the car and approached the house slowly. His steps dragged, because he dreaded what was coming. He went up and rang the doorbell. A plump, smiling elderly woman opened the door.

"May I help you?" she asked politely.

"I'm Hayden Grant," he said in a subdued tone. "My wife lives here, I believe. Her name is Dana."

"Miss Mobry is your wife?" she asked, puzzled. "But I'm sure she said she wasn't married."

"She's very much married," he replied. He removed his cream-colored Stetson, belatedly, and let the hand holding it drop to his side. "I'd like to see her."

She gnawed on her lip, frowning. "Well, she's not here at the moment," she said. "She went to see that new adventure movie playing at the shopping center. With Mr. Coleman, that is."

He looked vaguely homicidal. "Who's Mr. Coleman?" he asked shortly.

"He lives here, too," she stammered, made nervous by the black glitter of his eyes. "He's a very nice young man…"

"Which shopping center and which movie?" he demanded.

She told him. She didn't dare not to.

He stomped back to his car, slammed into it and skidded on his way out the driveway.

"Oh, dear, oh, dear," Mrs. Harper mumbled. "I wonder if I shouldn't have mentioned that David is eleven years old…"

Sadly unaware of the age of Dana's "date," Hank drove to the shopping center, parked the car and went straight to the theater. As luck would have it, the feature was just ending, so people were pouring out of three exits. He stood, glaring, until he spotted Dana.

She was talking to a small boy in a baseball cap, her face animated, smiling. His heart jumped as he watched her come out of the big building. He loved her. He hadn't known. He honestly hadn't known. His heart accelerated wildly, but his eyes began to glow from within, quiet and watchful and adoring.

Dana was too far away to see his expression. But she spotted him at once and stopped dead in her tracks. The boy was saying something, but she wasn't listening. Her face was stark white.

Hank approached her, alert to any sudden movement. If she tried to run, he'd have her before she got three steps.

But she didn't run. She lifted her chin as if in preparation for battle and her hands clenched the small purse she was holding against the waist of her denim skirt.

"Hello, Dana," he said when he was within earshot.

She looked at him warily. "How did you find me?" she asked.

"I didn't. A detective agency did."

She looked paler. "I signed all the necessary papers," she told him curtly. "You're free."

He stuck his hands deep into his pockets. "Am I?"

Dana turned to David and handed him a five-dollar bill. "Why don't you go back in there and play the arcade machine for a minute or two while I speak to this man, David?" she asked.

He grinned. "Sure, Miss Mobry, thanks!"

He was off at a lope.

"So you came with the boy, not with some other man," Hank murmured absently.

She flushed. "As if I'd trust my own judgment

about men ever again! David's mother is at work, so I offered to treat him to a movie."

"You do like kids, don't you?" he asked, and his eyes were very soft as they fell to her waistline. "That's fortunate."

"That isn't what I'd call it," she said stubbornly.

He sighed. He didn't know what to say, but this certainly wasn't the ideal place to talk. "Look, suppose you go fetch the boy and we'll go back to your boarding house? Did you drive here?"

She shook her head. "We got a city bus." She wanted to argue, but he looked as if he was going to dig his heels in. She couldn't understand why he was here, when Betty was free. Perhaps that's what he wanted to explain. She seemed to have no choice but to do as he said, for the time being, at least.

"A city bus!" he muttered, and in her condition! But he didn't dare mention that he knew about her pregnancy. Not yet. "Get the boy," he said shortly. "I'll take you home."

She went to find David, and Hank drove them back to the boarding house. David thanked her and deserted her. Mrs. Harper hovered, but a hard glare from Hank dispatched her soon enough. He closed the door behind her and sat down in the one chair in Dana's room, while she perched on the bed a little nervously.

"Where's Betty?" she wanted to know.

"In Corpus Christi, I guess," he said. "I'm alone."

"You won't be alone for long," she reminded him. "You're getting married again."

"I'm already married," he said quietly. "I have a young and very pretty wife."

She flushed. "I divorced you."

He shook his head. "I stopped it."

"Why?" she asked miserably, her eyes eloquent in a face like rice paper. "You don't have to stay married to me now that she's free!"

He winced. He reached over and touched her cheek, but she jerked away from him.

He averted his face and stared down at the floor. "I don't want to remarry Betty."

She stared at his averted features, unconvinced. "You've never gotten over her, Hank," she said sadly. "You said yourself that part of the reason you married me was so she wouldn't know how you'd grieved since she divorced you."

"Maybe it was the old story of wanting what I couldn't have, or the grass being greener on the other side of the fence," he ventured.

She drew in a long breath. "Or maybe it was just that you never stopped loving her," she added, and the eyes that searched his were wistful and sad. "Oh, Hank, we can't love to order. We have to settle for what we can have in this life." Her eyes went to the floor. "I'll go back to school and work toward my degree and I'll be happy."

His eyes slid up to hers. "Without me?" he asked bluntly.

She wasn't sure how much he knew. She blinked and gathered her scattered wits. "Doesn't Betty want to marry you?" she asked suspiciously.

"More than ever," he affirmed.

"Then what's the problem?"

"I told you. The problem is that I don't want to marry her."

"I don't understand," she said uneasily.

He smiled wistfully. "I used to envy other men taking their sons on camping and fishing trips with them. I never thought I might have one of my own. But a girl would be nice, too. I guess girls can fish and hunt as well as boys can, if they're so inclined." His eyes lifted to hers. "You like to shoot, as I recall."

"I don't like to hunt," she replied, uneasy at the way he was talking about kids. He couldn't possibly *know…*

He shrugged. "I'll teach you to shoot skeet."

"Okay, but I won't cook them."

He chuckled. "Concrete won't tenderize."

"I know what a skeet target is made of." She drew in another breath. The way he was touching her made her toes tingle. "Betty might change her mind about having a child."

He shook his head. "And even if she did, she wouldn't want it, or love it. You will. You'll want our kids and spoil them rotten if I don't watch out." His eyes lifted. "Tilly's already looking forward to it. She's bought a food processor so she can make fresh baby food for him."

She flushed. "She's jumping the gun."

"No, she isn't," he said with a grin. "Tilly's kin to Dr. Lou Coltrain's office nurse."

"Oh, my God!" she said in a burst.

He shrugged. "So I know. The world won't end because you didn't tell me." His eyes darkened. "I'm sorry that I made it so rough on you that you didn't feel you could tell me."

She glared at him. "I'm not going back."

His shoulders seemed to fall. "I know I've made a lot of mistakes," he said. "You have to make allowances. Until a couple of weeks ago, I thought I was still in love with my ex-wife. I had to get to know her again to realize that she was an illusion. The reality of Betty was pretty harsh, after you."

"I don't understand."

"Don't you?" He sighed. "Well, Dana, I suppose I made an idol of her after she left. The one that got away is always better than anything that's left."

"You didn't act like someone who wasn't in love with his ex-wife," she reminded him as all the painful things he'd said to her returned in a flash of anger.

"All it took was two weeks in Corpus Christi to cure me," he returned. He leaned forward with his forearms resting on his knees and stared at the floor. "She's shallow," he said, glancing at Dana. "Shallow and selfish and spoiled. And I'd been away from her so long that I forgot. It cut the heart out of me when I realized that you went away because you thought I wanted Betty instead of you. I'm sorry for that."

"You can't help wanting someone else..."

"I want you, Dana," he said with a quizzical smile.

She clasped her hands hard at her waist. "You're just making the best of it, aren't you? You know about the baby and how I feel about you and you're sorry for me."

His heart jumped. "How you feel?" he prompted.

"You know that I'm in love with you," she said, avoiding his penetrating gaze. "That I have been since I was seventeen."

His heart wasn't jumping anymore, it had stopped. He barely could breathe. He certainly was robbed of speech.

She jerked one shoulder as she assumed his silence was one of regret for her sake, because he had nothing to give her. "Shameful, isn't it? I was still a kid. I couldn't even let boys kiss me, because I kept thinking about you. I've lived like a nun all these years, waiting and hoping, and it has to happen like this…you have to be forced into marriage just when your ex-wife is free again."

He hadn't known that she loved him. He'd known she wanted him, which was a very different thing altogether. He was stunned for a moment, and then overwhelmed, overjoyed.

"I'm sorry," she said on a long breath. "I guess we're both trapped."

"You'll need some maternity clothes," he remarked, clearing his throat. "Things to wear when we give parties. After all, I'm a rich man. We wouldn't want people to think I couldn't afford to dress you properly, would we?"

She frowned. "I'm not coming back…"

"We can turn that third guest room into a nursery," he continued, as if she hadn't spoken. "It's next door to the master bedroom, and we can leave the door open at night. I'll get a monitor, too," he added thoughtfully. "So if the baby has any problems at night, it will set off an alarm next to our bed. Or we could get a nurse for the first month or two. Would you like that?"

He'd made her speechless with plans. "I haven't thought about any of that," she stammered.

"Don't you want a settled life for our baby, with a mother and father who love him?" he persisted.

He cut the ground right out from under her with that last question. What could she say? Of course, she wanted a settled life for their child. But if Hank still loved Betty, what kind of life would it be?

Her eyes mirrored all her worries. He touched her cheek, and then smoothed back her disheveled hair. "I was trying to live in the past because I didn't have much of a present, or a future, unless you count making money. That's no longer true. I have something to look forward to now, something to challenge me, keep me going." He smiled. "I guess Tilly will make me miserable for a week, paying me back for the way I treated you. I won't be allowed to forget one rotten thing I said to you, and she'll burn the banana pudding every time I ask her to make it." He sighed. "But it will be worth it, if you'll just come home, Dana. Tilly's all aglow at the thought of having a baby in the house."

"We've already discussed this," she began.

He bent and drew his lips tenderly across hers. "Not really," he murmured. "Open your lips a little, I can't taste you like this."

"I don't wa…"

"Ummm, that's it," he whispered gently, and deepened the kiss.

She forgot what she was trying to think to say to him. Her arms curled up around his neck and she let him lift her over his legs, so that he could hold her gently across his body. He was gentle and slow, and very thorough. When he finally lifted his head, she couldn't think at all.

"I'm going to like being a father," he assured her. "I won't mind sitting up with you when he's teething or giving bottles or changing diapers."

"That's nice."

He smiled. "Do you have a lot to pack?"

"Just a few skirts and blouses and shoes. But I haven't said I'm going with you."

"What's holding you back?" he asked gently.

"You haven't explained why you don't want Betty back."

"Oh. That." He shrugged. "I don't love her. I'm not sure I ever did. I wanted her, but there's a big difference in lust and love."

"Are you sure?"

"Considering the sort of man I am—and I think you know me pretty well by now—do you think I'm capable of making love to one woman when I'm in love with someone else?"

She searched his eyes. "Well, no, I don't think so. You're pretty old-fashioned like that."

He nodded. "So how could I have made love to you so completely that one time if I'd really been in love with Betty?"

"I'm sure most men wouldn't have refused something that was offered."

"We're talking about me. Would I?"

She grimaced. "No."

"That being the case, making love to you was something of a declaration of my feelings, wasn't it?"

It was. She caught her breath. "Oh, my goodness. I never considered that."

"Neither did I until I was well on my way to Corpus Christi," he admitted. "I called it guilt and remorse and misplaced emotion, I denied it to you and myself. But in the end, I came back because I loved you. And you weren't there." He smiled sadly. "I thought you'd fight Betty. I never expected you to run."

"I didn't think you wanted me. Women only fight when they know they're loved. I didn't." She searched his eyes, fascinated. "I don't guess you'd like to…say it?"

He grimaced. "Not really."

"Oh."

"But I could. If it matters that much." He looked down at her stomach. "I guess kids like to hear it, too, don't they?"

She nodded. "All the time."

He cleared his throat. "Okay. Give me a minute to get used to the idea."

She smiled with excitement and growing delight. "You can have as much as you need."

"Okay. I…love you."

Her eyebrows rose.

"I love you," he repeated, and this time it sounded as if he meant it. He stared down at her with wonder. "By God, I do," he whispered huskily. "With all my heart, Dana, even if I didn't realize it."

She moved closer and slid her face into his hot throat, curling into him like a kitten. "I love you, too, Hank."

He smiled crookedly, staring past her head to the door. He hadn't expected it to be so easy to confess his deepest emotions. He'd never done it before, not even with Betty. His arms contracted. "I guess we're not the first people who ever fell in love."

"It feels like it, though, doesn't it?" she asked drowsily. "Oh, Hank, I wish my dad was still alive, so he'd know."

His hand smoothed over her hair. "He knows, Dana," he said at her temple, his voice deep and quiet and loving. "Somehow, I'm sure he knows."

She curled closer. "Perhaps he does."

Chapter Seven

The baby was born at two o'clock in the morning. Tilly sat in the emergency room cubicle in her robe and slippers, her hair in curlers, glaring at the disheveled man across from her who was sitting up, pale-faced, on the examination table thanking the doctor for his new son.

"It's a boy!" he exclaimed when the doctor moved out of sight. "And Dana's fine! I can see her as soon as they bring her out of the recovery room!"

"You saw her already," she muttered at him and cocked an eyebrow at his red face. "Just before you fainted…"

"I never!" he said. "I tripped over that gown they made me wear in the delivery room!"

"The one that only came to your knees?" she asked knowingly. "Dana was laughing so hard, she didn't even have to push. The baby just popped right out."

"I've had a hectic night," he began defensively.

"Sure, denying that it was labor pains, right up until her water broke. 'It's just false labor, sweetheart, you're only eight months and three weeks along,' you said. And there we were, rushing her to the hospital because you were afraid to wait for an ambulance, me in my nightgown, too! And then we no sooner get her into the delivery room when you see the baby coming out and faint dead away!"

He glared at her. "I didn't faint, I tripped…!"

She opened her mouth to argue just as a nurse peeked around the corner. "Mr. Grant, your wife is asking for you."

"I'll be right there."

"Are you feeling all right now?" she asked.

"I tripped," he said firmly.

The nurse and Tilly exchanged amused glances, but he didn't see them. "Yes, sir, I know you did, but we can't overlook any fall in a hospital."

"Sure. I knew that."

He followed the nurse down the hall until she stopped at a private room and stood aside to let him enter.

Dana was sitting up in bed with their son in her

arms, tears of pure joy in her eyes as she watched the nurse stuff Hank into a gown and mask.

"Hospital rules," he muttered.

"Yes, sir, but all for baby's protection, and we know you don't mind," she replied with a grin.

He chuckled. "Of course not."

She tied the last tie and left him with his small family.

"Are you okay?" she asked.

He nodded. "Just a little shaky, and I did not faint," he added.

"Of course you didn't, darling," she agreed. "Come see what I've got."

She pulled back the flannel and exposed a perfect little boy. His eyes weren't even open just yet, and he looked tiny.

"He's going to grow, isn't he?" Hank asked worriedly.

"Of course he is!"

He touched the tiny head, fascinated. The baby was smaller than he'd expected, so fragile, so new. Tears stung his eyes as he looked at his very own son.

Seconds later, the tiny mouth opened and began to cry. Dana chuckled as she fumbled with the gown and got it off one shoulder, exposing a firm, swollen breast. While Hank watched, spellbound, she guided the tiny mouth to a hard nipple and caught her breath as he began to suckle.

Flushed, she looked up to find an expression of pure wonder on her husband's face.

"I know we talked about bottle feeding," she began.

"Forget we said a word," he replied. He stood over her, his eyes so full of love that they sparkled with it. "I hope you can do that for a year or so, because I love watching it."

She laughed a little self-consciously. "I love feeling it," she confessed, stroking the tiny head. "Oh, Hank, we've got a baby," she breathed ecstatically. "A real, live, healthy little boy!"

He nodded. He was too choked for speech.

"I love you."

He took a steadying breath. "I love you, honey," he replied. His eyes searched hers hungrily. "With all my heart."

"My paper husband," she murmured.

"Remembering?" he teased. "Me, too. But I feel pretty flesh and blood right now."

"You look it, too." She drew him down and kissed him through the mask. "Have you forgotten what day it is?"

He frowned. "Well, in all the excitement…"

"It's your birthday!"

His eyebrows arched. "It is?"

"Yes, it is." She grinned at him. "Like your present?" she added, nodding toward the baby feeding at her breast.

"I love it," he returned. "Do I get one of these every year?" he teased.

"I won't make any promises, but we'll see."

"That's a deal."

Tilly joined them minutes later, still in her gown and robe with her hair in curlers.

"Good Lord, haven't you gone home yet?" Hank asked, aghast.

She gave him an amused grin. "How?"

"You could…" He pursed his lips. "No money for a cab, and you can't drive."

"Got it."

He looked sheepish. "I'll drive you home right now." He bent and kissed Dana and his child. "I'll be back as soon as I drop off Tilly. Anything you want me to bring you?"

She nodded. "Strawberry ice cream."

"I'll be back in a flash!"

And he was. For years afterward, the small hospital staff talked about the day young Donald Mandel Grant was born, when his proud dad satisfied Dana's craving for strawberry ice cream by having a truckload of the most expensive made delivered to the hospital. Dana said that it was a shame their baby was too young to enjoy it, but Hank promised

that he wouldn't miss out. Hank had just purchased
an ice cream company, and he was waiting for their
son's first birthday party with pure glee!

* * * * *

CHRISTMAS COWBOY

To the men and women
of the Cornelia Police Department

Chapter One

It was the holiday season in Jacobsville, Texas. Gaily colored strands of lights crisscrossed the main street, and green garlands and wreaths graced each telephone pole along the way. In the center of town, all the small maple trees that grew out of square beds at intervals along the sidewalk were decorated with lights as well.

People were bundled in coats, because even in south Texas it was cold in late November. They rushed along with shopping bags full of festively wrapped presents to go under the tree. And over on East Main Street, the Optimist Club had its yearly Christmas tree lot open already. A family of four was browsing its sawdust-covered grounds, early enough to have the pick of the beautifully shaped fir trees, just after Thanksgiving.

Dorie Wayne gazed at her surroundings the way a child would look through a store window at toys she couldn't afford. Her hand went to the thin scar down an otherwise perfect cheek and she shivered. How long ago it seemed that she stood right here on this street corner in front of the Jacobsville Drugstore, and backed away from Corrigan Hart. It had been an instinctive move; at eighteen, he'd frightened her. He was so very masculine, a mature man with a cold temper and an iron will. He'd set his sights on Dorie, who found him fearful instead of attractive, despite the fact that any single woman hereabouts would have gone to him on her knees.

She recalled his jet black hair and pale, metallic eyes. She'd wondered at first if it wasn't her fairness that attracted him, because he was so dark. Dorie had hair so blond it was almost platinum, and it was cut short, falling into natural thick waves. Her complexion was delicate and fair, and she had big gray eyes, just a shade darker than Corrigan's. He was very handsome—unlike his brothers. At least, that was what people said. Dorie hadn't gotten to meet the others when she left Jacobsville. And only Corrigan and three of his brothers lived in Jacobsville. The fifth Hart male wasn't talked about, ever. His name wasn't even known locally.

Corrigan and three of his four brothers had come down to Jacobsville from San Antonio eight years ago to take over the rich cattle operation their grandfather had left to them in his will.

It had been something of a local joke that the Harts had no hearts, because they seemed immune to women. They kept to themselves and there was no gossip about them with women. But that changed when Dorie attended a local square dance and found herself whirling around the floor in Corrigan Hart's arms.

Never one to pull his punches, he made his intentions obvious right at the start. He found her attractive. He was drawn to her. He wanted her. Just like that.

There was never any mention of marriage, engagement or even some furtive live-in arrangement. Corrigan said often that he wasn't the marrying kind. He didn't want ties. He made that very clear, because there was never any discussions of taking her to meet his brothers. He kept her away from their ranch.

But despite his aversion to relationships, he couldn't seem to see enough of Dorie. He wanted her and with every new kiss Dorie grew weaker and hungrier for him.

Then one spring day, he kissed her into oblivion,

picked her up in his arms and carried her right into her own bedroom the minute her father left for his weekly poker game.

Despite the drugging effect of masterful kisses and the poignant trembling his expert hands aroused, Dorie had come to her senses just barely in time and pushed him away. Dazed, he'd looked down at her with stunned, puzzled eyes, only belatedly realizing that she was trying to get away, not closer.

She remembered, red-faced even now, how he'd pulled away and stood up, breathing raggedly, eyes blazing with frustrated desire. He'd treated her to a scalding lecture about girls who teased. She'd treated him to one about confirmed bachelors who wouldn't take no for an answer, especially since she'd told him she wasn't the sleep-around sort.

He didn't buy that, he'd told her coldly. She was just holding out for marriage, and there was no hope in that direction. He wanted to sleep with her, and she sure seemed to want him, too. But he didn't want her for keeps.

Dorie had been in love with him, and his emotional rejection had broken something fragile inside her. But she hadn't been about to let him see her pain.

He'd gone on, in the same vein. One insult had led to another, and once he'd gotten really worked up, he'd stormed out the door. His parting shot had been that she must be nuts if she thought he was going to buy her being a virgin. There was no such thing anymore, even at the young age of eighteen.

His rejection had closed doors between them. Dorie couldn't bear the thought of staying in Jacobsville and having everybody know that Corrigan Hart had thrown her aside because she wouldn't sleep with him. And everybody *would* know, somehow. They always knew the secret things in small towns.

That very night Dorie had made up her mind to take up her cousin Belinda's offer to come to New York and get into modeling. Certainly Dorie had the looks and figure for it. She might be young, but she had poise and grace and an exquisite face framed by short, wavy blond hair. Out of that face, huge gray eyes shone like beacons, mirroring happiness or sorrow.

After that sordid evening, Dorie cut her losses and bought a bus ticket.

She'd been standing right here, on this very corner, waiting for the bus to pick her up in front of this drugstore, when Corrigan had found her.

Her abrupt withdrawal from him had halted him in his tracks. Whatever he'd been going to say, her shamed refusal to look at him, combined with her backward steps, stopped him. She was still smarting from his angry words, as well as from her own uninhibited behavior. She was ashamed that she'd given him such license with her body now that she knew there had only been desire on his part.

He hadn't said a single word before the bus stopped for her. He hadn't said a word as she hurriedly gave her ticket to the driver, got on the bus and waited for it to leave without looking his way again. He'd stood there in the trickling rain, without even a raincoat, with his hands deep in his jean pockets, and watched the bus pull away from the curb. That was how Dorie had remembered him all the long years, a lonely fading figure in the distance.

She'd loved him desperately. But her own self-respect wouldn't let her settle for a furtive affair in the goldfish-bowl atmosphere of Jacobsville. She'd wanted a home, a husband, children, everything.

Corrigan had only wanted to sleep with her.

She'd gone, breathless and sick at heart, all the way to New York City, swearing her father to absolute secrecy about her movements.

There had been a letter, a few weeks after her arrival, from her father. In it, he told her that he'd seen Corrigan only once since her departure, and that he was now hot in pursuit of a rich divorcée with sophistication dripping from her fingers. If Dorie had any parting regrets about her decision to leave town, that was the end of them. Corrigan had made his feelings plain, if he was seeing some woman already.

Dorie wondered if her father hadn't said something unpleasant to Corrigan Hart about his daughter's sudden departure from home. It would have been like him. He was fiercely protective of his only child, especially since the death of her mother from heart disease some years past. And his opinion about philandering men was obvious to everyone.

He believed in the old-fashioned sort of courtship, the kind that ended in marriage. Only a handful of conventional people were left, he told Dorie over and over. Such people were the cornerstones of social order. If they all fell, chaos reigned. A man who loved a woman would want to give her, and his children, his name. And Corrigan, he added, had made it clear to the whole town that he wanted no part of marriage or a family. Dorie would have been asking for heartbreak if she'd given in to Corrigan's selfish demands.

Her father was dead now. Dorie had come home for the funeral as well as to dispose of the house and property and decide her own future. She'd started out with such hopes of becoming a successful model. Her eyes closed and she shivered unconsciously at the memories.

"Dorie?"

She turned at the hesitant sound of her name. The face took a little longer to recognize. "Abby?" she said. "Abby Clark!"

"Abby Ballenger," the other woman corrected with a grin. "I married Calhoun."

"Calhoun!" Dorie was momentarily floored. The younger Ballenger brother had been a rounder and a half, and he was married? And to Abby, of all people, the shy and sweet girl for whom Calhoun and Justin had shared guardianship following the death of their parents.

"Surprising, isn't it?" Abby asked, hugging the other woman. "And there's more. We have three sons."

"I haven't been away that long, have I?" Dorie asked hesitantly.

"Eight years," came the reply. Abby was a little older, but she still had the same pretty gray-blue eyes and dark hair, even if it had silver threads now. "Justin married Shelby Jacobs just after I married Calhoun. They have three sons, too," she added on a sigh. "Not a girl in the bunch."

Dorie shook her head. "For heaven's sake!"

"We heard that you were in modeling…" Her voice trailed away as she saw the obvious long scar on the once-perfect cheek. "What happened?"

Dorie's eyes were all but dead. "Not much. I decided that modeling wasn't for me." She laughed at some private joke. "I went back to school and completed a course in business. Now I work for a group of attorneys. I'm a stenographer." Her gaze fell. "Jacobsville hasn't changed a bit."

"Jacobsville never changes," Abby chuckled. "I find it comforting." The laughter went out of her eyes. "We all heard about your father. I'm sorry. It must have been a blow."

"He'd been in the nursing home near me for some time, but he always said he wanted to be buried here. That's why I brought him home. I appreciated so many people coming to the funeral. It was kind."

"I suppose you noticed one missing face in the crowd?" Abby asked carefully, because she knew how persistent Corrigan Hart had been in his pursuit of Dorie.

"Yes." She twisted her purse in her hands. "Are they still making jokes about the Hart boys?"

"More than ever. There's never been the slightest hint of gossip about any of them and a woman. I guess they're all determined to die single. Especially Corrigan. He's turned into a recluse. He stays out at the ranch all the time now. He's never seen."

"Why?"

Abby seemed evasive. "He doesn't mix and nobody knows much about his life. Odd, isn't it, in a town this small, where we mostly know each other's business, that he isn't talked about? But he stays out of sight and none of the other boys ever speak about him. He's become the original local mystery."

"Well, don't look at me as if I'm the answer. He couldn't get rid of me fast enough," she said with a twinge of remaining bitterness.

"That's what you think. He became a holy terror in the weeks after you left town. Nobody would go near him."

"He only wanted me," Dorie said doggedly.

Abby's eyes narrowed. "And you were terrified of him," she recalled. "Calhoun used to joke about it. You were such an innocent and Corrigan was a rounder. He said it was poetic justice that rakes got caught by innocents."

"I remember Calhoun being a rake."

"He was," Abby recalled. "But not now. He's reformed. He's the greatest family man I could have imagined, a doting father and a wonderful husband." She sobered. "I'm sorry things didn't work out for you and Corrigan. If you hadn't taken off like that, I think he might have decided that he couldn't live without you."

"God forbid," she laughed, her eyes quick and nervous. "He wasn't a marrying man. He said so, frequently. And I was raised…well, you know how Dad was. Ministers have a decidedly conventional outlook on life."

"I know."

"I haven't had such a bad time of it," she lied,

grateful that her old friend couldn't read minds. She smiled. "I like New York."

"Do you have anyone there?"

"You mean a boyfriend, or what do they call it, a significant other?" she murmured. "No. I...don't have much to do with men."

There was a strangely haunted look about her that Abby quickly dispelled with an offer of coffee and a sandwich in the local café.

"Yes, thanks, I'm not hungry but I'd love some hot chocolate."

"Great!" Abby said. "I've got an hour to kill before I have to pick my two oldest boys up at school and the youngest from kindergarten. I'll enjoy your company."

The café was all but empty. It was a slow day, and except for a disgruntled looking cowboy sitting alone at a corner table, it was deserted.

Barbara, the owner, took their orders with a grin. "Nice to have pleasant company," she said, glaring toward the cowboy in the corner. "He brought a little black cloud in with him, and it's growing." She leaned closer. "He's one of the Hart employees," she whispered. "Or, he was until this morning. It seems that Corrigan fired him."

The sound of the man's name was enough to make Dorie's heart race, even after so many years. But she steeled herself not to let it show. She had nothing left to offer Corrigan, even if he was still interested in her. And that was a laugh. If he'd cared even a little, he'd have come to New York looking for her all those years ago.

"Fired him?" Abby glanced at the man and scowled. "But that's Buck Wyley," she protested. "He's the Harts' foreman. He's been with them since they came here."

"He made a remark Corrigan didn't like. He got knocked on his pants for his trouble and summarily fired." Barbara shrugged. "The Harts are all high-tempered, but until now I always thought Corrigan was fair. What sort of boss fires a man with Christmas only three weeks away?"

"Ebenezer Scrooge?" Abby ventured dryly.

"Buck said he cut another cowboy's wages to the bone for leaving a gate open." She shook her head. "Funny, we've heard almost nothing about Corrigan for years, and all of a sudden he comes back into the light like a smoldering madman."

"So I noticed," Abby said.

Barbara wiped her hands on a dishcloth. "I don't know what happened to set him off after so many years. The other brothers have been more visible lately, but not Corrigan. I'd wondered if he'd moved away for a while. Nobody even spoke of him." She glanced at Dorie with curious eyes. "You're Dorothy

Wayne, aren't you?" she asked then, smiling. "I thought I recognized you. Sorry about your pa."

"Thanks," Dorie said automatically. She noticed how Barbara's eyes went to the thin scar on her cheek and flitted quickly away.

"I'll get your order."

Barbara went back behind the counter and Abby's puzzled gaze went to the corner.

"Having a bad day, Buck?" she called.

He sipped black coffee. "It couldn't get much worse, Mrs. Ballenger," he replied in a deep, pleasant tone. "I don't suppose Calhoun and Justin are hiring out at the feedlot?"

"They'd hire you in a minute, and you know it," Abby told him. She smiled. "Why don't you go out there and…"

"Oh, the devil!" Buck muttered, his black eyes flashing. He got to his feet and stood there, vibrating, as a tall, lean figure came through the open door.

Dorie actually caught her breath. The tall man was familiar to her, even after all those years. Dressed in tight jeans, with hand-tooled boots and a chambray shirt and a neat, spotless white Stetson atop his black hair, he looked formidable, even with the cane he was using for support.

He didn't look at the table where Dorie was sitting, which was on the other side of the café from Buck.

"You fired me," Buck snapped at him. "What do

you want, another punch at me? This time, you'll get it back in spades, gimpy leg or not!"

Corrigan Hart just stared at the man, his pale eyes like chrome sparkling in sunlight.

"Those purebred Angus we got from Montana are coming in by truck this morning," he said. "You're the only one who knows how to use the master program for the computerized herd records."

"And you need me," Buck agreed with a cold smile. "For how long?"

"Two weeks," came the curt reply. "You'll work that long for your severance pay. If you're still of a mind to quit."

"Quit, hell!" Buck shot back, astonished. "You fired me!"

"I did not!" the older man replied curtly. "I said you could mind your own damned business or get out."

Buck's head turned and he stared at the other man for a minute. "If I come back, you'd better keep your fists to yourself from now on," he said shortly.

The other man didn't blink. "You know why you got hit."

Buck glanced warily toward Dorie and a ruddy color ran along his high cheekbones. "I never meant it the way you took it," he retorted.

"You'll think twice before you presume to make such remarks to me again, then, won't you?"

Buck made a movement that his employer took for assent.

"And your Christmas bonus is now history!" he added.

Buck let out an angry breath, almost spoke, but crushed his lips together finally in furious submission.

"Go home!" the older man said abruptly.

Buck pulled his hat over his eyes, tossed a dollar bill on the table with his coffee cup and strode out with barely a tip of the hat to the women present, muttering under his breath as he went.

The door closed with a snap. Corrigan Hart didn't move. He stood very still for a moment, as if steeling himself.

Then he turned, and his pale eyes stared right into Dorie's. But the anger in them eclipsed into a look of such shock that Dorie blinked.

"What happened to you?" he asked shortly.

She knew what he meant without asking. She put a hand self-consciously to her cheek. "An accident," she said stiffly.

His chin lifted. The tension in the café was so thick that Abby shifted uncomfortably at the table.

"You don't model now," he continued.

The certainty in the statement made her miserable. "No. Of course I don't."

He leaned heavily on the cane. "Sorry about your father," he said curtly.

She nodded.

His face seemed pinched as he stared at her. Even across the room, the heat in the look was tangible to Dorie. Her hands holding the mug of hot chocolate went white at the knuckles from the pressure of them around it.

He glanced at Abby. "How are things at the feed-lot?"

"Much as usual," she replied pleasantly. "Calhoun and Justin are still turning away business. Nice, in the flat cattle market this fall."

"I agree. We've culled as many head as possible and we're venturing into new areas of crossbreeding. Nothing but purebreds now. We're hoping to pioneer a new breed."

"Good for you," Abby replied.

His eyes went back to Dorie. They lingered on her wan face, her lack of spirit. "How long are you going to stay?" he asked.

The question was voiced in such a way it seemed like a challenge. Her shoulders rose and fell. "Until I tie up all the loose ends, I suppose. They've given me two weeks off at the law firm where I work."

"As an attorney?"

She shook her head. "A stenographer."

He scowled. "With your head for figures?" he asked shortly.

Her gaze was puzzled. She hadn't realized that he was aware of her aptitude for math.

"It's a waste," he persisted. "You'd have been a natural at bookkeeping and marketing."

She'd often thought so, too, but she hadn't pursued her interest in that field. Especially after her first attempt at modeling.

He gave her a calculating stare. "Clarisse Marston has opened a boutique in town. She designs women's clothes and has them made up at a local textile plant. She sells all over the state."

"Yes," Abby added. "In fact, she's now doing a lot of designing for Todd Burke's wife, Jane—you know, her signature rodeo line of sportswear."

"I've heard of it, even in New York," Dorie admitted.

"The thing Clarisse doesn't have is someone to help her with marketing and bookkeeping." He shook his head. "It amazes me that she hasn't gone belly-up already."

Abby started to speak, but the look on Corrigan's face silenced her. She only smiled at Dorie.

"This is your home," Corrigan persisted quietly. "You were born and raised in Jacobsville. Surely having a good job here would be preferable to being a stenographer in New York. Unless," he added slowly, "there's some reason you want to stay there."

His eyes were flashing. Dorie looked into the film on her cooling hot chocolate. "I don't have anyone in New York." She shifted her legs. "I don't have anyone here, either, now."

"But you do," Abby protested. "All your friends."

"Of course, she may miss the bright lights and excitement," Corrigan drawled.

She looked at him curiously. He was trying to goad her. Why?

"Is Jacobsville too small for you now, city girl?" he persisted with a mocking smile.

"No, it isn't that at all," she said. She cleared her throat.

"Come home," Abby coaxed.

She didn't answer.

"Still afraid of me?" Corrigan asked with a harsh laugh when her head jerked up. "That's why you left. Is it why you won't come back?"

She colored furiously, the first trace of color that had shown in her face since the strange conversation began.

"I'm not...afraid of you!" she faltered.

But she was, and he knew it. His silver eyes narrowed and that familiar, mocking smile turned up his thin upper lip. "Prove it."

"Maybe Miss Marston doesn't want a book-keeper."

"She does," he returned.

She hesitated. "She might not like me."

"She will."

She let out an exasperated sigh. "I can't make a decision that important in a few seconds," she told him. "I have to think about it."

"Take your time," he replied. "Nobody's rushing you."

"It would be lovely if you came back, though," Abby said with a smile. "No matter how many friends we have, we can always use one more."

"Exactly," Corrigan told her. His eyes narrowed. "Of course, you needn't consider me in your decision. I'm not trying to get you to come back for my sake. But I'm sure there are plenty of other bachelors left around here who'd be delighted to give you a whirl, if you needed an incentive."

His lean face was so hard and closed that not one flicker of emotion got away from it.

Abby was eyeing him curiously, but she didn't say a word, not even when her gaze fell to his hand on the silver knob of the cane and saw it go white from the pressure.

He eased up on the handle, just the same. "Well?"

"I'd like to," Dorie said quietly. She didn't look at

him. Odd, how his statement had hurt, after all those years. She looked back on the past with desperation these days, wondering how her life would have been if she hadn't resisted him that night he'd tried to carry her to bed.

She hadn't wanted an affair, but he was an honorable man, in his fashion. Perhaps he would have followed up with a proposal, despite his obvious distaste for the married state. Or perhaps he wouldn't have. There might have been a child…

She grimaced and lifted the cup of chocolate to her lips. It was tepid and vaguely distasteful.

"Go see Clarisse, why don't you?" he added. "You've nothing to lose, and a lot to gain. She's a sweet woman. You'll like her."

Did he? She didn't dare wonder about that, or voice her curiosity. "I might do that," she replied.

The tap of the cane seemed unusually loud as he turned back to the door. "Give the brothers my best," Corrigan told Abby. He nodded and was gone.

Only then did Dorie look up, her eyes on his tall, muscular body as he walked carefully back to the big double-cabbed black ranch pickup truck he drove.

"What happened to him?" Dorie asked.

Abby sipped her own hot chocolate before she answered. "It happened the week after you left town. He went on a hunting trip in Montana with some other men. During a heavy, late spring snow, Corrigan and another man went off on their own in a four-wheel-drive utility vehicle to scout another section of the hunting range."

"And?" Dorie prompted.

"The truck went over a steep incline and overturned. The other man was killed outright. Corrigan was pinned and couldn't get free. He lay there most of the night and into the next day before the party came looking for them and found him. By that time, he was unconscious. The impact broke his leg in two places, and he had frostbite as well. He almost died."

Dorie caught her breath. "How horrible!"

"They wanted to amputate the leg, but…" she shrugged. "He refused them permission to operate, so they did the best they could. The leg is usable, just, but it will always be stiff. They said later that it was a miracle he didn't lose any toes. He had just enough sense left to wrap himself in one of those thin thermal sheets the men had carried on the trip. It saved him from a dangerous frostbite."

"Poor man."

"Oh, don't make that mistake," Abby mused. "Nobody is allowed to pity Corrigan Hart. Just ask his brothers."

"All the same, he never seemed the sort of man to lose control of anything, not even a truck."

"He wasn't himself but he didn't lose control, either."

"I beg your pardon?"

Abby grimaced. "He and the other man, the one who was driving, had been drinking. He blamed himself not only for the wreck, but for the other man's death. He knew the man wasn't fit to drive but he didn't try to stop him. They say he's been punishing himself ever since. That's why he never comes into town, or has any social life. He's withdrawn into himself and nobody can drag him back out. He's become a hermit."

"But, why?"

"Why was he drinking, you mean?" Abby said, and Dorie nodded. Still, Abby hesitated to put it into words.

"Tell me," came the persistent nudge from Dorie.

Abby's eyes were apologetic. "Nobody knows, really. But the gossip was that he was trying to get over losing you."

Chapter Two

"But he wanted to lose me," Dorie exclaimed, shocked. "He couldn't get out of my house fast enough when I refused...refused him," she blurted. She clasped her hands together. "He accused me of being frigid and a tease..."

"Corrigan was a rounder, Dorie," Abby said gently. "In this modern age, even in Jacobsville, a lot of girls are pretty sophisticated at eighteen. He wouldn't have known about your father being a minister, because he'd retired from the church before the Harts came to take over their grandfather's ranch. He was probably surprised to find you less accommodating than other girls."

"Surprised wasn't the word," Dorie said miserably. "He was furious."

"He did go to the bus depot when you left."

"How did you know that?"

"Everybody talked about it," Abby admitted. "It was generally thought that he went there to stop you."

"He didn't say a word," came the quiet reply. "Not one word."

"Maybe he didn't know what to say. He was probably embarrassed and upset about the way he'd treated you. A man like that might not know what to do with an innocent girl."

Dorie laughed bitterly. "Sure he did. You see her off and hope she won't come back. He told me that he had no intention of marrying."

"He could have changed his mind."

Dorie shook her head. "Not a chance. He never talked about us being a couple. He kept reminding me that I was young and that he liked variety. He said that we shouldn't think of each other in any serious way, but just enjoy each other while it lasted."

"That sounds like a Hart, all right," Abby had to admit. "They're all like Corrigan. Apparently they have a collective bad attitude toward women and think of them as minor amusements."

"He picked on the wrong girl," Dorie said. She finished her hot chocolate. "I'd never even had a real boyfriend when he came along. He was so forceful and demanding and inflexible, so devoid of tenderness when he was with me." She huddled closer into her sweater. "He came at me like a rocket. I couldn't run, I couldn't hide, he just kept coming." Her eyes closed on a long sigh. "Oh, Abby, he scared me to death. I'd been raised in a such a way that I couldn't have an affair, and I knew that was all he wanted. I ran, and kept running. Now I can't stop."

"You could, if you wanted to."

"The only way I'd come back is with a written guarantee that he wanted nothing more to do with me," she said with a cold laugh. "Otherwise, I'd never feel safe here."

"He just told you himself that he had no designs on you," Abby reminded her. "He has other interests."

"Does he? Other…women interests?"

Abby clasped her fingers together on the table. "He goes out with a rich divorcée when he's in need of company," she said. "That's been going on for a long time now. He probably was telling the truth when he said that he wouldn't bother you. After all, it's been eight years." She studied the other woman. "You want to come home, don't you?"

Caught off guard, Dorie nodded. "I'm so alone," she confessed. "I have bolts and chains on my door and I live like a prisoner when I'm not at work. I rarely ever go outside. I miss trees and green grass."

"There's always Central Park."

"You can't plant flowers there," she said, "or have a dog or cat in a tiny apartment like mine. I want to sit out in the rain and watch the stars at night. I've dreamed of coming home."

"Why haven't you?"

"Because of the way I left," she confessed. "I didn't want any more trouble than I'd already had. It was bad enough that Dad had to come and see me, that I couldn't come home."

"Because of Corrigan?"

"What?" For an instant, Dorie's eyes were frightened. Then they seemed to calm. "No, it was for another reason altogether, those first few years. I couldn't risk coming here, where it's so easy to find people…" She closed up when she realized what she was saying. "It was a problem I had, in New York. That's all I can tell you. And it's over now. There's no more danger from that direction. I'm safe."

"I don't understand."

"You don't need to know," Dorie said gently. "It wouldn't help matters to talk about it now. But I would like to come back home. I seem to have spent most of my life on the run."

What an odd turn of phrase, Abby thought, but she didn't question it. She just smiled. "Well, if you decide to come back, I'll introduce you to Clarisse. Just let me know."

Dorie brightened. "All right. Let me think about it for a day or two, and I'll be in touch with you."

"Good. I'll hold you to that."

For the next two days, Dorie thought about nothing else except coming back to her hometown. While she thought, she wandered around the small yard, looking at the empty bird feeders and the squirrel feeder nearby. She saw the discarded watering pot, the weed-bound flower beds. Her father's long absence had made its mark on the little property. It needed a loving hand to restore it.

She stood very still as an idea formed in her mind. She didn't have to sell the property. She could keep it. She could live here. With her math skills, and the bookkeeping training she'd had in business school, she could open a small bookkeeping service of her own. Clarisse could be a client. She could have others. She could support herself. She could leave New York.

The idea took wing. She was so excited about it that she called Abby the next morning when she was sure that the boys would be in school.

She outlined the idea to her friend. "Well, what do you think?" she asked enthusiastically.

"I think it's a great idea!" Abby exclaimed. "And the perfect solution. When are you going to start?"

"Next week," she said with absolute certainty. "I'll

use the Christmas vacation I would have had as my notice. It will only take a couple of days to pack up the few things I have. I'll have to pay the rent, because I signed a lease, but if things work out as I hope they will, that won't be a problem. Oh, Abby, it's like a dream!"

"Now you sound more like the Dorothy I used to know," Abby told her. "I'm so glad you're coming home."

"So am I," Dorie replied, and even as she said it, she tried not to think of the complications that could arise. Corrigan was still around. But he'd made her a promise of sorts, and perhaps he'd keep it. Anyway, she'd worry about that situation later.

A week later, Dorie was settled into her father's house, with all her bittersweet memories of him to keep her company. She'd shipped her few big things, like her piano, home by a moving service. Boxes still cluttered the den, but she was beginning to get her house into some sort of order.

It needed a new roof, and some paint, as well as some plumbing work on the leaky bathtub faucet. But those were minor inconveniences. She had a good little nest egg in her savings account and it would tide her over, if she was careful, until she could be self-supporting in her business again.

She had some cards and stationery printed and put an ad in the Jacobsville weekly newspaper. Then she settled in and began to work in the yard, despite the cold weather. She was finding that grief had to be worked through. It didn't end at the funeral. And the house was a constant reminder of the old days when she and her father had been happy.

So it was a shock to find Corrigan Hart on her doorstep the first Saturday she was in residence.

She just stared at him at first, as if she'd been stunned. In fact, she was. He was the last person she'd have expected to find on her doorstep.

He had a bouquet of flowers in the hand that wasn't holding the cane and his hat. He proferred them brusquely.

"Housewarming present," he said.

She took the pretty bouquet and belatedly stood aside. "Would you like to come in? I could make coffee."

He accepted the invitation, placing his hat on the rack by the door. He kept the cane and she noticed that he leaned on it heavily as he made his way to the nearest easy chair and sat down in it.

"They say damp weather is hard on injured joints," she remarked.

His pale eyes speared into her face, with an equal mixture of curiosity and irritation. "They're right," he drawled. "Walking hurts. Does it help to have me admit it?"

"I wasn't trying to score points," she replied quietly. "I didn't get to say so in the café, but I'm sorry you got hurt."

His own eyes were pointed on the scar that ran the length of her cheek. "I'm sorry you did," he said gruffly. "You mentioned coffee?"

There it was again, that bluntness that had frightened her so much at eighteen. Despite the eight years in between, he still intimidated her.

She moved into the small kitchen, visible from the living room, and filled the pot with water and a premeasured coffee packet. After she'd started it dripping, and had laid a tray with cups, saucers and the condiments, she rejoined him.

"Are you settling in?" he asked a minute after she'd dropped down onto the sofa.

"Yes," she said. "It's strange, after being away for so many years. And I miss Dad. But I always loved this house. Eventually it will be comforting to live here. Once I get over the worst of the grieving."

He nodded. "We lost both our parents at once, in a flood," he said tersely. "I remember how we felt."

He looked around at the high ceilings and marked walls, and the open fireplace. He nodded toward it. "That isn't efficient. You need a stove in here."

"I need a lot of things in here, but I have to eat, too," she said with a faint smile. She pushed back her short, wavy platinum hair and curled up on the sofa in her jeans and gray sweatshirt and socks. Her shoes were under the sofa. Even in cold weather, she hated wearing shoes around the house.

He seemed to notice that and found it amusing, judging by the twinkle in his pale eyes.

"I hate shoes," she said.

"I remember."

That was surprising. She hardly remembered the girl she'd been eight years ago. It seemed like a lifetime.

"You had a dog, that damned little spaniel, and you were out in the front yard washing him one day when I drove by," he recalled. "He didn't like a bath, and you were soaked, bare feet, cutoffs, tank top and all." His eyes darkened as he looked at her. "I told you to go in the house, do you remember?"

"Yes." The short command had always puzzled her, because he'd seemed angry, not amused as he did now.

"I never said why," he continued. His face tautened as he looked at her. "You weren't wearing anything under that tank top and it was plastered to you," he added quietly. "You can't imagine what it did to me... And there was that damned Bobby Harris standing on the sidewalk gawking at you."

Bobby had asked her out later that day, and she'd refused, because she didn't like him. He was an older boy; her father never had liked him.

"I didn't realize," she said, amazed that the memory should be so tame now, when his odd behavior had actually hurt in the past. She actually flushed at the thought that he'd seen her that way so early in their relationship.

"I know that, now, eight years too late," he said abruptly.

She cocked her head, studying him curiously.

He saw her gaze and lifted his eyes. "I thought you were displaying your charms brazenly for my benefit, and maybe even for Bobby's," he said with a mocking smile. "That's why I acted the way I did that last night we dated."

Her face thinned with distress. "Oh, no!"

"Oh, yes," he said, his voice deep with bitterness. "I thought you were playing me for a sucker, Dorie. That you were pretending to be innocent because I was rich and you wanted a wedding ring instead of an affair."

The horror she felt showed in her wan face.

"Yes, I know," he said when she started to protest. "I only saw what I wanted to see. But the joke was on me. By the time I realized what a hell of a mistake I'd made about you, you were halfway on a bus out of town. I went after you. But I couldn't manage the right words to stop you. My pride cut my throat. I was never that wrong about anyone before."

She averted her gaze. "It was a long time ago. I was just a kid."

"Yes. Just a kid. And I mistook you for a woman." He studied her through narrow lids. "You don't look much older even now. How did you get that scar?"

Her fingers went to it. The memories poured over her, hot and hurting. She got to her feet. "I'll see about the coffee."

She heard a rough sound behind her, but apparently it wasn't something he wanted to put words to. She escaped into the kitchen, found some cookies to put in a bowl and carried the coffee back to the coffee table on a silver tray.

"Fancy stuff," he mused.

She knew that he had equally fancy stuff at his place. She'd never been there, but she'd certainly heard about the Hart heirlooms that the four brothers displayed with such pride. Old Spanish silver, five generations old, dating all the way back to Spain graced their side table. There was crystal as well, and dozens of other heirlooms that would probably never be handed down. None of the Harts, it was rumored, had any ambitions of marrying.

"This was my grandmother's," she said. "It's all I had of her. She brought this service over from England, they said."

"Ours came from Spain." He waited for her to pour the coffee. He picked up his cup, waving away cream and sugar. He took a sip, nodded and took another. "You make good coffee. Amazing how many people can't."

"I'm sure it's bad for us. Most things are."

He agreed. He put the cup back into the saucer and studied her over its rim. "Are you planning to stay for good?"

"I guess so," she faltered. "I've had stationery and cards printed, and I've already had two offers of work."

"I'm bringing you a third—our household accounts. We've been sharing them since our mother died. Consequently each of us insists that it's not our turn to do them, so they don't get done."

"You'd bring them to me?" she asked hesitantly.

He studied her broodingly. "Why shouldn't I? Are you afraid to come out to the ranch and do them?"

"Of course not."

"Of course not," he muttered, glaring at her. He sat forward, watching her uneasy movement. "Eight years, and I still frighten you."

She curled up even more. "Don't be absurd. I'm twenty-six."

"You don't look or act it."

"Go ahead," she invited. "Be as blunt as you like."

"Thanks, I will. You're still a virgin."

Coffee went everywhere. She cursed roundly,

amusing him, as she searched for napkins to mop up the spill, which was mostly on her.

"Why are you?" he persisted, baiting her. "Were you waiting for me?"

She stood up, slamming the coffee cup to the floor. It shattered with a pleasantly loud crash, and she thanked goodness that it was an old one. "You son of a...!"

He stood up, too, chuckling. "That's better," he mused, watching her eyes flash, her face burn with color.

She kicked at a pottery shard. "Damn you, Corrigan Hart!"

He moved closer, watching her eyelids flutter. She tried to back up, but she couldn't go far. Her legs were against the sofa. There was no place to run.

He paused a step away from her, close enough that she could actually feel the heat of his body through her clothing and his. He looked down into her eyes without speaking for several long seconds.

"You're not the child you used to be," he said, his voice as smooth as velvet. "You can stand up for yourself, even with me. And everything's going to be all right. You're home. You're safe."

It was almost as if he knew what she'd been through. His eyes were quiet and full of secrets, but he smiled. His hand reached out and touched her short hair.

"You still wear it like a boy's," he murmured. "But it's silky. Just the way I remember it."

He was much too close. He made her nervous. Her hands went out and pressed into his shirtfront, but instead of moving back, he moved forward. She shivered at the feel of his chest under her hands, even with the shirt covering it.

"I don't want a lover," she said, almost choking on the words.

"Neither do I," he replied heavily. "So we'll be friends. That's all."

She nibbled on her lower lip. He smelled of spice and leather. She used to dream about him when she first left home. Over the years, he'd assumed the image of a protector in her mind. Strange, when he'd once frightened her so much.

Impulsively she laid her cheek against his chest with a little sigh and closed her eyes.

He shivered for an instant, before his lean hands pressed her gently to him, in a nonthreatening way. He stared over her head with eyes that blazed, eyes that he was thankful she couldn't see.

"We've lost years," he said half under his breath. "But Christmas brings miracles. Maybe we'll have one of our own."

"A miracle?" she mused, smiling. She felt ever so safe in his arms. "What sort?"

"I don't know," he murmured, absently stroking

her hair. "We'll have to wait and see. You aren't going to sleep, are you?"

"Not quite." She lifted her head and looked up at him, a little puzzled at the familiarity she felt with him. "I didn't expect that you'd ever be comfortable to be around."

"How so?"

She shrugged. "I wasn't afraid."

"Why should you be?" he replied. "We're different people now."

"I guess."

He brushed a stray hair from her eyebrow with a lean, sure hand. "I want you to know something," he said quietly. "What happened that night…I wouldn't have forced you. Things got a little out of hand, and I said some things, a lot of things, that I regret. I guess you realize now that I had a different picture of you than the one that was real. But even so, I wouldn't have harmed you."

"I think I knew that," she said. "But thank you for telling me."

His hand lay alongside her soft cheek and his metallic eyes went dark and sad. "I mourned you," he said huskily. "Nothing was the same after you'd gone."

She lowered her eyes to his throat. "I didn't have much fun in New York at first, either."

"Modeling wasn't all it was cracked up to be?"

She hesitated. Then she shook her head. "I did better as a stenographer."

"And you'll do even better as a financial expert, right here," he told her. He smiled, tilting up her chin. "Are you going to take the job I've offered you?"

"Yes," she said at once. Her gaze drew slowly over his face. "Are your brothers like you?"

"Wait and see."

"That sounds ominous."

He chuckled, moving slowly away from her to retrieve his cane from the chair. "They're no worse, at least."

"Are they as outspoken as you?"

"Definitely." He saw her apprehension. "Think of the positive side. At least you'll always know exactly where you stand with us."

"That must be a plus."

"Around here, it is. We're hard cases. We don't make friends easily."

"And you don't marry. I remember."

His face went hard. "You have plenty of reason to remember that I said that. But I'm eight years older, and a lot wiser. I don't have such concrete ideas anymore."

"You mean, you're not still a confirmed bachelor?" She laughed nervously. "They say you're taken with the gay divorcée, just the same."

"How did you hear about her?" he asked curtly.

His level, challenging gaze made her uneasy. "People talk," she said.

"Well, the gay divorcée," he emphasized, his expression becoming even more remote, "is a special case. And we're not a couple. Despite what you may have heard. We're friends."

She turned away. "That's no concern of mine. I'll do your bookkeeping on those household accounts, and thank you for the work. But I have no interest in your private life."

He didn't return the compliment. He reached for his hat and perched it on his black hair. There were threads of gray at his temples now, and new lines in his dark, lean face.

"I'm sorry about your accident," she said abruptly, watching him lean heavily on the cane.

"I'll get by," he said. "My leg is stiff, but I'm not crippled. It hurts right now because I took a toss off a horse, and I need the cane. As a rule, I walk well enough without one."

"I remember the way you used to ride," she recalled. "I thought I'd never seen anything in my life as beautiful as you astride a horse at a fast gallop."

His posture went even more rigid. "You never said so."

She smiled. "You intimidated me. I was afraid of you. And not only because you wanted me." She averted her eyes. "I wanted you, too. But I hadn't been raised to believe in a promiscuous life-style. Which," she added, looking up at his shocked face, "was all you were offering me. You said so."

"God help me, I never knew that your father was a minister and your mother a missionary," he said heavily. "Not until it was far too late to do me any good. I expected that all young women were free with their favors in this age of no-consequences intimacy."

"It wouldn't be of no consequence to me," she said firmly. "I was never one to go with the crowd. I'm still not."

"Yes, I know," he murmured dryly, giving her a long, meaningful glance. "It's obvious."

"And it's none of your business."

"I wouldn't go that far." He tilted his hat over his eyes. "I haven't changed completely, you know. I still go after the things I want, even if I don't go as fast as I used to."

"I expect you do," she said. "Does the divorcée know?"

"Know what? That I'm persistent? Sure she does."

"Good for her."

"She's a beauty," he added, propping on his stick. "Of an age to be sophisticated and good fun."

Her heart hurt. "I'm sure you enjoy her company."

"I enjoy yours as much," he replied surprisingly. "Thanks for the coffee."

"Don't you like cookies?" she asked, noting that he hadn't touched them.

"No," he said. "I don't care for sweets at all."

"Really?"

He shrugged. "We never had them at home. Our mother wasn't the homey sort."

"What was she like?" she had to ask.

"She couldn't cook, hated housework and spouted contempt for any woman who could sew and knit and crochet," he replied.

She felt cold. "And your father?"

"He was a good man, but he couldn't cope with us alone." His eyes grew dark. "When she took off and deserted him, part of him died. She'd just come back, out of money and all alone, from her latest lover. They were talking about a reconciliation when the flood took the house where she was living right out from under them." His face changed, hardened. He leaned heavily on the cane. "Simon and Cag and I were grown by then. We took care of the other two."

"No wonder you don't like women," she murmured quietly.

He gave her a long, level look and then dropped his gaze. She missed the calculation in his tone when he added, "Marriage is old-fashioned, anyway. I have a dog, a good horse and a houseful of modern appliances. I even have a housekeeper who can cook. A wife would be redundant."

"Well, I never," she exclaimed, breathless.

"I know," he replied, and there was suddenly a wicked glint in his eyes. "You can't blame that on me," he added. "God knows, I did my best to bring you into the age of enlightenment."

While she was absorbing that dry remark, he tipped his hat, turned and walked out the door.

She darted onto the porch after him. "When?" she called after him. "You didn't say when you wanted me to start."

"I'll phone you." He didn't look back. He got into his truck laboriously and drove away without even a wave of his hand.

At least she had the promise of a job, she told herself. She shouldn't read hidden messages into what he said. But the past he'd shared with her, about his mother, left her chilled. How could a woman have five sons and leave them?

And what was the secret about the fifth brother, Simon, the one nobody had ever seen? She wondered if he'd done something unspeakable, or if he was in trouble with the law. There had to be a reason why the brothers never spoke of him much. Perhaps she'd find out one day.

Chapter Three

It was the next day before she realized she hadn't thanked Corrigan for the flowers he'd brought. She sent a note out to the ranch on Monday, and got one back that read, simply, "You're welcome." So much for olive branches, if one had been needed.

She found plenty to keep her busy in the days that followed. It seemed that all her father's friends and the people she'd gone to school with wanted her to come home. Everyone seemed to know a potential client. It wasn't long before she was up to her ears in work.

The biggest surprise came Thursday morning when she heard the sound of many heavy footsteps and looked up from her desk to find three huge, intimidating men standing on her porch just beyond the glass-fronted door. They'd come in that big double-cabbed pickup that Corrigan usually drove, and she wondered if these were his brothers.

She went to open the door and felt like a midget when they came tromping inside her house, their spurs jingling pleasantly on boots that looked as if they'd been kept in a swamp.

"We're the Harts," one of them said. "Corrigan's brothers."

As she'd guessed. She studied them curiously. Corrigan was tall, but these men were giants. Two were dark-haired like Corrigan, and one had blond-streaked brown hair. All were dark-eyed, unlike him. None of them would have made any lists of handsome bachelors. They were rugged-looking, lean and tanned, and they made her nervous. The Hart boys made most people nervous. The only other local family that had come close to their reputations for fiery tempers were the Tremayne boys, who were all married and just a little tamer now. The Harts were relative newcomers in Jacobsville, having only been around eight years or so. But they kept to themselves and seemed to have ties to San Antonio that were hard to break. What little socializing they did was all done there, in the city. They didn't mix much in Jacobsville.

Not only were they too rugged for words, but they also had the most unusual first names Dorie could remember hearing. They introduced themselves abruptly, without even being asked first.

Reynard was the youngest. They called him Rey. He had deep-set black eyes and a thin mouth and, gossip said, the worst temper of the four.

The second youngest was Leopold. He was broader than the other three, although not fat, and the tallest. He never seemed to shave. He had blond-streaked brown hair and brown eyes and a mischievous streak that the others apparently lacked.

Callaghan was the eldest, two years older than Corrigan. He had black eyes like a cobra. He didn't blink. He was taller than all his brothers, with the exception of Leopold, and he did most of the bronc-breaking at the ranch. He looked Spanish, more than the others, and he had the bearing and arrogance of royalty, as if he belonged in another century. They said he had the old-fashioned attitudes of the past, as well.

He gave the broader of the three a push toward Dorie. He glared over his shoulder, but took off his hat and forced a smile as he stood in front of Dorie.

"You must be Dorothy Wayne," Leopold said with a grin. "You work for us."

"Y…yes, I guess I do," she stammered. She felt

surrounded. She moved back behind the desk and just stared at them, feeling nervous and inadequate.

"Will you two stop glaring?" Leopold shot at his taciturn brothers. "You're scaring her!"

They seemed to make an effort to relax, although it didn't quite work out.

"Never mind," Leopold muttered. He clutched his hat in his hand. "We'd like you to come out to the ranch," he said. "The household accounts are about to do us in. We can't keep Corrigan still long enough to get him to bring them to you."

"He came over Saturday," she said.

"Yeah, we heard," Leo mused. "Roses, wasn't it?"

The other two almost smiled.

"Roses," she agreed. Her gray eyes were wide and they darted from one giant to another.

"He forgot to bring you the books. The office is in a hel…heck of a mess," Leo continued. "We can't make heads nor tails of it. Corrigan scribbles, and we've volunteered him to do it mostly, but we can't read his writing. He escaped to a herd sale in Montana, so we're stuck." He shrugged and managed to look helpless. "We can't see if we've got enough money in the account to buy groceries." He looked hungry. He sighed loudly. "We'd sure appreciate it if you could come out, maybe in the morning, about nine? If that's not too early."

"Oh, no," she said. "I'm up and making breakfast by six."

"Making breakfast? You can cook, then?" Leopold asked.

"Well, yes." She hesitated, but he looked really interested. "I make biscuits and bacon and eggs."

"Pig meat," the one called Reynard muttered.

"Steak's better," Callaghan agreed.

"If she can make biscuits, the other stuff doesn't matter," Reynard retorted.

"Will you two shut up?" Leopold asked sharply. He turned back to Dorie and gave her a thorough appraisal, although not in the least sexual. "You don't look like a bookkeeper."

"Nice hair," Reynard remarked.

"Bad scar on that cheek," Callaghan remarked. "How did it happen?"

Heavens, he was blunt! She was almost startled enough to tell him. She blurted that it had been in an accident.

"Tough," he said. "But if you can cook, scars don't matter much."

Her mouth was open, and Leopold stomped on his big brother's foot, hard.

Callaghan popped him one on the arm with a fist the size of a ham. "Cut it out!"

"Don't insult her, she won't come!"

"I didn't!"

Reynard moved forward, elbowing the other two out of the way. He had his own hat in his hand. He tried to smile. It looked as if he hadn't had much practice at it.

"We'd like you to come tomorrow. Will you?"

She hesitated.

"Now see what you've done!" Leopold shot at Callaghan. "She's scared of us!"

"We wouldn't hurt you," Reynard said gently. He gave up trying to smile; it was unnatural anyway. "We have old Mrs. Culbertson keeping house for us. She carries a broomstick around with her. You'll be safe."

She bit back a laugh. But her eyes began to twinkle.

"She carries the broomstick because of him," Reynard added, indicating Leopold. "He likes to…"

"Never mind!" Leopold said icily.

"I was only going to say that you…"

"Shut up!"

"If you two don't stop, I'm going to lay you both out right here," Callaghan said, and looked very much as if he meant it. "Apologize."

They both murmured reluctant apologies.

"All right, that's that." He put his hat back on. "If you can come at nine, we'll send one of the boys for you."

"Thank you, I'd rather drive my own car."

"I've seen your car. That's why I'm sending one of the boys for you," Callaghan continued doggedly.

Her mouth fell open again. "It's a…a nice old car! And it runs fine!"

"Everybody knows Turkey Sanders sold it to you," Callaghan said with a disgusted look. "He's a pirate. You'll be lucky if the wheels don't fall off the first time you go around a curve."

"That's right," Rey agreed.

"We'll stop by on our way out of town and talk to him," Leopold said. "He'll bring your car back in and make sure it's perfectly safe to drive. He'll do it first thing tomorrow."

"But…"

They put their hats back on, gave her polite nods and stomped back out the way they'd come.

Callaghan paused at the front door, with the screen open. "He may talk and act tough, but he's hurt pretty bad, inside where it doesn't show. Don't hurt him again."

"Him?"

"Corrigan."

She moved forward, just a step. "It wasn't like that," she said gently. "He didn't feel anything for me."

"And you didn't, for him?"

She averted her gaze to the floor. "It was a long time ago."

"You shouldn't have left."

She looked back up, her eyes wide and wounded. "I was afraid of him!"

He let out a long breath. "You were just a kid. We tried to tell him. Even though we hadn't seen you, we knew about you from other people. We were pretty sure you weren't the sort of girl to play around. He wouldn't listen." He shrugged. "Maybe we corrupted him. You might ask him sometimes about our parents," he added coldly. "Kids don't grow up hating marriage without reason."

There was a lot of pain in his lean face. He was telling her things she'd never have dared ask Corrigan. She moved forward another step, aware of the other two talking out on the porch in hushed whispers.

"Is he still...like that?"

His eyes were cold, but as they looked into hers, they seemed to soften just a little. "He's not the same man he was. You'll have to find out the rest for yourself. We don't interfere in each other's lives, as a rule." His gaze went over her wan face. "You've been to hell and back, too."

He was as perceptive as his brother. She smiled. "I suppose it's part of becoming an adult. Losing illusions and dreams and hope, I mean." She locked her fingers together and looked up at him quietly. "Growing up is painful."

"Don't let go," he said suddenly. "No matter what he says, what he does, don't let go."

Her surprise widened her eyes. "Why?"

He pulled his hat lower over his forehead. "They don't make women like you anymore."

"Like me?" She frowned.

His dark eyes glittered. He smiled in a way that, if she hadn't been half-crazy about Corrigan, would have curled her toes. "I wish we'd met you before," he said. "You'd never have gotten on that bus." He tilted the hat. "We'll send Joey for you in the morning."

"But…"

The door closed behind him. He motioned to the other two and they followed him down the steps to the four-door pickup truck. It had a big cab. It was streamlined and black, and it had a menacing look not—unlike Corrigan Hart's brothers!

She wondered why they'd all come together to ask her to go out to the ranch, and why they'd done it when Corrigan was gone. She supposed she'd find out. She did wonder again about the fifth brother, the mysterious one that Corrigan had mentioned. None of these men were named Simon.

Later, the telephone rang, and it was Turkey Sanders. "I just wanted you to know that I'm going to have that car I sold you picked up in the morning and put to rights," he said at once. "I guarantee, it's going to be the best used car you've ever driven! If you would, just leave the keys in it, and I'll have it picked up first thing. And if there's anything else I can do for you, little lady, you just ask!"

He sounded much more enthusiastic than he had when he'd sold her the rusty little car. "Why, thank you," she said.

"No problem. None at all. Have a nice day, now."

He hung up and she stared blankly at the receiver. Well, nobody could say that living in Jacobsville wasn't interesting, she told herself. Apparently the brothers had a way with other businessmen, too. She'd never have admitted that the car had worried her from the time Turkey had talked her into buying it, for what seemed like a high price for such a wreck. She had a driver's license, which she had to have renewed. But never having owned a car in New York, it was unique to have one of her own, even if it did look like ten miles of bad road.

It was a cold, blustery morning when a polite young man drove up in a black Mercedes and held the door open for her.

"I'm Joey," he told her. "The brothers sent me to fetch you. I sure am glad you took on this job," he added. "They won't give me any money for gas until that checkbook's balanced. I've been having to syphon it out of their trucks with a hose." He shook his head ruefully as he waited for her to move her long denim skirt completely out of the door frame so that he could close the door. "I hate the taste of gasoline."

He closed the door, got in under the wheel and took off in a cloud of dust.

She smiled to herself. The brothers were strange people.

The ranch was immaculate, from its white wood fences to the ranch house itself, a long elegant brick home with a sprawling manicured lawn and a swimming pool and tennis court. The bunkhouse was brick, too, and the barn was so big that she imagined it could hold an entire herd of horses.

"Big, huh?" Joey grinned at her. "The brothers do things on a big scale, but they're meticulous— especially Cag. He runs the place, mostly."

"Cag?"

"Callaghan. Nobody calls him that in the family." He glanced in her direction, amused. "They said you're the reason Corrigan never married."

Her heart jumped. "No kidding?"

"Oh, yeah. He doesn't even look at women these days. But when he heard that you were coming back, he shaved and bought new clothes." He shook his head. "Shocked us all, seeing him without a beard."

"I can't imagine him with one," she said with some confusion.

"Pity about his leg, but he's elegant on a horse, just the same."

"I think he gets around very well."

"Better than he used to." He pulled up in front of the house, turned off the engine and went around to help her out.

"It's right in here."

He led her in through the front door and down a carpeted hall to a pine-paneled office. "Mrs. Culbertson will be along any minute to get you some coffee or tea or a soft drink. The brothers had to get to work or they'd have been here to meet you. No worry, though, Corrigan's home. He'll be here shortly and show you the books. He's trying to doctor a colt, down in the barn."

"Thank you, Joey."

He tipped his hat. "My pleasure, ma'am." He gave her a cursory appraisal, nodded and went back out again.

He'd no sooner gone than a short, plump little woman with twinkling blue eyes and gray hair came in, rubbing her hands dry on her apron. "You'd be Miss Wayne. I'm Betty Culbertson," she introduced herself. "Can I get you a cup of coffee?"

"Oh, yes, please."

"Cream, sugar?"

"I like it black," she said.

The older woman grinned. "So do the boys. They don't like sweets, either. Hard to get fat around here, except on gravy and biscuits. They'd have those every meal if I'd cook them."

The questions the brothers had asked about her cooking came back to haunt her.

"None of them believe in marriage, do they?" she asked.

Mrs. Culbertson shook her head. "They've been bachelors too long now. They're set in their ways and none of them have much to do with women. Not that they aren't targeted by local belles," she added with a chuckle. "But nobody has much luck. Corrigan, now, he's mellowed. I hear it's because of you."

While Dorie flushed and tried to find the right words to answer her, a deep voice did it for her.

"Yes, it is," Corrigan said from the doorway. "But she isn't supposed to know it."

"Oops," Mrs. Culbertson said with a wicked chuckle. "Sorry."

He shrugged. "No harm done. I'll have coffee. So will she. And if you see Leopold…"

"I'll smash his skull for him, if I do," the elderly woman said abruptly, and her whole demeanor changed. Her blue eyes let off sparks. "That devil!"

"He did it again, I guess?"

She made an angry noise through her nose. "I've told him and told him…"

"You'd think he'd get tired of having that broomstick thrown at him, wouldn't you?" Corrigan asked pleasantly.

"One of these days he won't be quick enough," Mrs. Culbertson said with an evil smile.

"I'll talk to him."

"Everybody's already talked to him. It does no good."

"What does he do?" Dorie asked curiously.

Mrs. Culbertson looked at Corrigan, who'd started to answer, with eyes that promised culinary retribution.

"Sorry," he said abruptly. "I can't say."

Mrs. Culbertson nodded curtly and smiled at Dorie. "I'll just get that coffee. Be back in a jiffy."

She left and Corrigan's dark eyes slid over Dorie's pretty figure.

"You look very nice," he said. His eyes lifted to her wavy hair and he smiled appreciatively. "I always loved your hair. That was a first for me. Usually I like a woman's hair long. Yours suits you just as it is."

Her slender hand went to the platinum waves self-consciously. "It's easy to keep like this." She shifted to the other foot. "Your brothers came to the house yesterday and asked me to come out here and look at the household accounts. They say they're starving."

"They look like it, too, don't they?" he asked disgustedly. "Good God, starving!"

"They were very nice," she continued. "They talked to Turkey Sanders and he's repairing my car."

"His *mechanic's* repairing your car," he told her. "Turkey's having a tooth fixed."

She knew she shouldn't ask. But she had to. "Why?"

"He made a remark that Cag didn't like."

"Cag. Oh, yes, he's the eldest."

He brightened when he realized that she remembered that. "He's thirty-eight, if you call that old." Anticipating her next question, he added blithely, "Leo's thirty-four. I'm thirty-six. Rey's thirty-two."

"So Cag hit Turkey Sanders?"

He shook his head.

"Then who broke his tooth?"

"Leo."

"Cag got mad, but Leo hit Turkey Sanders?" she asked, fascinated.

He nodded. "He did that to save him from Cag."

"I don't understand."

"Cag was in the Special Forces," he explained. "He was a captain when they sent him to the Middle East some years back." He shrugged. "He knows too much about hand-to-hand combat to be let loose in a temper. So we try to shield people from him." He grinned. "Leo figured that if he hit Turkey first, Cag wouldn't. And he didn't."

She just shook her head. "Your brothers are... unique," she said finally, having failed to find a good word to describe them.

He chuckled. "You don't know the half of it."

"Do they really hate women?"

"Sometimes," he said.

"I'll bet they're sought after," she mentioned, "especially when people get a good look at this ranch."

"The ranch is only a part of the properties we own," he replied. "Our people are fourth-generation Texans, and we inherited thousands of acres of land and five ranches. They were almost bankrupt when the old man died, though," he mused. "He didn't really have a head for figures. Broke Grandad's heart. He saw the end of his empire. But we pulled it out of the fire."

"So I see," she agreed.

"The only problem is, none of us are married. So if we don't have descendants, who's going to keep the empire going?"

She thought of the most terrible answer to that question, and then got the giggles.

He raised an eyebrow.

She put a hand over her mouth until she got herself

back under control. "Sorry. I was only thinking of that movie about the man who got pregnant…!"

He gave her a level look, unsmiling.

She cleared her throat. "Where are the accounts?"

He hesitated for a minute, and then opened the desk drawer and took out a set of ledgers, placing them on the spotless cherry wood desk.

"This is beautiful," she remarked, stroking the silky, high-polished surface.

"It was our grandfather's," he told her. "We didn't want to change things around too much. The old gentleman was fond of the office just the way it is."

She looked around, puzzled by the plain wood paneling. There were no deer heads or weapons anywhere. She said so.

"He didn't like trophies," he told her. "Neither do we. If we hunt, we use every part of the deer, but we don't have the heads mounted. It doesn't seem quite sporting."

She turned as she pulled out the desk chair, and looked at him with open curiosity.

"None of your brothers are like I pictured them."

"In what way?"

She smiled. "You're very handsome," she said, averting her eyes when his began to glitter. "They aren't. And they all have very dark eyes. Yours are gray, like mine."

"They favor our mother," he said. "I favor him." He nodded toward the one portrait, on the wall behind the desk. It looked early twentieth century and featured a man very like Corrigan, except with silver hair.

"So that's what you'll look like," she remarked absently.

"Eventually. Not for a few years, I hope."

She glanced at him, because he'd come to stand beside her. "You're going gray, just at the temples."

He looked down into her soft face. His eyes narrowed as he searched every inch of her above the neck. "Gray won't show in that beautiful mop on your head," he said quietly. "It'll blend in and make it even prettier."

The comment was softly spoken, and so poetic that it embarrassed her. She smiled self-consciously and her gaze fell to his shirt. It was open at the collar, because it was warm in the house. Thick black hair peered over the button, and unwanted memories of that last night they'd been together came flooding back. He'd taken his shirt off, to give her hands total access to his broad, hair-roughened chest. He liked her lips on it…

She cleared her throat and looked away, her color high. "I'd better get to work."

His lean hand caught her arm, very gently, and he pulled her back around. His free hand went to the snaps that held the shirt together. He looked into her startled eyes and slowly, one by one, he flicked the snaps apart.

"What…are you…doing?" she faltered. She couldn't breathe. He was weaving spells around her. She felt weak-kneed already, and the sight of that broad chest completely bare drew a faint gasp from her lips.

He had her by the elbows. He drew her to him, so that her lips were on a level with his collarbone. She could hear his heartbeat, actually hear it.

"It was like this," he said in a raw, ragged tone. "But I had your blouse off, your breasts bare. I drew you to me, like this," he whispered unsteadily, drawing her against the length of him, "and I bent, and took your open mouth under my own…like this…"

It was happening all over again. She was eight years older, but apparently not one day less vulnerable. He put her cold hands into the thick hair on his chest and moved them while his hard mouth took slow, sweet possession of her lips.

He nudged her lips apart and hesitated for just a second, long enough to look into her eyes and see the submission and faint hunger in them. There was just the hint of a smile on his lips before he parted them against her soft mouth.

Chapter Four

She had no pride at all, she decided in the hectic seconds that followed the first touch of his hard mouth. She was a total washout as a liberated woman.

His hands had gone to her waist and then moved up to her rib cage, to the soft underside of her breasts. He stroked just under them until she shivered and moaned, and then his hands lifted and took possession; blatant possession.

He felt her mouth open. His own answered it while he touched her, searched over her breasts and found the hard nipples that pushed against his palms.

His mouth grew rougher. She felt his hands move

around her, felt the catch give. Her blouse was pushed up with a shivering urgency, and seconds later, her bare breasts were buried in the thick hair that covered his chest and abdomen.

She cried out, dragging her mouth from his.

He looked into her eyes, but he wouldn't let her go. His hard face was expressionless. Only his eyes were alive, glittering like gray fires. He deliberately moved her from side to side and watched her face as he did it, enjoying, with a completely masculine delight, the pleasure she couldn't hide.

"Your nipples are like rocks against me." He bit off the words, holding her even closer. "I took your breasts inside my mouth the night we made love, and you arched up right off the bed to give them to me. Do you remember what you did next?"

She couldn't speak. She looked at him with mingled desire and fear.

"You slid your hands inside my jeans," he whispered roughly. "And you touched me. That's when I lost control."

Her moan was one of shame, not pleasure. She found his chest with her cheek and pressed close to him, shivering. "I'm sorry," she whispered brokenly. "I'm so sorry…!"

His mouth found her eyes and kissed them shut. "Don't," he whispered roughly. "I'm not saying it to shame you. I only want you to remember why it ended the way it did. You were grass green and I didn't know it. I encouraged you to be uninhibited, but I'd never have done it if I'd known what an innocent you were." His mouth slid over her forehead with breathless tenderness while his hands slid to her lower back and pulled her even closer. "I was going to take you," he whispered. His hands contracted and his body went rigid with a surge of arousal that she could feel. His legs trembled. "I still want to, God help me," he breathed at her temple. "I've never had the sort of arousal I feel with you. I don't even have to undress you first." His hands began to tremble as he moved her sensually against his hips. His mouth slid down to hers and softly covered it, lifting and touching and probing until she shivered again with pleasure.

"I thought you knew," she whimpered.

"I didn't." His hands moved to the very base of her spine and lifted her gently into the hard thrust of his body. He caught his breath at the wave of pleasure that washed over him immediately. "Dorie," he breathed.

She couldn't think at all. When he took one of her hands and pressed it to his lower body, she didn't even have the will to protest. Her hand opened and she let him move it gently against him, on fire with the need to touch him.

"Eight years," she said shakily.

"And we're still starving for each other," he whispered at her mouth. His hand became insistent. "Harder," he said and his breath caught.

"This…isn't wise," she said against his chest.

"No, but it's sweet. Dorie…!" He cried out hoarsely, his whole body shuddering.

Her hand stilled at once. "I'm sorry," she whispered frantically. "Did I hurt you?"

He wasn't breathing normally at all. His face was buried in her throat and he was shaking like a leaf. She brushed her mouth over his cheek, his chin, his lips, his nose, whispering his name as she clung to him.

His hand gripped her upper thigh, and it was so bruising that she was afraid she was going to have to protest. He fought for sanity, embarrassed by his weakness.

She was still kissing him. He felt her breasts moving against his chest, intensifying the throbbing, hellish ache below his belt.

He held her firmly in place with hands that shook.

She subsided and stood quietly against him. She knew now, as she hadn't eight years ago, what was wrong with him. She felt guilty and ashamed for pushing him so far out of control.

Her fingers touched his thick, cool hair lovingly. Her lips found his eyelids and brushed softly against them. He was vulnerable and she wanted to protect him, cherish him.

The tenderness was doing strange things to him. He still wanted her to the point of madness, but those comforting little kisses made his heart warm. He'd never been touched in such a way by a woman; he'd never felt so cherished.

She drew back, and he pulled her close again.

"Don't stop," he whispered, calmer now. His hands had moved up to the silken skin of her back, and he smiled under the whisper of her lips on his skin.

"I'm so sorry," she whispered.

His fingers slid under the blouse again and up to explore the softness of her breasts. "Why?" he asked.

"You were hurting," she said. "I shouldn't have touched you…"

He chuckled wickedly. "I made you."

"I still can't go to bed with you," she said miserably. "I don't care if the whole world does it, I just can't!"

His hands opened and enfolded her breasts tenderly. "You want to," he murmured as he caressed them.

"Of course I want to!" Her eyes closed and she swayed closer to his hands. "Oh, glory," she managed to say tightly, shivering.

"Your breasts are very sensitive," he said at her

lips. "And soft like warm silk under my hands. I'd like to lay you down on my grandfather's desk and take your blouse off and put my lips on you there. But Mrs. Culbertson is making coffee." He lifted his head and looked into her dazed, soft gray eyes. "Thank God," he whispered absently as he searched them.

"Thank God for what?" she asked huskily.

"Miracles, maybe," he replied. He smoothed the blouse up again and his eyes sketched her pretty pink breasts with their hard dark pink crowns. "I could eat you like taffy right now," he said in a rough tone.

The office was so quiet that not a sound could be heard above the shiver of her breath as she looked up at him.

His pale eyes were almost apologetic. "I think I have a death wish," he began huskily as he bent.

She watched his mouth hover over her breast with a sense of shocked wonder. Her eyes wide, her breath stopped in her throat, she waited, trembling.

He looked up, then, and saw her eyes. He made a sound in the back of his throat and his mouth opened as he propelled her closer, so that he had her almost completely in that warm, moist recess.

She wept. The pleasure grew to unbearable heights. Her fingers tangled in his hair and she pulled him closer. She growled sharply at the sensations she felt. Her hips moved involuntarily, searching for his body.

The suction became so sweet that she suddenly arched backward, and would have fallen if it hadn't been for his supporting arm. She caught her breath and convulsed, her body frozen in an arc of pure ecstasy.

He felt the deep contractions of her body under his mouth with raging pride. His mouth grew a little rough, and the convulsions deepened.

Only when he felt her begin to relax did he lift his head and bring her back into a standing position, so that he could look at her face.

She couldn't breathe. She sobbed as she looked up into his pale eyes. The tears came, hot and quick, when she realized what had happened. And he'd seen it!

"Don't," he chided tenderly. He reached for a handkerchief and dried her red eyes and wiped her nose. "Don't be embarrassed."

"I could die of shame," she wept.

"For what?" he asked softly. "For letting me watch you?"

Her face went red. "I never, never…!"

He put a long forefinger against her lips. "I've never seen a woman like that," he whispered. "I've never known one who could be satisfied by a man's mouth suckling at her breast. It was the most beautiful experience I've ever had."

She wasn't crying now. She was staring at him, her eyes wide and soft and curious.

He brushed back her wild hair. "It was worth what I felt earlier," he murmured dryly.

She colored even more. "I can't stay here," she told him wildly. "I have to go away…"

"Hell, no, you don't," he said tersely. "You're not getting away from me a second time. Don't even think about running."

"But," she began urgently.

"But what?" he asked curtly. "But you can't give yourself to me outside marriage? I know that. I'm not asking you to sleep with me."

"It's like torture for you."

"Yes," he said simply. "But the alternative is to never touch you." His hand slid over her blouse and he smiled gently at the immediate response of her body. "I love this," he said gruffly. "And so do you."

She grimaced. "Of course I do," she muttered. "I've never let anyone else touch me like that. It's been eight years since I've even been kissed!"

"Same here," he said bluntly.

"Ha! You've been going around with a divorcée!" she flung at him out of frustration and embarrassment.

"I don't have sex with her," he said.

"They say she's very pretty."

He smiled. "She is. Pretty and elegant and kind.

But I don't feel desire for her, any more than she feels it for me. I told you we were friends. We are. And that's all we are."

"But…but…"

"But what, Dorie?"

"Men don't stop kissing women just because they get turned down once."

"It was much worse than just getting turned down," he told her. "I ran you out of town. It was rough living with that, especially when your father took a few strips off me and told me all about your past. I felt two inches high." His eyes darkened with the pain of the memory. "I hated having made an enemy of him. He was a good man. But I'd never had much interest in marriage or let anyone get as close to me as you did. If you were afraid, so was I."

"Cag said your parents weren't a happy couple."

His eyebrow lifted. "He never talks about them. That's a first."

"He told me to ask you about them."

"I see." He sighed. "Well, I told you a little about that, but we're going to have to talk more about them sooner or later, and about some other things." He lifted his head and listened and then looked down at her with a wicked grin. "But for the present, you'd better fasten your bra and tuck your blouse back in and try to look as if you haven't just made love with me."

"Why?"

"Mrs. Culbertson's coming down the hall."

"Oh, my gosh!"

She fumbled with catches and buttons, her face red, her hair wild as she raced to put herself back together. He snapped his shirt up lazily, his silvery eyes full of mischief as he watched her frantic efforts to improve her appearance.

"Lucky I didn't lay you down on the desk, isn't it?" he said, chuckling.

There was a tap on the half-closed door and Mrs. Culbertson came in with a tray. She was so intent on getting it to the desk intact that she didn't even look at Dorie.

"Here it is. Sorry I took so long, but I couldn't find the cream pitcher."

"Who drinks cream?" Corrigan asked curiously.

"It was the only excuse I could think of," she told him seriously.

He looked uneasy. "Thanks."

She grinned at him and then looked at Dorie. Her eyes were twinkling as she went back out. And this time she closed the door.

Dorie's face was still flushed. Her gray eyes were wide and turbulent. Her mouth was swollen and when she folded her arms over her chest, she flinched.

His eyes went to her blouse and back up again.

"When I felt you going over the edge, it excited me, and I got a little rough. Did I hurt you?"

The question was matter-of-fact, and strangely tender.

She shook her head, averting her eyes. It was embarrassing to remember what had happened.

He caught her hand and led her to the chairs in front of the desk. "Sit down and I'll pour you a cup of coffee."

She looked up at him a little uneasily. "Is something wrong with me, do you think?" she asked with honest concern. "I mean, it's unnatural…isn't it?"

His fingers touched her soft cheek. He shook his head. "People can't be pigeonholed. You might not be that responsive to any other man. Maybe it's waiting so long. Maybe it's that you're perfectly attuned to me. I might be able to accomplish the same thing by kissing your thighs, or your belly."

She flushed. "You wouldn't!"

"Why not?"

The thought of it made her vibrate all over. She knew that men kissed women in intimate places, but she hadn't quite connected it until then.

"The inside of your thighs is very vulnerable to being caressed," he said simply. "Not to mention your back, your hips, your feet," he added with a gentle smile. "Lovemaking is an art. There are no set rules."

She watched him turn and pour coffee into a ceramic cup. He handed it to her and watched the way her fingers deliberately touched his as he drew them away.

He wanted her so much that he could barely stand up straight, but it was early days yet. He had to go slowly this time and not push her too hard. She had a fear not only of him, but of real intimacy. He couldn't afford to let things go too far.

"What sort of things are we going to talk about later?" she asked after she'd finished half her coffee.

"Cabbages and kings," he mused. He sat across from her, his long legs crossed, his eyes possessive and caressing on her face.

"I don't like cabbage and I don't know any kings."

"Then suppose we lie down together on the sofa?"

Her eyes flashed up to see the amusement in his and back down to her cup. "Don't tease. I'm not sophisticated enough for it."

"I'm not teasing."

She sighed and took another sip of coffee. "There's no future in it. You know that."

He didn't know it. She was living in the past, convinced that he had nothing more than an affair in mind for them. He smiled secretively to himself as he thought about the future. Fate had given him a second chance; he wasn't going to waste it.

"About these books," he said in a businesslike tone. "I've made an effort with them, but although I can do math, my penmanship isn't what it should be. If you can't read any of the numbers, circle them and I'll tell you what they are. I have to meet a prospective buyer down at the barn in a few minutes, but I'll be somewhere close by all day."

"All right."

He finished his coffee and put the cup back on the tray, checking his watch. "I'd better go." He looked down at her with covetous eyes and leaned against the arms of her chair to study her. "Let's go dancing tomorrow night."

Her heart jumped. She was remembering how it was when they were close together and her face flushed.

His eyebrow lifted and he grinned. "Don't look so apprehensive. The time to worry is when nothing happens when I hold you."

"It always did," she replied.

He nodded. "Every time," he agreed. "I only had to touch you." He smiled softly. "And vice versa," he added with a wicked glance.

"I was green," she reminded him.

"You still are," he reminded her.

"Not so much," she ventured shyly.

"We both learned something today," he said quietly. "Dorie, if you can be satisfied by so small a caress, try to imagine how it would feel if we went all the way."

Her eyelids flickered. Her breath came like rustling leaves.

He bent and drew his mouth with exquisite tenderness over her parted lips. "Or is that the real problem?" he asked at her mouth. "Are you afraid of the actual penetration?"

Her heart stopped dead and then ran away. "Corrigan!" She ground out his name.

He drew back a breath so that he could see her eyes. He wasn't smiling. It was no joke.

"You'd better tell me," he said quietly.

She drew her lower lip in with her teeth, looking worried.

"I won't tell anyone."

"I know that." She took a long breath. "When my cousin Mary was married, she came to visit us after the honeymoon was over. She'd been so happy and excited." She grimaced. "She said that it hurt awfully bad, that she bled and bled, and he made fun of her because she cried. She said that he didn't even kiss her. He just...pushed into her...!"

He cursed under his breath. "Didn't you talk to anyone else about sex?"

"It wasn't something I could discuss with my

father, and Mary was the only friend I had," she told him. "She said that all the things they write about are just fiction, and that the reality is just like her mother once said—a woman deals with it for the pleasure of children."

He leaned forward on his hands, shaking his head. "I wish you'd told me this eight years ago."

"You'd have laughed," she replied. "You didn't believe I was innocent anyway."

He looked up into her eyes. "I'm sorry," he said heavily. "Life teaches hard lessons."

She thought about her own experience with modeling. "Yes, it does."

He got to his feet and looked down at her with a worried scowl. "Don't you watch hot movies?"

"Those women aren't virgins," she returned.

"No. I don't guess they are." His eyes narrowed as he searched her face. "And I don't know what to tell you. I'd never touched an innocent woman until you came along. Maybe it does hurt. But I promise you, it would only be one time. I know enough to make it good for you. And I would."

"It isn't going to be that way," she reminded him tersely, denying herself the dreams of marriage and children that she'd always connected with him. "We're going to be friends."

He didn't speak. His gaze didn't falter. "I'll check back with you later about the books," he said quietly.

"Okay."

He started to turn, thought better of it and leaned down again with his weight balanced on the chair arms. "Do you remember what happened when I started to suckle you?"

She went scarlet. "Please..."

"It will be like that," he said evenly. "Just like that. You won't think about pain. You may not even notice any. You go in headfirst when I touch you. And I wasn't even taking my time with you today. Think about that. It might help."

He pushed away from her again and went to the desk to pick up his hat. He placed it on his head and smiled at her without mockery.

"Don't let my brothers walk over you," he said. "If one of them gives you any trouble, lay into him with the first hard object you can get your hands on."

"They seem very nice," she said.

"They like you," he replied. "But they have plans."

"Plans?"

"Not to hurt you," he assured her. "You should never have told them you could cook."

"I don't understand."

"Mrs. Culbertson wants to quit. They can't make biscuits. It's what they live for, a plateful of home-made buttered biscuits with half a dozen jars of jam and jelly."

"How does that concern me?"

"Don't you know?" He perched himself against the desk. "They've decided that we should marry you."

"We?"

"We're a family. Mostly we share things. Not women, but we do share cooks." He cocked his head and grinned at her shocked face. "If I marry you, they don't have to worry about where their next fresh biscuit is coming from."

"You don't want to marry me."

"Well, they'll probably find some way around that," he said pointedly.

"They can't force you to marry me."

"I wouldn't make any bets on that," he said. "You don't know them yet."

"You're their brother. They'd want you to be happy."

"They think you'll make me happy."

She lowered her eyes. "You should talk to them."

"And say what? That I don't want you? I don't think they'd believe me."

"I meant, you should tell them that you don't want to get married."

"They've already had a meeting and decided that I do. They've picked out a minister and a dress that they think you'll look lovely in. They've done a rough draft of a wedding invitation…"

"You're out of your mind!"

"No, I'm not." He went to the middle desk drawer,

fumbled through it, pulled it farther out and reached for something pushed to the very back of the desk. He produced it, scanned it, nodded and handed it to her. "Read that."

It was a wedding invitation. Her middle name was misspelled. "It's Ellen, not Ellis."

He reached behind him for a pen, took the invitation back, made the change and handed it back to her.

"Why did you do that?" she asked curiously.

"Oh, they like everything neat and correct."

"Don't correct it! Tear it up!"

"They'll just do another one. The papers will print what's on there, too. You don't want your middle name misspelled several thousand times, do you?"

She was all but gasping for breath. "I don't understand."

"I know. Don't worry about it right now. There's plenty of time. They haven't decided on a definite date yet, anyway."

She stood up, wild-eyed. "You can't let your brothers decide when and who you're going to marry!"

"Well, you go stop them, then," he said easily. "But don't say I didn't tell you so."

He pulled his hat over his eyes and walked out the door, whistling softly to himself.

Chapter Five

First she did the accounts. Her mind was still reeling from Corrigan's ardor, and she had to be collected when she spoke to his brothers. She deciphered his scribbled numbers, balanced the books, checked her figures and put down a total.

They certainly weren't broke, and there was enough money in the account to feed Patton's Third Army. She left them a note saying so, amused at the pathetic picture they'd painted of their finances. Probably, the reason for that was part of their master plan.

She went outside to look for them after she'd done the books. They were all four in the barn, standing close together. They stopped talking the minute she came into view, and she knew for certain that they'd been talking about her.

"I'm not marrying him," she told them clearly, and pointed at Corrigan.

"Okay," Leo said easily.

"The thought never crossed my mind," Rey remarked.

Cag just shrugged.

Corrigan grinned.

"I'm through with the books," she said uneasily. "I want to go home now."

"You haven't eaten lunch," Rey said.

"It's only eleven o'clock," she said pointedly.

"We have an early lunch, because we work until dark," Cag volunteered.

"Mrs. Culbertson just left," Rey said. He sighed. "She put some beef and gravy in the oven to warm. But she didn't make us any biscuits."

"We don't have anything to put gravy on," Leo agreed.

"Can't work all afternoon without a biscuit," Cag said, nodding.

Corrigan grinned.

Dorie had thought that Corrigan was making up that story about the brothers' mania for biscuits. Apparently it was the gospel truth.

"Just one pan full," Leo coaxed. "It wouldn't take

five minutes." He eyed her warily. "If you can really make them. Maybe you can't. Maybe you were just saying you could, to impress us."

"That's right," Rey added.

"I can make biscuits," she said, needled. "You just point me to the kitchen and I'll show you."

Leo grinned. "Right this way!"

Half an hour later, the pan of biscuits were gone so fast that they might have disintegrated. Leo and Corrigan were actually fighting over the last one, pulled it apart in their rush, and ended up splitting it while the other two sat there gloating. They'd had more than their share because they had faster hands.

"Next time, you've got to make two pans," Corrigan told her. "One doesn't fill Leo's hollow tooth."

"I noticed," she said, surprisingly touched by the way they'd eaten her biscuits with such enjoyment. "I'll make you a pan of rolls to go with them next time."

"Rolls?" Leo looked faint. *"You can make home-made rolls?"*

"I'll see about the wedding rings right now," Rey said, wiping his mouth and pushing away from the table.

"I've got the corrected invitation in my pocket," Cag murmured as he got up, too.

Leo joined the other two at the door. "They said they can get the dress here from Paris in two weeks," Leo said.

Dorie gaped at them. But before she could say a word, all three of them had rushed out the door and closed it, talking animatedly among themselves.

"But, I didn't say…!" she exclaimed.

"There, there," Corrigan said, deftly adding another spoonful of gravy to his own remaining half of a biscuit. "It's all right. They forgot to call the minister and book him."

Just at that moment, the door opened and Leo stuck his head in. "Are you Methodist, Baptist or Presbyterian?" he asked her.

"I'm…Presbyterian," she faltered.

He scowled. "Nearest Presbyterian minister is in Victoria," he murmured thoughtfully, "but don't worry, I'll get him here." He closed the door.

"Just a minute!" she called.

The doors of the pickup closed three times. The engine roared. "Too late," Corrigan said imperturbably.

"But didn't you hear him?" she burst out. "For heaven's sake, they're going to get a minister!"

"Hard to get married in church without one," he insisted. He gestured toward her plate with a fork to the remaining chunk of beef. "Don't waste that. It's one of our own steers. Corn fed, no hormones, no antibiotics, no insecticides. We run a clean, environmentally safe operation here."

She was diverted. "Really?"

"We're renegades," he told her. "They groan when they see us coming at cattle conventions. Usually we go with Donavan. He's just like us about cattle. He and the Ballenger brothers have gone several rounds over cattle prods and feed additives. He's mellowed a bit since his nephew came to live with him and he got married. But he likes the way we do things."

"I guess so." She savored the last of the beef. "It's really good."

"Beats eating pigs," he remarked, and grinned.

She burst out laughing. "Your brother Cag had plenty to say on that subject."

"He only eats beef or fish. He won't touch anything that comes from a pig. He says it's because he doesn't like the taste." He leaned forward conspiratorially. "But I say it's because of that movie he went to see. He used to love a nice ham."

"What movie?"

"The one with the talking pig."

"Cag went to see *that?*"

"He likes cartoons and sentimental movies." He shrugged. "Odd, isn't it? He's the most staid of us. To look at him, you'd never know he had a sense of humor or that he was sentimental. He's like the others in his lack of conventional good looks, though. Most women can't get past that big nose and those eyes."

"A cobra with a rabbit," she said without thinking.

He chuckled. "Exactly."

"Does he hate women as much as the rest of you?"

"Hard to tell. You haven't seen him in a tuxedo at a social bash. Women, really beautiful women, followed him around all night dropping their room keys at his feet."

"What did he do?"

"Kept walking."

She put down her fork. "What do you do?"

He smiled mockingly. "They don't drop room keys at my feet anymore. The limp puts them off."

"Baloney," she said. "You're the handsomest of the four, and it isn't just looks."

He leaned back in his chair to look at her. His eyes narrowed thoughtfully. "Does the limp bother you?"

"Don't be ridiculous," she said, lifting her gaze. "Why should it?"

"I can't dance very well anymore."

She smiled. "I don't ever go to dances."

"Why not?"

She sipped coffee. "I don't like men touching me."

His eyes changed. "You like me touching you."

"You aren't a stranger," she said simply.

"Maybe I am," he murmured quietly. "What do you know about me?"

She stared at him. "Well, you're thirty-six, you're a rancher, you've never married, you come from San Antonio."

"And?"

"I don't know any more than that," she said slowly.

"We were a couple for several weeks before you left town. Is that all you learned?"

"You were always such a private person," she reminded him. "You never talked about yourself or your brothers. And we never really talked that much when we were together."

"We spent more time kissing," he recalled. "I was too wrapped up in trying to get you into bed to care how well we knew each other," he said with self-contempt. "I wasted a lot of time."

"You said that we shouldn't look back."

"I'm trying not to. It's hard, sometimes." He moved forward to take her hands under his on the table. "I like classical music, but I'm just as happy with country or pop. I like a good chess game. I enjoy science fiction movies and old Westerns, the silent kind. I'm an early riser, I work hard and I don't cheat on my tax returns. I went to college to learn animal husbandry, but I never graduated."

She smiled. "Do you like fried liver?"

He made a horrible face. "Do you?"

She made the same face. "But I don't like sweets very much, either," she said, remembering that he didn't.

"Good thing. Nobody around here eats them."

"I remember." She looked around at the comfortably big kitchen. There was a new electric stove and a huge refrigerator, flanked by an upright freezer. The sink was a double stainless-steel one, with a window above it overlooking the pasture where the colts were kept. Next to that was a dishwasher. There was plenty of cabinet space, too.

"Like it?" he asked.

She smiled. "It's a dream of a kitchen. I'll bet Mrs. Culbertson loves working in here."

"Would you?"

She met his eyes and felt her own flickering at the intensity of his stare.

"If you can make homemade bread, you have to be an accomplished cook," he continued. "There's a high-tech mixer in the cabinet, and every gourmet tool known to man. Or woman."

"It's very modern."

"It's going to be very deserted in about three weeks," he informed.

"Why is Mrs. Culbertson quitting?"

"Her husband has cancer, and she wants to retire and stay at home with him, for as long as he's got," he said abruptly. He toyed with his coffee cup. "They've been married for fifty years." He took a sharp breath, and his eyes were very dark as they met hers. "I've believed all my life that no marriage could possibly last longer than a few years. People change. Situations change. Jobs conflict." He shrugged. "Then Mrs. Culbertson came here to work, with her husband. And I had to eat my words." He lowered his eyes back to the cup. "They were forever holding hands, helping each other, walking in the early morning together and talking. She smiled at him, and she was beautiful. He smiled back. Nobody had to say that they loved each other. It was obvious."

"My parents were like that," she recalled. "Dad and Mom loved each other terribly. When she died, I almost lost him, too. He lived for me. But the last thing he said on his deathbed—" she swallowed, fighting tears "—was her name."

He got up from the table abruptly and went to the window over the sink. He leaned against it, breathing heavily, as if what she'd said had affected him powerfully. And, in fact, it had.

She watched him through tears. "You don't like hearing about happy marriages. Why?"

"Because I had that same chance once," he said in a low, dull tone. "And I threw it away."

She wondered who the woman had been. Nobody had said that any of the Hart brothers had ever been engaged. But there could have been someone she hadn't heard about.

"You're the one who keeps saying we can't look back," she remarked, dabbing her eyes with her napkin.

"It's impossible not to. The past makes us the people we are." He sighed wearily. "My parents had five of us in ten years. My mother hadn't wanted the first child. She didn't have a choice. He took away her checkbook and kept her pregnant. She hated him and us in equal measure. When she left it was almost a relief." He turned and looked across the room at her. "I've never been held with tenderness. None of us have. It's why we're the way we are, it's why we don't have women around. The only thing we know about women is that they're treacherous and cold and cruel."

"Oh, Corrigan," she said softly, wincing.

His eyes narrowed. "Desire is a hot and unmanageable thing. Sex can be pleasant enough. But I'd gladly be impotent to have a woman hold me the way you did in my office and kiss my eyes." His face went as hard as stone. "You can't imagine how it felt."

"But I can," she replied. She smiled. "You kissed my eyes."

"Yes."

He looked so lost, so lonely. She got up from the table and went to him, paused in front of him. Her hands pressed gently against his broad chest as she looked up into his eyes.

"You know more about me than I've ever told anyone else," he said quietly. "Now don't you think it's time you told me what happened to you in New York?"

She sighed worriedly. She'd been ashamed to tell him how stupid she'd been. But now there was a bigger reason. It was going to hurt him. She didn't understand how she knew it, but she did. He was going to blame himself all over again for the way they'd separated.

"Not now," she said.

"You're holding back. Don't let's have secrets between us," he said solemnly.

"It will hurt," she said.

"Most everything does, these days," he murmured, and rubbed his thigh.

She took his hand and held it warmly. "Come and sit down."

"Not in here."

He drew her into the living room. It was warm

and dim and quiet. He led her to his big armchair, dropped into it and pulled her down into his arms.

"Now, tell me," he said, when her cheek was pillowed on his hard chest.

"It's not a nice story."

"Tell me."

She rubbed her hand against his shirt and closed her eyes. "I found an ad in the paper. It was one of those big ads that promise the stars, just the thing to appeal to a naive country girl who thinks she can just walk into a modeling career. I cut out the ad and called the number."

"And?"

She grimaced. "It was a scam, but I didn't know it at first. The man seemed very nice, and he had a studio in a good part of town. Belinda had gone to Europe for the week on an assignment for the magazine where she worked, and I didn't know anyone else to ask about it. I assumed that it was legitimate." Her eyes closed and she pressed closer, feeling his arm come around her tightly, as if he knew she was seeking comfort.

"Go ahead," he coaxed gently.

"He gave me a few things to try on and he took pictures of me wearing them. But then I was sitting there, just in a two-piece bathing suit, and he told me to take it off." His breathing stilled under her ear. "I couldn't," she snapped. "I just couldn't let him look at me like that, no matter how good a job I could get, and I said so. Then he got ugly. He told me that he was in the business of producing nude calendars and that if I didn't do the assignment, he'd take me to court and sue me for not fulfilling the contract I'd signed. No, I didn't read it," she said when he asked. "The fine print did say that I agreed to pose in any manner the photographer said for me to. I knew that I couldn't afford a lawsuit."

"And?" He sounded as cold as ice.

She bit her lower lip. "While I was thinking about alternatives, he laughed and came toward me. I could forget the contract, he said, if I was that prudish. But he'd have a return for the time he'd wasted on me. He said that he was going to make me sleep with him."

"Good God!"

She smoothed his shirt, trying to calm him. Tears stung her eyes. "I fought him, but I wasn't strong enough. He had me undressed before I knew it. We struggled there on the floor and he started hitting me." Her voice broke and she felt Corrigan stiffen against her. "He had a diamond ring on his right hand. That's how he cut my cheek. I didn't even feel it until much later. He wore me down to the point that I couldn't kick or bite or scream. I would never have been able to get away. But one of his girls, one of the ones who didn't mind posing nude, came into the studio. She was his lover and she was furious when she saw him with me…like that. She started screaming and throwing things at him. I grabbed my clothes and ran."

She shivered even then with the remembered humiliation, the fear that he was going to come after her. "I managed to get enough on to look halfway decent, and I walked all the way back to Belinda's apartment." She swallowed. "When I was rational enough to talk, I called the police. They arrested him and charged him with attempted rape. But he said that I'd signed a contract and I wasn't happy with the money he offered me, and that I'd only yelled rape because I wanted to back out of the deal."

He bit off a curse. "And then what?"

"He won," she said in a flat, defeated tone. "He had friends and influence. But the story was a big deal locally for two or three days, and he was furious. His brother had a nasty temper and he started making obscene phone calls to me and making threats as well. I didn't want to put Belinda in any danger, so I moved out while she was still in Europe and never told her a thing about what had happened. I got a job in New Jersey and worked there for two years. Then Belinda moved out to Long Island and asked me to come back. There was a good job going with a law firm that had an office pretty close to her house. I had good typing skills by then, so I took it."

"What about the brother?" he asked.

"He didn't know where to find me. I learned later that he and the photographer were having trouble with the police about some pornography ring they were involved in. Ironically they both went to prison soon after I left Manhattan. But for a long time, I was even afraid to come home, in case they had anyone watching me. I was afraid for my father."

"You poor kid," he said heavily. "Good God! And after what had happened here..." His teeth ground together as he remembered what he'd done to her.

"Don't," she said gently, smoothing out the frown between his heavy eyebrows. "I never blamed you. Never!"

He caught her hand and brought it to his mouth. "I wanted to come after you," he said. "Your father stopped me. He said that you hated the very mention of my name."

"I did, at first, but only because I was so hurt by the way things had worked out." She looked at his firm chin. "But I would have been glad to see you, just the same."

"I wasn't sure of that." He traced her mouth. "I thought that it might be as well to leave things the way they were. You were so young, and I was wary of complications in my life just then." He sighed softly. "There's one other thing you don't know about me."

"Can't you tell me?"

He smiled softly. "We're sharing our deepest secrets. I suppose I might as well. We have a fifth brother. His name is Simon."

"You mentioned him the first time you came over, with that bouquet."

He nodded. "He's in San Antonio. Just after you left town, he was in a wreck and afterward, in a coma. We couldn't all go back, and leave the ranch to itself. So I went. It was several weeks before I could leave him. By the time I got back, you weren't living with Belinda anymore and I couldn't make her tell me where you were. Soon after that, your father came down on my head like a brick and I lost heart."

"You called Belinda?"

"Yes."

"You wanted to find me?"

He searched her eyes quietly. "I wanted to know that you were safe, that I hadn't hurt you too badly. At least I found that much out. I didn't hope for more."

She traced his eyebrows, lost in the sudden intimacy. "I dreamed about you," she said. "But every time, you'd come toward me and I'd wake up."

He traced the artery in her throat down to her collarbone. "My dreams were a bit more erotic." His eyes darkened. "I had you in ways and places you can't imagine, each more heated than the one before. I couldn't wait to go to bed, so that I could have you again."

She blushed. "At first, you mean, just after I left."

His hand smoothed onto her throat. "For eight years. Every night of my life."

She caught her breath. She could hardly get it at all. His eyes were glittering with feeling. "All that time?"

He nodded. He looked at her soft throat where the blouse had parted, and his face hardened. His fingers trailed lightly down onto her bodice, onto her breast. "I haven't touched a woman since you left Jacobsville," he said huskily. "I haven't been a man since then."

Her wide eyes filled with tears. She had a good idea of what it would be like for a man like Corrigan to be incapable with a woman. "Was it because we fought, at the last?"

"It was because we made love," he whispered. "Have you forgotten what we did?"

She averted her eyes, hiding them in embarrassment.

"You left a virgin," he said quietly, "but only technically. We had each other in your bed," he reminded her, "naked in each other's arms. We did everything except go those last few aching inches. Your body was almost open to me, I was against you, we were moving together...and you cried out when you felt me there. You squirmed out from under me and ran."

"I was so afraid," she whispered shamefully. "It hurt, and I kept remembering what I'd been told..."

"It wouldn't have hurt for long," he said gently. "And it wouldn't have been traumatic, not for you. But you didn't know that, and I was too excited to coax you. I lost my temper instead of reassuring you. And we spent so many years apart, suffering for it."

She laid her hot cheek against his chest and closed her eyes. "I didn't want to remember how far we went," she said through a mist. "I hurt you terribly when I drew back..."

"Not that much," he said. "We'd made love in so many ways already that I wasn't that hungry." He smoothed her soft hair. "I wanted an excuse to make you leave."

"Why?"

His lips touched her hair. "Because I wanted to make you pregnant," he whispered, feeling her body jump as he said it. "And it scared me to death. You see, modern women don't want babies, because they're a trap. My mother taught me that."

Chapter Six

"That's not true!" She pressed closer. "I would have loved having a baby, and I'd never have felt trapped!" she said, her voice husky with feeling. Especially your baby, she added silently. "I didn't know any of your background, especially anything about your mother. You never told me."

His chest rose and fell abruptly. "I couldn't. You scared me to death. Maybe I deliberately upset you, to make you run. But when I got what I thought I wanted, I didn't want it. It hurt when you wouldn't even look at me, at the bus stop. I guess I'd shamed you so badly that you couldn't." He sighed. "I thought you were modern, that we'd enjoy each other and that would be the end of it. I got the shock of my life that last night. I couldn't even deal with it. I lost my head."

She lifted her face and looked into his eyes. "You were honest about it. You'd already said that you wanted no part of marriage or a family, that all you could offer me was a night in your arms with no strings attached. But I couldn't manage to stop, or stop you, until the very last. I was raised to think of sleeping around as a sin."

His face contorted. He averted his eyes to keep her from seeing the pain in them. "I didn't know that until it was much too late. Sometimes, you don't realize how much things mean to you until you lose them."

His fingers moved gently in her hair while she stood quietly, breathing uneasily. "It wasn't just our mother who soured us on women. Simon was married," he said after a minute. "He was the only one of us who ever was. His wife got pregnant the first time they were together, but she didn't want a child. She didn't really want Simon, she just wanted to be rich. He was crazy about her." He sighed painfully. "She had an abortion and he found out later, accidentally. They had a fight on the way home from one of her incessant parties. He wrecked the car, she died and he lost an arm. That's why he doesn't live on the ranch. He can't do the things he used to do. He's embittered and he's withdrawn from the rest of us." He laughed a little. "You think the four of us hate women. You should see Simon."

She stirred in his arms. "Poor man. He must have loved her very much."

"Too much. That's another common problem we seem to have. We love irrationally and obsessively."

"And reluctantly," she guessed.

He laughed. "And that."

He let her go with a long sigh and stared down at her warmly. "I suppose I'd better take you home. If you're still here when the boys get back, they'll tie you to the stove."

She smiled. "I like your brothers." She hesitated. "Corrigan, they aren't really going to try to force you to marry me, are they?"

"Of course not," he scoffed. "They're only teasing."

"Okay."

It was a good thing, he thought, that she couldn't see his fingers crossed behind his back.

He took her home, pausing to kiss her gently at the front door.

"I'll be along tomorrow night," he said softly. "We'll go to a movie. There's a new one every Saturday night at the Roxy downtown."

She searched his eyes and tried to decide if he was doing this because he wanted to or because his brothers were pestering him.

He smiled. "Don't worry so much. You're home, it's going to be Christmas, you have a job and plenty of friends. It's going to be the best Christmas you've ever had."

She smiled back. "Maybe it will be," she said, catching some of his own excitement. Her gaze caressed his face. They were much more like friends, with all the dark secrets out in the open. But his kisses had made her too hungry for him. She needed time to get her emotions under control. Perhaps a day would do it. He was throwing out broad hints of some sort, but he hadn't spoken one word of love. In that respect, nothing had changed.

"Good night, then," he said.

"Good night."

She closed the door and turned on the lights. It had been a strange and wonderful day. Somehow, the future looked unusually bright, despite all her worries.

The next morning, Dorie had to go into town to Clarisse's shop to help her with the bookkeeping. It was unfortunate that when she walked in, a beautiful woman in designer clothes should be standing at the counter, discussing Corrigan.

"It's going to be the most glorious Christmas ever!" she was telling the other woman, pushing back her red-gold hair and laughing. "Corrigan is taking me to the Christmas party at the Coltrains' house, and afterward we're going to Christmas Eve services at the Methodist Church." She sighed. "I'm glad to be home. You know, there's been some talk about Corrigan and a woman from his past who just came back recently. I asked him about it, if he was serious about her." She laughed gaily. "He said that he was just buttering her up so that she'd do some bookkeeping for him and the brothers, that she'd run out on him once and he didn't have any intention of letting her get close enough to do it again. I told him that I could find it in my heart to feel sorry for her, and he said that he didn't feel sorry for her at all, that he had plans for her..."

Clarisse spotted Dorie and caught her breath. "Why, Dorothy, I wasn't expecting you...quite so soon!"

"I thought I'd say hello," Dorie said, frozen in the doorway. She managed a pasty smile. "I'll come back Monday. Have a nice weekend."

"Who was that?" she heard the other woman say as she went quickly back out the door and down the street to where she'd parked the car Turkey Sanders had returned early in the morning, very nicely fixed.

She got behind the wheel, her fingers turning white as she gripped it. She could barely see for the tears. She started the engine with shaking fingers and backed out into the street. She heard someone call to her and saw the redhead standing on the sidewalk, with an odd expression on her face, trying to get Dorie's attention.

She didn't look again. She put the car into gear and sped out of town.

She didn't go straight home. She went to a small park inside the city and sat down among the gay lights and decorations with a crowd that had gathered for a Christmas concert performed by the local high-school band and chorus. There were so many people that one more didn't matter, and her tears weren't as noticeable in the crush of voices.

The lovely, familiar carols were oddly soothing. But her Christmas spirit was absent. How could she have trusted Corrigan? She was falling in love all over again, and he was setting her up for a fall. She'd never believe a word he said, ever again. And now that she'd had a look at his beautiful divorcée, she knew she wouldn't have a chance with him. That woman was exquisite, from her creamy skin to her perfect figure and face. The only surprising thing was that he hadn't married her years ago. Surely a woman like that wouldn't hang around waiting, when she could have any man she wanted.

Someone offered her a cup of hot apple cider, and she managed a smile and thanked the child who held it out to her. It was spicy and sweet and tasted good against the chill. She sipped it, thinking how horrible it was going to be from now on, living in Jacobsville with Corrigan only a few miles away and that woman hanging on his arm. He hadn't mentioned anything about Christmas to Dorie, but apparently he had his plans all mapped out if he was taking the merry divorcée to a party. When had he been going to tell her the truth? Or had he been going to let her find it out all for herself?

She couldn't remember ever feeling quite so bad.

She finished the cider, listened to one more song and then got up and walked through the crowd, down the long sidewalk to where she'd parked her car. She sat in it for a moment, trying to decide what to do. It was Saturday and she had nothing planned for today. She wasn't going to go home. She couldn't bear the thought of going home.

She turned the car and headed up to the interstate, on the road to Victoria.

Corrigan paced up and down Dorie's front porch for an hour until he realized that she wasn't coming home. He drove back to town and pulled up in front of Tira Beck's brick house.

She came out onto the porch, in jeans and a sweatshirt, her glorious hair around her shoulders. Her arms were folded and she looked concerned. Her frantic phone call had sent him flying over to Dorie's house hours before he was due to pick her up for the movie. Now it looked as if the movie, and anything else, was off.

"Well?" she asked.

He shook his head, with his hands deep in his jacket pockets. "She wasn't there. I waited for an hour. There's no note on the door, no nothing."

Tira sighed miserably. "It's all my fault. Me and my big mouth. I had no idea who she was, and I didn't know that what I was telling Clarisse was just a bunch of bull that you'd handed me to keep me from seeing how much you cared for the woman."

She looked up accusingly. "See what happens when you lie to your friends?"

"You didn't have to tell her that!"

"I didn't know she was there! And we had agreed to go to the Coltrains' party together, you and me and Charles Percy."

"You didn't mention that you had a date for it, I guess?" he asked irritably.

"No. I didn't realize anyone except Clarisse was listening, and she already knew I was going with Charles."

He tilted his hat farther over his tired eyes. "God, the webs we weave," he said heavily. "She's gone and I don't know where to look for her. She might have gone back to New York for all I know, especially after yesterday. She had every reason to think I was dead serious about her until this morning."

Tira folded her arms closer against the cold look he shot her. "I said I'm sorry," she muttered. "I tried to stop her and tell her that she'd misunderstood me about the party, that I wasn't your date. But she wouldn't even look at me. I'm not sure she saw me. She was crying."

He groaned aloud.

"Oh, Corrigan, I'm sorry," she said gently. "Simon always says you do everything the hard way. I guess he knows you better than the others."

He glanced at her curiously. "When have you seen Simon?"

"At the cattle convention in San Antonio last week. I sold a lot of my Montana herd there."

"And he actually spoke to you?"

She smiled wistfully. "He always speaks to me," she said. "I don't treat him like an invalid. He feels comfortable with me."

He gave her an intent look. "He wouldn't if he knew how you felt about him."

Her eyes narrowed angrily. "I'm not telling him. And neither are you! If he wants me to be just a friend, I can settle for that. It isn't as if I'm shopping for a new husband. One was enough," she added curtly.

"Simon was always protective about you," he recalled. "Even before you married."

"He pushed me at John," she reminded him.

"Simon was married when he met you."

Her expression closed. She didn't say a word, but it was there, in her face. She'd hated Simon's wife, and the feeling had been mutual. Simon had hated her husband, too. But despite all the turbulence between Tira and Simon, there had never been a hint of infidelity while they were both married. Now, it was as if they couldn't get past their respective bad marriages to really look at each other romantically. Tira loved Simon, although no one except Corrigan knew it. But Simon kept secrets. No one was privy to them anymore, not even his own brothers. He kept to himself in San Antonio. Too much, sometimes.

Tira was watching him brood. "Why don't you file a missing persons report?" she suggested suddenly.

"I have to wait twenty-four hours. She could be in Alaska by then." He muttered under his breath. "I guess I could hire a private detective to look for her."

She gave him a thoughtful look and her eyes twinkled. "I've got a better idea. Why not tell your brothers she's gone missing?"

His eyebrows lifted, and hope returned. "Now that's a constructive suggestion," he agreed, nodding, and he began to grin. "They were already looking forward to homemade biscuits every morning. They'll be horrified!"

And they were. It was amazing, the looks that he got from his own kinfolk when he mentioned that their prized biscuit maker had gone missing.

"It's your fault," Rey said angrily. "You should have proposed to her."

"I thought you guys had all that taken care of," Corrigan said reasonably. "The rings, the minister, the gown, the invitations..."

"Everything except the most important part," Cag told him coldly.

"Oh, that. Did we forget to tell her that he loved her?" Leo asked sharply. "Good Lord, we did! No wonder she left!" He glared at his brother. "You could have told her yourself if you hadn't been chewing on your hurt pride. And speaking of pride, why didn't you tell Tira the truth instead of hedging your bets with a bunch of lies?"

"Because Tira has a big mouth and I didn't want the whole town to know I was dying of unrequited love for Dorie!" he raged. "She doesn't want to marry me. She said so! A man has to have a little pride to cling to!"

"Pride and those sort of biscuits don't mix," Rey stressed. "We've got to get her back. Okay, boys, who do we know in the highway patrol? Better yet, don't we know at least one Texas Ranger? Those boys can track anybody! Let's pool resources here…"

Watching them work, Corrigan felt relieved for himself and just a little sorry for Dorie. She wouldn't stand a chance.

She didn't, either. A tall, good-looking man with black hair wearing a white Stetson and a Texas Ranger's star on his uniform knocked at the door of her motel room in Victoria. When she answered it, he tipped his hat politely, smiled and put her in handcuffs.

They were halfway back to Jacobsville, her hastily packed suitcase and her purse beside her, before she got enough breath back to protest.

"But why have you arrested me?" she demanded.

"Why?" He thought for a minute and she saw him scowl in the rearview mirror. "Oh, I remember. Cattle rustling." He nodded. "Yep, that's it. Cattle rustling." He glanced at her in the rearview mirror.

"You see, rustling is a crime that cuts across county lines, which gave me the authority to arrest you."

"Whose cattle have I rustled?" she demanded impertinently.

"The Hart Brothers filed the charges."

"Hart...Corrigan Hart?" She made a furious sound under her breath. "No. Not Corrigan. Them. It was them! Them and their damned biscuits! It's a put-up job," she exclaimed. "They've falsely accused me so that they can get me back into their kitchen!"

He chuckled at the way she phrased it. The Hart brothers and their mania for biscuits was known far and wide. "No, ma'am, I can swear to that," he told her. His twinkling black eyes shone out of a lean, darkly tanned face. His hair was black, too, straight and thick under that wide-brimmed white hat. "They showed me where it was."

"It?"

"The bull you rustled. His stall was empty, all right."

Her eyes bulged. "Didn't you look for him on the ranch?"

"Yes, ma'am," he assured her with a wide smile. "I looked. But the stall was empty, and they said he'd be in it if he hadn't been rustled. That was a million-dollar bull, ma'am." He shook his head. "They could shoot you for that. This is Texas, you know. Cattle rustling is a very serious charge."

"How could I rustle a bull? Do you have any idea how much a bull weighs?" She was sounding hysterical. She calmed down. "All right. If I took that bull, where was he?"

"Probably hidden in your room, ma'am. I plan to phone back when we get to the Hart place and have the manager search it," he assured her. His rakish grin widened. "Of course, if he doesn't find a bull in your room, that will probably mean that I can drop the charges."

"Drop them, the devil!" she flared, blowing a wisp of platinum hair out of her eyes. "I'll sue the whole damned state for false arrest!"

He chuckled at her fury. "Sorry. You can't. I had probable cause."

"What probable cause?"

He glanced at her in the rearview mirror with a rakish grin. "You had a hamburger for lunch, didn't you, ma'am?"

She was openly gasping by now. The man was a lunatic. He must be a friend of the brothers, that was the only possible explanation. She gave up arguing, because she couldn't win. But she was going to do some serious damage to four ugly men when she got back to Jacobsville.

The ranger pulled up in front of the Harts' ranch house and all four of them came tumbling out of the living room and down to the driveway. Every one of them was smiling except Corrigan.

"Thanks, Colton," Leo said, shaking the ranger's

hand. "I don't know what we'd have done without you."

The man called Colton got out and opened the back seat to extricate a fuming, muttering Dorie. She glared at the brothers with eyes that promised retribution as her handcuffs were removed and her suitcase and purse handed to her.

"We found the bull," Cag told the ranger. "He'd strayed just out behind the barn. Sorry to have put you to this trouble. We'll make our own apologies to Miss Wayne, here."

Colton stared at the fuming ex-prisoner with pursed lips. "Good luck," he told them.

Dorie didn't know where to start. She looked up at Colton and wondered how many years she could get for kicking a Texas Ranger's shin.

Reading that intent in her eyes, he chuckled and climbed back into his car. "Tell Simon I said hello," he called to them. "We miss seeing him around the state capital now that he's given up public office."

"I'll tell him," Cag promised.

That barely registered as he drove away with a wave of his hand, leaving Dorie alone with the men.

"Nice to see you again, Miss Wayne," Cag said, tipping his hat. "Excuse me. Cows to feed."

"Fences to mend," Leo added, grinning as he followed Cag's example.

"Right. Me, too." Rey tipped his own hat and lit out after his brothers.

Which left Corrigan to face the music, and it was all furious discord and bass.

She folded her arms over her breasts and glared at him.

"It was their idea," he said pointedly.

"Arrested for rustling. Me! He…that man…that Texas Ranger tried to infer that I had a bull hidden in my motel room, for God's sake! He handcuffed me!" She held up her wrists to show them to him.

"He probably felt safer that way," he remarked, observing her high color and furious face.

"I want to go home! Right now!"

He could see that it would be useless to try to talk to her. He only made one small effort. "Tira's sorry," he said quietly. "She wanted to tell you that she's going to the Coltrains' party with Charles Percy. I was going to drive, that's all. I'd planned to take you with me."

"I heard all about your 'plan.'"

The pain in her eyes was hard to bear. He averted his gaze. "You'd said repeatedly that you wanted no part of me," he said curtly. "I wasn't about to let people think I was dying of love for you."

"Wouldn't that be one for the record books?" she said furiously.

His gaze met hers evenly. "I'll get Joey to drive you home."

He turned and walked away, favoring his leg a little. She watched him with tears in her eyes. It was just too much for one weekend.

* * *

Joey drove her home and she stayed away from the ranch. Corrigan was back to doing the books himself, because she wouldn't. Her pride was raw, and so was his. It looked like a complete stalemate.

"We've got to do something," Cag said on Christmas Eve, as Corrigan sat in the study all by himself in the dark. "It's killing him. He won't even talk about going to the Coltrains' party."

"I'm not missing it," Leo said. "They've got five sets of Lionel electric trains up and running on one of the most impressive layouts in Texas."

"Your brother is more important than trains," Rey said grimly. "What are we going to do?"

Cag's dark eyes began to twinkle. "I think we should bring him a Christmas present."

"What sort of present?" Rey asked.

"A biscuit maker," Cag said.

Leo chuckled. "I'll get a bow."

"I'll get out the truck," Rey said, shooting out the front door.

"Shhh!" Cag called to them. "It wouldn't do to let him know what we're up to. We've already made one monumental mistake."

They nodded and moved more stealthily.

Corrigan was nursing a glass of whiskey. He heard the truck leave and come back about an hour later, but he wasn't really interested in what his brothers were doing. They'd probably gone to the Christmas party over at Coltrain's ranch.

He was still sitting in the dark when he heard curious muffled sounds and a door closing.

He got up and went out into the hall. His brothers looked flushed and flustered and a little mussed. They looked at him, wide-eyed. Leo was breathing hard, leaning against the living-room door.

"What are you three up to now?" he demanded.

"We put your Christmas present in there," Leo said, indicating the living room. "We're going to let you open it early."

"It's something nice," Cag told him.

"And very useful," Leo agreed.

Rey heard muffled noises getting louder. "Better let him get in there. I don't want to have to run it down again."

"Run it down?" Corrigan cocked his head. "What the hell have you got in there? Not another rattler...!"

"Oh, it's not that dangerous," Cag assured him. He frowned. "Well, not quite that dangerous." He moved forward, extricated Leo from the door and opened it, pushing Corrigan inside. "Merry Christmas," he added, and locked the door.

Corrigan noticed two things at once—that the door was locked, and that a gunnysack tied with a ribbon was sitting in a chair struggling like crazy.

Outside the door, there were muffled voices.

"Oh, God," he said apprehensively.

He untied the red ribbon that had the top securely tied, and out popped a raging mad Dorothy Wayne.

"I'll kill them!" she yelled.

Big booted feet ran for safety out in the hall.

Corrigan started laughing and couldn't stop. Honest to God, his well-meaning brothers were going to be the death of him.

"I hate them, I hate this ranch, I hate Jacobsville, I hate you...*mmmfff!*"

He stopped the furious tirade with his mouth. Amazing how quickly she calmed down when his arms went around her and he eased her gently out of the chair and down onto the long leather couch.

She couldn't get enough breath to continue. His mouth was open and hungry on her lips and his body was as hard as hers was soft as it moved restlessly against her.

She felt his hands on her hips and, an instant later, he was lying between her thighs, moving in a tender, achingly soft rhythm that made her moan.

"I love you," he whispered before she could get a word out.

And then she didn't want to get a word out.

His hands were inside her blouse and he was fighting his way under her skirt when they dimly heard a key turn in the lock.

The door opened and three pair of shocked, delighted eyes peered in.

"You monsters!" she said with the last breath

she had. She was in such a state of disarray that she couldn't manage anything else. Their position was so blatant that there was little use in pretending that they were just talking.

"That's no way to talk to your brothers-in-law," Leo stated. "The wedding's next Saturday, by the way." He smiled apologetically. "We couldn't get the San Antonio symphony orchestra to come, because they have engagements, but we did get the governor to give you away. He'll be along just before the ceremony." He waved a hand at them and grinned. "Carry on, don't mind us."

Corrigan fumbled for a cushion and flung it with all his might at the door. It closed. Outside, deep chuckles could be heard.

Dorie looked up into Corrigan's steely gray eyes with wonder. "Did he say the governor's going to give me away? Our governor? The governor of Texas?"

"The very one."

"But, how?"

"The governor's a friend of ours. Simon worked with him until the wreck, when he retired from public office. Don't you ever read a newspaper?"

"I guess not."

"Never mind. Just forget about all the details." He bent to her mouth. "Now, where were we...?"

The wedding was the social event of the year. The governor did give her away; along with all four brothers, including the tall, darkly distinguished

Simon, who wore an artificial arm just for the occasion. Dorie was exquisite in a Paris gown designed especially for her by a well-known couturier. Newspapers sent representatives. The whole world seemed to form outside the little Presbyterian church in Victoria.

"I can't believe this," she whispered to Corrigan as they were leaving on their Jamaica honeymoon. "Corrigan, that's the vice president over there, standing beside the governor and Simon!"

"Well, they sort of want Simon for a cabinet position. He doesn't want to leave Texas. They're coaxing him."

She just shook her head. The Hart family was just too much altogether!

That night, lying in her new husband's arms with the sound of the ocean right outside the window, she gazed up at him with wonder as he made the softest, sweetest love to her in the dimly lit room.

His body rose and fell like the tide, and he smiled at her, watching her excited eyes with sparks in his own as her body hesitated only briefly and then accepted him completely on a gasp of shocked pleasure.

"And you were afraid that it was going to hurt," he chided as he moved tenderly against her.

"Yes." She was gasping for air, clinging, lifting to him in shivering arcs of involuntary rigor. "It's… killing me…!"

"Already?" he chided, bending to brush his lips

over her swollen mouth. "Darlin', we've barely started!"

"Barely...? Oh!"

He was laughing. She could hear him as she washed up and down on waves of ecstasy that brought unbelievable noises out of her. She died half a dozen times, almost lost consciousness, and still he laughed, deep in his throat, as he went from one side of the bed to the other with her in a tangle of glorious abandon that never seemed to end. Eventually they ended up on the carpet with the sheet trailing behind them as she cried out, sobbing, one last time and heard him groan as he finally shuddered to completion.

They were both covered with sweat. Her hair was wet. She was trembling and couldn't stop. Beside her, he lay on his back with one leg bent at the knee. Incredibly he was still as aroused as he'd been when they started. She sat up gingerly and stared at him, awed.

He chuckled up at her. "Come down here," he dared her.

"I can't!" She was gasping. "And you can't...you couldn't...!"

"If you weren't the walking wounded, I sure as hell could," he said. "I've saved it all up for eight years, and I'm still starving for you."

She just looked at him, fascinated. "I read a book."

"I'm not in it," he assured her. He tugged her down

on top of him and brushed her breasts with his lips. "I guess you're sore."

She blushed. "You *guess?*"

He chuckled. "All right. Come here, my new best friend, and we'll go to sleep, since we can't do anything else."

"We're on the floor," she noted.

"At least we won't fall off next time."

She laughed because he was outrageous. She'd never thought that intimacy would be fun as well as pleasurable. She traced his nose and bent to kiss his lips. "Where are we going to live?"

"At the ranch."

"Only if your brothers live in the barn," she said. "I'm not having them outside the door every night listening to us."

"They won't have to stand outside the door. Judging from what I just heard, they could hear you with the windows closed if they stood on the town squa... Ouch!"

"Let that be a lesson to you," she told him dryly, watching him rub the nip she'd given his thigh. "Naked men are vulnerable."

"And you aren't?"

"Now, Corrigan...!"

She screeched and he laughed and they fell down again in a tangle, close together, and the laughter gave way to soft conversation. Eventually they even slept.

When they got back to the ranch, the three brothers

were gone and there was a hastily scrawled note on the door.

"We're sleeping in the bunkhouse until we can build you a house of your own. Congratulations. Champagne is in the fridge." It was signed with love, all three brothers—and the name of the fourth was penciled in.

"On second thought," she said, with her arm around her husband, "maybe those boys aren't so bad after all!"

He tried to stop her from opening the door, but it was too late. The bucket of water left her wavy hair straight and her navy blue coat dripping. She looked at Corrigan with eyes the size of plates, her arms outstretched, her mouth open.

Corrigan looked around her. On the floor of the hall were two towels and two new bathrobes, and an assortment of unmentionable items.

He knew that if he laughed, he'd be sleeping in the barn for the next month. But he couldn't help it. And after a glance at the floor—neither could she.

* * * * *

THE
Essential
COLLECTION

by Diana Palmer

YES! Please send me *The Essential Collection* by Diana Palmer. This collection will begin with 3 FREE BOOKS and 2 FREE GIFTS in my very first shipment—and more valuable free gifts will follow! My books will arrive in 8 monthly shipments until I have the entire 51-book *Essential Collection* by Diana Palmer. I will receive 2 free books in each shipment and I will pay just $4.49 U.S./$5.39 CDN for each of the other 4 books in each shipment, plus $2.99 for shipping and handling.* If I decide to keep the entire collection, I'll only have paid for 32 books because 19 books are free. I understand that accepting the 3 free books and gifts places me under no obligation to buy anything. I can always return a shipment and cancel at any time. My free books and gifts are mine to keep no matter what I decide.

279 HDK 9860   479 HDK 9860

Name	(PLEASE PRINT)

Address	Apt. #

City	State/Prov.	Zip/Postal Code

Signature (if under 18, a parent or guardian must sign)

Mail to the **Reader Service:**
IN U.S.A.: P.O. Box 1867, Buffalo, NY 14240-1867
IN CANADA: P.O. Box 609, Fort Erie, Ontario L2A 5X3

ECDPBPA11